IN-HOUSE WEDDINGS

Writings from an Unbound Europe

■ □ ■ □ ■

BOHUMIL HRABAL

IN-HOUSE WEDDINGS

Translated from the Czech
by Tony Liman

NORTHWESTERN UNIVERSITY PRESS

EVANSTON, ILLINOIS

Northwestern University Press
www.nupress.northwestern.edu

English translation copyright © 2007 by Northwestern University Press. Published
2007 by Northwestern University Press. Originally published in Czech in 1987
under the title *Svatby v dome*. Copyright © Bohumil Hrabal Estate, Zurich,
Switzerland. All rights reserved.

In-House Weddings is the first volume in a trilogy that includes
Vita Nuova and *Vacant Lots*.

Printed in the United States of America

10   9   8   7   6   5   4   3

Library of Congress Cataloging-in-Publication Data

Hrabal, Bohumil, 1914–1997.
    [Svatby v dome. English]
    In-house weddings / Bohumil Hrabal ; translated from the Czech by
Tony Liman.
        p. cm. — (Writings from an unbound Europe)
    ISBN-13: 978-0-8101-2429-5 (cloth : alk. paper)
    ISBN-10: 0-8101-2429-7 (cloth : alk. paper)
    ISBN-13: 978-0-8101-2430-1 (pbk. : alk. paper)
    ISBN-10: 0-8101-2430-0 (pbk. : alk. paper)
    1. Hrabal, Bohumil, 1914–1997—Fiction. I. Liman, Tony, 1966–
II. Title. III. Series.
PG5039.18.R2S8513 2007
891.8'635—dc22

                                                              2007017819

∞The paper used in this publication meets the minimum requirements of the American
National Standard for Information Sciences—Permanence of Paper for Printed Library
Materials, ANSI Z39.48-1992.

■ □ ■ □ ■

IN-HOUSE WEDDINGS

■ □ ■ □ ■

CHAPTER ONE

THE BUILDING I WAS LOOKING FOR WAS QUITE FINE— OUT IN FRONT of its main entrance stood a gas lamppost; the sidewalk, once checkered, had most certainly been torn up ages ago and most recently filled in again. The gas lamp was already lit, so I was able to decipher the house number correctly: twenty-four. When I stepped inside, the hallway smelled of the cold and spilled wine. The walls were damp, peeling like puff pastry. When I walked through the hallway, out into the small courtyard, I had to jump back. A blonde in violet panties and bra was splashing bucketfuls of water around the yard, up as high as the windows, then brushing the water away into the gutter. She was in a sweat, scowling, focused on her work. Again she took a bucket of water, a bucket into which the water gushed from an open tap, hung the empty bucket on the brass tap, and again splashed water onto the cement yard. I said, "Is Miss Liza home?"

"She's not, but ask the doctor, he's washing floors, too, you see we need to keep it clean here, the whole building walks past my windows, and I'm a neat woman!" So said the saturnine blonde, and perhaps in an effort to prove what she said, she collided with my shoulder in pushing by into the hallway to flick the switch on in her room, and I could actually see her place was unbelievably clean: a polished stove and a polished wardrobe, atop which lay an ostrich-feather fan, and under the window was a plushly upholstered couch decorated with velvet pillows, and a table laid with a tablecloth, in the center of which glowed a vase full of artificial flowers, wild poppies.

I shrugged my shoulders, waded down the long puddle toward the stairway, and took six steps to the next courtyard, on the right spread a long shed, buried up to its windows in dirt that had been dropped there once to create an upper courtyard. Along the blanked-out windows I set out toward a one-story building, next to the ground floor a balcony, silhouetted, decorated with cast-iron railings; an adjoining structure's wall rose over the shed into the sky, nothing but this tall wall, a wall with peeling plaster, a gigantic windowless wall, so vast it dwarfed the building with the balcony and lighted windows. To the left was a stand for beating carpets on, then an open door to the laundry, through which detergent and dirty water stank. And drawn by a light on the ground floor, the cold glow of a droplight, I kept on going. And while it was pleasant in the small courtyard, a draft of air so cold came from an open ground-floor window that it made me shiver.

I stood around for a while, Should I go in, should I not go in? Should I ask, or should I merely leave? Down in the lower courtyard I could hear the blonde splash another bucket onto the cement, then I heard the sound of water rising in the gush from the open tap into the bucket; I stood at the dirt pile by the wire-mesh window, that blanked-out window of the long shed above, where the high wall rose to the sky, out of the dirt pile grew two stalks of ivy which crept along wires strung across the courtyard, and tendrils fell from the branches of wild, creeping ivy, upturning halfway to the ground, those tendrils touched me lightly, and I mustered my courage and stepped up to the window.

There on the ground knelt a man with a scrub brush, scrubbing the floor. Not kneeling, but prone on all fours, scrubbing the floor, focused, dreamy, and quiet, now he straightened up and gazed with pleasure at another piece of scrubbed wooden floor. In the corner was a stove, a cast-iron stove with a roaring fire and a big pot of boiling water. I stood near the window, there was a candelabra unscrewed from an old piano with a board nailed underneath, and on it sat a huge asparagus, its branches dangling right to the floor, touching two mirrors that leaned against the window wall. In the corner of the room stood a brass art nouveau bed on brass castors. The rest of the furniture was outside, chairs and a table, and an oval stool, on which rested a split tree stump that probably had a beehive inside.

And the man dug the brush into the water again and continued focusing on scrubbing the floor, the scrub brush scratched and the droplight lit the way. And again down in the lower courtyard I heard the loud splash of water hitting cement, then someone on the second floor opened a door, light flew out into the yard and snapped off again as someone upstairs closed the door. I heard steps come down the winding stairs, quickly, I squeezed in behind the bathroom door, mortified that the one descending the stairs was coming to use this very bathroom, because in this building anything could be, but I relaxed only when the person coming down the stairs kept on going to the lower courtyard. I came out of the bathroom and heard the blonde splash another bucket of water, apparently, right under the feet of the person who'd just come down from the second floor, because he let out a horrible yell, and then I heard nothing but curses, one finer than the next, like the blonde had been in wait all night for the very moment when she could let fly at this person who'd stepped in the way of her bucket.

"I'm a neat woman, sure as hell a stickler for clean! Goddamn building, damn all the tenants and their guests! Goddamn home weddings!" griped the woman, got up in violet bra and panties. And I screwed up my courage, scared stiff the person who'd just come down from the second floor would have to go up again, and I heard, practically right under me, under the courtyard, way down in the depths of the cellar, someone shoveling coal, dropped down dully, off the shovel into a metal bucket.

"Doctor," I said, coughing, "do you hear me? Doctor, you wouldn't happen to know when Miss Liza and her husband are due back?"

And yes, the man I'd spoken to kept a hold on the scrub brush, and now he was tossing it into the bucket and starting to wipe down the floor with a rinsed rag.

I leaned against the two mirrors between the windows and saw the man had blue eyes. He wiped the sweat from his brow and then told me with a smile, Miss Liza went across the water, she'd be back soon, and if I wanted I could wait at his place, he'd put a chair next to the stove for me.

And then he straightened up heavily, and when his head glinted in the lamplight, I saw he didn't have much hair. Now he was spreading newspapers around so he could get to the door without messing up his floor, and I got the feeling he was a soccer player who'd given up playing a long time ago. He offered me his hand and led me over to the stove and then slapped himself on the forehead, walked back out over the newspapers, and back in with a chair. I sat down and it was nice, I'd started to get cold, and the stove gave off a pleasant heat. The doctor picked up the bucket easily, carried it out into the courtyard, I heard him pour the dirty water into the gutter, but the gutter wouldn't drain, it burbled, choked, drained slow, only to suddenly swig down everything the bucket had poured into it, in one gulp. Almost like the gutter had breathed a sigh of relief. And the man whom I'd called doctor, who'd accepted being called doctor, poured hot water into the bucket, then went out into the hallway to fill it the rest of the way with water from the tap. Then other steps echoed through the courtyard. I heard them stop, and I felt someone look into the room, I heard a bucket set down against the courtyard tiles, but then whoever it was picked it up and continued on their way, up the stairs to the second floor, where they let out a gasp, a sigh of relief, just like the little gutter that had hemmed and hawed and suddenly with a horrible sound slurped that entire bucket of grime.

"According to your tone of voice, you're from Moravia," the doctor said, kneeling down again, then he dropped to the floor on all fours and continued to scrub with his brush, sopping up the dirt with his rag, rinsing it off in the bucket.

"I am," I said.

"Remember, anything worth anything in Prague is from Moravia, I'm from Moravia, too . . . But look out! Everything that's classy about me comes from a small Czech town," he said laughing, inspected his floor with pleasure, and continued, "but I had to break from my small town, because I couldn't bear being at home anymore. One day I took a good look and threw up my hands. I hadn't even noticed I'd been the dandy for so long, that I'd been walking around in handsome made-in-Prague clothes for so long, walking around for so long in these fine shoes, bought at Poldi Gutman's, choosing handsome ties for so long to match the even more handsome shirts I bought up in Příkopy, wearing these hats bought at Čekan's and little deerskin gloves for ever so long, too. I threw up my hands because I saw I was living with my parents and my brother Břet'a in a palace and that I had my own beautiful library in the den, but, in short, had done nothing so far to deserve it, living it up like the French emperor, so I fled that beautiful apartment in the brewery, shame-faced, and didn't stop till I got here, to this downstairs room, a for-mer smithy, a room that had nothing, that I had to paint myself, fix up, find my own furniture for, so everything I have in here is mine, bought with cash I earned myself up at Kladno, in the Poldinka Steel Mill, in its beautiful head of smoke, ringlets seared with stars . . . And so I'm a fellow crowned with stars."

"And is that why you're washing the floor?" I asked, laughing.

"You know, that's exactly why. If you aspire to be stylistically pure, you must focus," the doctor said, and he held the rag dripping dirt and continued, rapt, "I want to have no more than anybody else, I want to get closer to everybody else by working, or by trying to live and work exactly as they do, that's exactly why this thing I'm doing right now is my poetic, my poetry, which makes me free, at least I believe makes me free. That's why I walked out on my library, on my brown-velvet-covered writing desk, walked out on the tile stove our maid kept stoked, walked out on the home-cooked meals Momma made for me and the cellar full of Daddy's beer and wine."

I raised my eyes, brightening at a memory, "Yes, I come from an eleven roomer, too, in fact, we had two maids and I had a nanny and Daddy had a Studebaker, his own chauffeur, and a cellar full of choice French wine and boxes of Irish and Scotch whisky, and my bedroom was Louis XIV, and Daddy had this English-style den, one whole wall of pleated drapes, Sèvres vases in every corner, walls full of Dutch originals, because Daddy traveled the world buying wood, because he was a court adviser, and Mom had a boudoir . . ."

The doctor splashed water onto the last scrap of dirty floor with his scrub brush and interrupted me, "And your villa, that apartment of yours, you left that of your own accord? Ran away from home?"

"No," I said, taken aback, "you know perfectly well yourself what it was like at the war's end . . . I was sixteen years old when they took me off to the camp, but not just me, even my parents. I didn't know where my brother Karli was, where my sister Wutzi was, only after I was in the camp did I get the news Karli'd been wounded near Stalingrad, he took it in the chin. Wutzi made off after her husband to some-where in Holland, and my little brother Heini was just a boy, so they sent us to work at the brickyard, and so even I was to blame for the Germans losing the war effort, me, who was sixteen years old."

He straightened up, shrugged his shoulders, sighed, then said, "Awful, but even the innocent suffer for a war lost. An eye for an eye, a tooth for a tooth, which was what was paid in the Old Testament, in this war, thanks to the cruelty of an all-out war, a new phrase was coined . . . For one eye, two eyes, for one tooth, the full jaw, ach! Do you see that? I'm done." He got up and gestured triumphantly at his wood floor, which smelled of soap and water.

Then I went out into the courtyard. On the second floor of the building opposite, where Liza was supposed to live, it was still dark, save on the ground floor, where a light shone out from the apartment of the saturnine blonde.

Then I helped the doctor lift his table into his clean room, then his chairs, we brought in the split tree stump with the beehive, and then we laid the tablecloth and the doctor brought out a glass yogurt tub that held three carnations, the doctor pulled down the droplight, took some newspaper and folded it around the wire for a shade that spotlighted just the white tablecloth and the beaming carnations, and then the doctor set a big pitcher down on the table, poured four pints of beer into it, and offered me a drink . . .

So I sat with a strange one, who sat across from me not looking directly at me, but sort of looking at me askance, off to one side, but I felt the sole reason he wasn't looking at me directly was actually kind of like a horse, to get a better look at me. And the beer was good, the stove roared because the doctor kept adding old, split-up boards.

"Beautiful here, isn't it?" said the doctor proudly. "Can you blame me? Sundays I go out to visit my mom, my parents, but coming back on the train, soon as I get off, I run back from the station as fast as I can and just let out a sigh of relief once I unlock my door, turn the light on, and I'm home again, once I get the fire here in the stove going, put a fresh flower into a glass, open a book on my white tablecloth, once I've brought myself a fresh pitcher of beer over from Vaništa's across the street, can you blame me?"

Through the open door came an alto voice. "Doctor, I've brought you something you'll smack your lips over today!" I jumped—there at the window stood the saturnine blonde—even the doctor gave a start, for there, from the waist up, she stood in her violet bra, arms raised, happily holding up a plate and a little steaming saucepan.

The doctor took the plate and the little saucepan and breathed it in, delighted.

"Oh, *magnat magyar* goulash, rump steak goulash—we'll have that right now. How'd you know I had nothing in, Mrs. Beranová? And 'specially since we're famished!"

And the neat blonde smiled and turned around, her massive neck threatening to burst, and she pushed aside the shoots of creeping vine, her shoes clicked across the little courtyard, and then, the sound of her footsteps slowed on the stairs down to her room.

"Who's that?" I said, gasping.

The doctor held a loaf of bread, but held it in such a weird way, sawing at the bread with a dull knife like it was something he wanted to say, so that he opted to set the bread and the knife down and said, "That lady was a waitress in Hamburg as a young woman, a waitress for twenty years, that's why she's so neat. Now she works as a dishwasher at the Golden Goose, they say they've never seen a neater woman, that's why they give her those little pots for all her fancy men. At the Golden Goose she washes dishes, all night here she washes down the courtyard and cleans her furniture, and she even washes those artificial flowers of hers. She's probably in love with me; that's why when she brings me a little pot, I don't know what to say, I'm embarrassed and shy."

"You still get shy?" I raised my eyes.

"Not so much anymore, those are just the shreds of shyness, but you know, I belong to a generation that was still shy, shy on up to twenty-five years of age. Probably because schools weren't co-ed . . . You know, when all's said and done, the one nice thing about me is I'm still likely to blush, still be shy . . . And the other thing that's me is I have an 'rr-j'—I, like, lisp when I pronounce 'er.' Last year, I went to see a doctor in hopes he'd rid me of it. And he listened for a while, and then he said, 'Now look, you have a few years on you already, starting to lose your hair, not a whole lot left of you. Only thing you got going for you is that "er," you hang onto it, and that'll be a hundred and fifty crowns for the advice.'" So said the doctor, and on the table he put the little pot, and he tried to cut another piece of bread, but somehow the loaf kept slipping out of his hands, and for the first time I noticed how worn his hands were, hands like country people had, like winegrowers, or people who dig for spuds and vegetables. When he finally managed a few slices, he picked all the little crumbs up off the tablecloth . . . He handed me a spoon and we ate with it. It felt a bit peculiar—first I took a little, handed him the spoon, then he ate a little, handed the spoon back over to me—we ate the bread along with it, ate like newlyweds at their wedding when they sup soup from the same plate with the same spoon. Ach, all that bread, my beautiful hunks of bread!

The doctor called out, "All the buttered bread I've eaten! If you lined all those slices up, thick as soles on hiking boots, I could walk on them all the way to Vienna—forget Vienna, all the way to Paris! My mother buttered my slices really thinly, see, so I preferred to do the buttering myself. I loved fat, as a boy when Mother wasn't home, I'd put goose or duck fat in a little pot. I'd have it with the bread, sup up the fat with a teaspoon, a little pepper and salt, and I'd crack open a beer, because, madame, I dwelled in a brewery for forty years."

And I said, "But I'm no madame!"

"All the better, anyway, I drank a beer to my goose-fat delight! You see, three times a year we would butcher a pig and, man, fat by the bucket load! But Mom buttered my slices so thinly I did them myself. When she wasn't looking, I'd butter them an inch thick in fat, then flip the bread over quick as can be so Mom wouldn't see, for if she'd caught me, she would have nagged, 'You're going to make yourself ill!' Well, for more than twenty years, I played this bread-and-butter game with Mom, and it's stayed with me even to this day, because I still like fat on my bread best, I even take two slices spread with fat to work with me, and even though Mom isn't here anymore, quick as can be, I flip them dry side up. Then, even in this life of mine it so happens, my slice falls, buttered-face down."

And right then, across the way, as we polished off that *magnat magyar* goulash, upstairs, above the neat woman's apartment, a light came on, and the veranda window flew open. I got up to go, shrugged my shoulders.

"Thank you," I said.

■ □ ■ □ ■

CHAPTER TWO

I STOOD IN THE COURTYARD IN THE DARK, DOWN THE STAIRS LED like on a steamship, down to where the neat lady's window shone, she now lying on the couch, under the window, stretched out, reading, her glasses casting big, glowing semicircles onto her face. At an open window on the second floor stood Liza, arms propped on its double wings that had just flown open.

"Pipsi," Liza called, "a bit farther on there's a door, it leads into the hallway for this gruesome building of ours."

Arms out in front of me I felt for the doorknob and wasn't able to get the door open, but Liza's voice called, "You gotta give it a good yank, give that bloody door the knee! Better still, wait a sec, Wulli's coming down!"

And then I heard someone run down the stairs, the silhouette of a man appeared in the frosted door pane, rattled the doorknob a few times, and the door flew open, trailing out deposits of sand and plaster, and from the hallway into the warm evening flowed a draft of air from somewhere deep in the cellar, cool air reeking of sauerkraut, and there stood Wulli, the one we'd been friends with even in wartime, but we hadn't set eyes on each other since. He looked a little paler, but it was him. By "we'd been friends" I mean he'd been with Father, who didn't actually like him much, because Liza, Wulli's wife, worked at Father's as a bookkeeper. Daddy liked her because she used to do all his correspondence. Wulli hugged me in the hallway, then went up the staircase ahead of me, I followed. We got to the balcony, up to where the open window was, I stepped over to the window and saw the entire courtyard below, that tall wall, the building with the second-floor balcony, and down on the ground floor, a room with a light on, where, hung on a board, a giant asparagus created a beautiful basket in the window. And now Liza came up, hugged me, and kissed me, and started to cry.

"A wretched reunion, eh? Where did all the golden days go?"

And she invited me into her apartment, into the kitchen partitioned off by a wardrobe, behind which a bed and a window onto the balcony, and then all that was left, to usher me into the tiny living room.

We sat on the couch, the windows to their room faced the street, in one window the gas lamp shone dully, cars rumbled by. Wulli brought up some Moravian wine from the cellar, and with a shaking hand he poured the glasses. I looked at Liza and Wulli uncomprehendingly, because they were whining horribly, one stumbling over the other in an effort to tell me the only reason they'd ended up this way was because Liza was German, Austrian, and because Wulli, even though he was from Moravia, had married her at the exact moment Czech patriots were being executed for Heydrich's assassination. When the war ended, they were both in the clink, Wulli, half a year, Liza, a year, and even though they escaped to Prague, they were found there in the end and punished, too, and for what? Liza for working as a secretary for the Oberlandrat and chucking every denunciation written by one Czech against another into the fire.

"But I know who's to blame, stab me in the neck if it wasn't the Jews," Wulli called, and jabbed a finger under his chin.

Liza nodded and glared as she always glared when the subject of the Jews came up. It was the Jews responsible for bankrupting Wulli's business, it was the Jews responsible for triggering the Germans into a war, and in the end, it was the Jews responsible for the Reich losing the war, even though in the final days, when the German soldiers were still up in Hodonín, in those last days, Liza claimed the Germans would win the war on account of they had a secret weapon. Now they both sat here on the couch in front of me, not having changed a bit, and Liza went on about the same old stuff, and Wulli puffed up at the idea of payback coming, the world couldn't let it be like this, if nothing else, there was going to be a nuclear-free zone at least, and he'd be a traveling chocolate salesman again, dealing with all the biggest Western clients, but for now it wasn't to be because the Jews were on top again and had all the power. I sat there watching these two people, and all their bellyaching stuck in my craw. After all, they were together. Their apartment was a bit smaller than the one they had before, it's not like they were living it up, but they certainly hadn't ended up the way my parents and my sister Wutzi and my brother Karli and I had. In fact, I became a bit disconcerted by what they were saying, because it started to dawn on me that the only reason they were whining that much was to discourage me from asking if I might stay with them, if they might help me get back on my feet. I had dropped by, after all, out of the blue and unannounced. Then it was quiet for a while, Wulli topped off the wine and the neck of the bottle clinked against the glass, and Liza placed her hand over mine and said, "Pipsi, what's up with you, what's happened to you? We received news you've been in Prague for two months already, but we don't hear from you, didn't hear from you, so we don't know, what are we supposed to think?"

Wulli said, "After all, me and Papa used to sit in the cellar, we drank champagne together, ach Pipsi, how Papa liked me, if only back then we had left in time, if only we had bought those two villas side-by-side at Mondsee, ach what a shame we believed the Reich would win it, if only . . ."

But Liza interrupted him, "Leave it, we're a product of the times, what do you expect Pipsi here to say? She lost everything, even Losiny, she lost everything, even all the Swiss bank accounts, but I'll bet you the Jews got hold of those. After all, Papa did business with Jewish companies, I should know, but who's going to step up now asking to be paid back, since the war ended up badly for the Germans and since your father died and where all the paperwork is, nobody knows . . . But what's up with you, Pipsi?"

"What should be up with me?" I asked, "I didn't want to live, it's been downhill with me ever since I was sixteen, I couldn't adjust, like some . . ."

"What do you mean, like some? What are you saying, Pipsi? I work as a clerk and for all my slaving make eight hundred, and Wulli here's slaving away as a smith's hand for a measly three thousand a month, and you're trying to make us feel guilty about it?"

"No, no," I said, "what I mean by I can't adjust like some is, I fell in love with this jazz guitarist, and when we were about to make the wedding announcements, when he'd already packed me off to Prague to his mother's to prepare for the wedding, about a month later I found out my jewel, my jazz guitarist, had hooked up with a jazz singer and run off with her to Vienna, where they got married . . . and so I didn't want to live anymore, I still don't, but in any case, when my suicide attempt didn't work, I threw up all the pills, I stayed alive, not that I wanted to, but I don't have the strength left to try to kill myself all over again."

I sat on the edge of the couch, hands in my lap, sat there like a lump on a log, like bad luck. Why, in fact, had I come here? I saw I was a stranger, same as with that second mother of mine, my gorgeous jazz-stinker's mother. He'd sent me to Žižkov, to the mother's, to start preparations for my wedding—to him, who ran off to Vienna with his lover and married her there. I saw these two former friends of Father's were on edge, worried I might ask them for something. You see, I realized back then they'd been nice to our whole family only because they had been honored by Papa's invitations to the villa, back then Wulli would have bent over backward trying to do us favors, he was even nice to me, and because Daddy had a huge fortune and his word meant something, not just in the wood business world, but everywhere. And there I sat now, run down. In fact, all of a sudden I saw myself, but before I could get up to go, Liza started in on me.

"Look, Pipsi, you can't go on like this, Pipsi, poor thing, just look at you. Okay, for God's sake, he ran off with someone else—so! So you'll find or fate'll find you another, but listen, you don't mean to go out in public with your hair like that! Just have a look at yourself, do you intend to get on a tram in that torn dress? And look at your shoes, you don't put on a pair of shoes as down-at-heel as that and traipse off to work. After all, you're working at the Hotel Paris, right? You still have that apartment in Píšťany, don't you? So go back, your home is there, find something to do there, after all, the apartment furniture was designed by Papa, wasn't it?"

And from outside, from the courtyard rose a sound like a quarry blast, followed by a cascade of small crashes. Wulli ran out into the hall and called me, he was delighted by what was taking place out there, because while we'd been sitting around he'd got scared stiff, not that I might ask for help with where to live, but with help on how to live. Now dust and smoke rose out there in the courtyard, all the lights came on, even the doctor ran outside to stand in his doorway, to listen and watch stone and plaster as it slid off the roof of the shed, plaster off the tall wall that towered into the sky. And Wulli shouted and pointed out the open window, "So this here's how we live! Every week this plaster tears off and, sometimes predawn, comes crashing down this way, onto the shed first and then the courtyard, we keep the bedroom furniture packed up in one of those sheds, buried in dust already, because over there, behind that wall, is a gigantic machine shop where they test how strong drive shafts are, they cut into them, and once the shaft splits in two, the shock shakes our whole building." So said Wulli, a traveling salesman during the first republic, when Jews used to still own businesses, when he went to cafés, when he went to Sokol, when he lived it up in the city with the other Moravians, till he fell for Liza, a German, and waged his money on the Reich's winning the war and he'd be the guy he always wanted to be, a big wheel with a Mercedes. Now here he was, yelling, and I watched him, and he made me sick right about then, I mean, Liza had always been German, in fact, my mother and she went to Vienna to see Hitler roll in with his armada . . . But Wulli, who's surname was Slávek, Moravian Slávek, in fact couldn't even speak German all that well, Liza had to translate everything for him, so this Slávek, seeing as he got hitched during the Protectorate, must have been convinced the Germans would win and so didn't even see it coming, this thing he couldn't even acknowledge, his being wrong, that he should have stayed a Sokol and a Moravian, just like he'd been back when he'd been in business and Jews were like anybody else in the country.

And Wulli shut the windows, coughed theatrically, and then continued, "The only one who likes it is the doctor, soon as there's anything bad, he's there, did you see him down in the courtyard? Now he'll go ambling about the yard, picking up bricks and bits of plaster . . . But who lives like this? Sure the masons will come out and throw the plaster back up, but in a week it'll be down again, a crash and a wall torn off, a courtyard full, just like the doctor ordered, he loves it, just like those in-house wedding fests of his. He'll invite friends over and they'll drink till they can't stand, drink so much people living above him are afraid of making their way down to the cellar for milk, coal, that's right, the milk and the coal." And then it struck me, the only reason Wulli was rambling on was just so I wouldn't get a chance to say what hadn't even occurred to me till then, so now I went ahead and said it. I said, "You see, I'm in an awful position, I'm just in Prague, like . . . I have no sublet."

Liza clapped her hands together, "What, you're unregistered?"

Wulli was too petrified to even entertain the implications, and on he yelled, "We don't deserve to live in a freezing building like this! In winter, we gotta walk out across the landing or adjoining balcony to get to the bathroom, where even the water freezes to the bucket on us—that's right, we flush our toilet with a bucket! The doctor's toilet's outside as well, he has to go out to the courtyard, but he praises that shit house, praises everything in here, loves the lot, outdoor toilet and all! And, Pipsi, if you just saw when the rain comes down, when there's a downpour! The whole upper courtyard is under water, we can't even make it to the laundry, we have to walk around on boards and sweep the water out with brooms, as if this building were our very own, but, Pipsi, we're here on a sublet, haven't even a deed for the apartment, actually we're about in the same boat as you, doctor's the only one likes it all here, room next to his used to be full of painters, performers, thought they were going to be artists, but they had to leave here, too, because none of them had jobs, so they couldn't get a permit to live here either."

Liza breathed a sigh of relief and then again feigned concern, "I'm scared to even think what it means if you're not registered, then actually you can't even get a permit to work in Prague."

And Wulli kept on yelling, came running into the kitchen, veering around the wardrobe like he was circling the net in a hockey game, and on he lamented, "Pipsi, we're in here living on a hope and a prayer, on borrowed time, on the fact we're related to the building owner, our aunt, but rest assured, if this were our permanent dwelling, if only we had that deed we dream of, we'd sign you up, all your worries'd be taken care of, but cross my heart, this apartment doesn't even do for us, much less you. In summer when the drafts and the stormy wind come, this courtyard turns into a whirling vortex, all the papers next door, all the leaves from as far away as Kotlaska, all gets sucked into the vortex and whirled around in here, plus all the muck that comes flying off that horrible wall, it all rises up to the rim of the roof but can't go farther, and so the vortex sucks it back down, and the hallway's full of papers and dust and sand, and the hallway's full of leaves. And the doctor he's living it up, off to the library every Friday for the wedding announcements, then inviting his guests over here for his in-house weddings, they drink and don't give a damn about the wind or if the courtyard is buried in paper and dust or if the courtyard is under water, they put on their own in-house weddings and drink and carry on, and when the wind stops, the courtyard looks like a garbage bin, there's so much crap. In fact, neighbors even have to come over to collect their laundry, towels, diapers—it all comes flying over here and it can't ever get out again. It's horrendous how many times I come home from work and already the wind'll slap me in the face with a diaper in the doorway, a wet one, and I'll get this rash, I detest wet diapers. Sometimes on those wind-whipped nights, it's like somebody up above's dumping a giant container out on us, that courtyard of ours and those sheds and buildings turn into this gigantic garbage bin, and the wind whistles and howls at the roofs—we can't sleep for all the howling, and when there is no howling, well then we've got the doctor and friends across the way hollering, carrying on with those in-house weddings of theirs, and though we live in the same house, we're not even a sublet, 'cause we don't even have a deed for this damnable apartment."

Liza laughed and said, "If we had a deed, we'd be long gone, swapped this place long since and been living somewhere else, anyplace but here, for cross my heart, the only reason we do live here is so they won't take away Auntie's whole apartment. It's above her regulation size, so basically the reason we have no deed is because we sacrifice for our family, we're not just after a deed . . . But, Pipsi, I'm an accountant and I know the rules, you're employed but don't have your registration, and I'm scared to even think it through. What do they say down at work?"

"They say they're going to keep me on one more week, but I must get myself a permit to live in Prague," and then when I saw my friends blanche, I grew bolder and added, "and that's why I came to visit you, that's why I came here today."

It was quiet, through the floor came the sound of someone on the ground floor yawning like crazy—actually, it was more like a long, woeful howl than a yawn, from somewhere deep down inside.

Wulli looked like he was going to be sick, "So on top of everything else, there's this. When the building finally settles down, when there're no home weddings, that woman down there is so beat from work she howls in her sleep . . . Like I said, this building is a curse."

And I smiled—somehow what I was hearing made me happy. I knew perfectly well these friends of mine had a sublet, that they could sign someone on if they wanted to, but they were scared of me, they knew my whole situation now. They'd always prided themselves on being upstanding people, and I'd deserted the ranks of the upstanding, because of the way my life was, someone had written to tell them all about me, all about what had brought me to Prague, the wedding that never was, my groom running off with that other one and leaving me at his mother's, with that second mother of mine, whom I lived with but who couldn't get me a permit because she only had a sublet, that second mother of mine, a cashier at the Two Cats, me a cashier at the Hotel Paris, where she found me work. After our shifts, we'd both come home to the apartment house in Žižkov, leaning on the banister, climbing to the fifth floor, tired, dusty, sweaty, when we got in, we'd shake out the blankets and just sit there on the footboard, then loosely pull down our stockings and stare at our dusty feet, examining our awful feet, sighing, till we found the strength to go wash off those feet of ours, and then we'd lie around, yawning, even till beyond midnight we went on with the awful yawning, just like the lady there downstairs, who'd begun to yawn again, that neat blonde who worked as a dishwasher at the Golden Goose. It was quiet, on the carpet a pin lay glittering, I picked up the pin, set it on the tablecloth, and rose to go.

And then those erstwhile friends of mine had to give me a hand, because I could barely get to my own two feet, and only just then did I notice why, there was so much furniture lumped around the room that there were just these little passages between the tables and shelves, couch and chairs, in fact, it was so tight I had to squeeze sideways to get out of the room to the kitchen and then to the enclosed balcony, where a door lit onto the spiral stair. We said good-bye, kissed each other, in fact Liza even got teary eyed, and Wulli squeezed his fingers together so hard his knuckles cracked, but I saw that looking like this, I could never come back, like this, never turn up again wearing these clothes and these shoes, in fact, couldn't turn up again before I had a permit to live in Prague and a regular job. I descended the spiral stair, in the dull light of a bare bulb the wall glittered and wept beads of moisture, maybe that whole stairwell sweated from its insides, beads of moisture weeping through the wall. I touched the wall with my finger, and it was cold and wet, like a dying man's brow, I turned about and saw two heads up there in the doorway, watching me, eyes wide, smiling, but behind the smiles I saw them shaken, and they'd both breathe a sigh of relief as soon as this building was quit of me.

And I stood by the same door I'd used to enter this stairwell, the door that led out to the small courtyard. I pressed my whole body to the door and leaned against the handle, into the yard the door opened, sweeping fallen mortar and brick before it. "Not that way!" Wulli called from upstairs.

"No matter," I yelled back, "I just want to see what your courtyard's like, what your sad little yard is like." And then I stood amid the rubble, all the lights on the second floor on, but down there on the ground floor a bulb shone from a swag lamp, and in the open window hung a huge asparagus. I walked by carefully, stepping quietly. There, inside, a white tablecloth glowed, and on top of that stood a glass of carnations and a pitcher of beer. The doctor sat next to the stove, sat stretched out, hands behind his head, gazing off into a corner of his room, the room he was so proud of, the room he could be by himself in, alone.

I backed out quietly, walked along past the shed through some debris and tripped over a brick. Then I stood by those six steps that led downstairs, down there in the half-light lay the neat lady on her couch, hair in curlers, breathing deeply, open book rising and falling on her chest, artificial flowers in the half-shadow of a lampshade glowed on the table, and then all of a sudden that lady let go a horrible yawn, a groan from somewhere down in her toes . . . I went quietly out to the corridor, in the alcoves over the apartment doors little gas lamps glowed, I stumbled a couple of times and grazed the wet wall, disgusted, I stepped out into the street, it was nice out there, I turned to look, and sure enough, both my sleeves looked like they'd been painted with a brush dipped in a bucket of lime. The gas lamps lit my way nice and clearly, the street was empty, I relaxed when I got to the main street, where people were, pedestrians and trams, lit-up shops and a tram island lit with nice purple lights . . .

■ □ ■ □ ■

CHAPTER THREE

I LIKE GOING TO THAT HOTEL OF MINE MAYBE AN HOUR OR TWO early. In Žižkov, where I live on the fifth floor, the halls reek of sauerkraut, Ema, that second mother of mine, ever since her husband died, out of grief she's quit cleaning up or even looking after herself, even the cashier job wears her out, so in the room where, as she likes to say, there always used to be flowers, there on the buffet is an urn with her husband's ashes, sometimes I get the feeling that not just the flat but the entire apartment building is one big urn, that all the hallways and flats are covered in ash, moist, sopping ash, that the light bulbs in the hallways glow just like the poorly lit gravestones in Olšany on All Saints' Day. But it's a lot different at the Hotel Paris. The restaurants and cafés, salons and hallways leading up to the rooms, everything is sparklingly beautiful and decorated with flowers, just like in the house we lived in until the end of the war. Here in the hotel the lights are always blazing, there are chandeliers and sconces on the walls in the shape of candles, everything here has style and the style makes you feel right at home. I am happy here at the Hotel Paris, that's why sometimes I come to work two hours early, I sit here like a guest, drinking coffee, eating Parisian torte and whipped cream with gusto, and smoking, waiters serve me, smile at me, because they know in a while I'll be back in the kitchen behind the counter again, in the heat and smoke and acrid smells, and everything the cooks put on the waiters' plates, everything will have to pass by me so I can mark down the prices of the food on the plates. I'm happy at this hotel, the hallways are swathed in red carpets, the bathrooms have tiled walls and are decorated with mirrors set in brass moldings, and tall windows facing the street are muffled with curtains, it's magnificent and proud, this Hotel Paris.

Here I forget about the present, this hotel brings me back to our villa, back to Daddy, whom I love even though he's dead, and who loved me and bought me presents like I was his sweetheart, Papa, who was a gentleman and knew how to live like a *Lebeman,* as they used to say in Vienna, Papa, who liked to dress well, and who carried a silver-tipped cane and always had one clean shirt for the afternoon and one for the evening.

I'm happy at this hotel, I sit and look around and always find something new on the walls, only just now I noticed the tapestries are beige-colored and ornamented with little flowers, like a dirndl skirt, and only just now I remarked how this hotel abhors empty space, the walls adorned with lit little chandeliers, big mirrors and small mirrors, and in the center of everything dangles a giant Venetian chandelier, just like the one we had in our dining room at home. I'm happy at this hotel, and before my shift I sit here and smile to myself, because Daddy, when he conducted business with his partners, used to stay either here or sometimes at the Hotel du Sax, or friends from abroad would live here at the Hotel Paris, and he'd purchase from them, or sell them wood or specialty plywood . . .

Ever since I visited Liza over in Libeň, I began to feel even worse. Shouldn't have gone there and showed myself when I was at rock bottom, I shouldn't have told them everything about myself like in a confessional, because I gave them a glimpse at my cards and they were horrified and wanted nothing but to see me out, I let them see me in my torn dress and trampled shoes, my matted hair . . . Now I sit in the restaurant of the Hotel Paris, here in the corner, and in the open salon there's a wedding in progress, flowers everywhere, the wedding bouquet juts out the center of the bride and groom's table like a geyser, the wedding party is happy, the bride and groom have already supped their soup from the one bowl with the one spoon, I came in just as maître d' Mašek smashed the two plates for the newlyweds to have lifelong good luck. So here I sit and see our waiters come out of the kitchen carrying ten plates of food on their trays, see them tilt to balance the weight on the one hand while steadying themselves with the other, see all the mirrors reflecting the wedding party, waiters, and guests. So here I sit, just a while longer, just two cigarettes more and then off to the kitchen for my afternoon shift, which runs until eleven, I'll sit into the night in the gigantic kitchen with the huge exhaust fans and gas stoves, burnt grease rising and mingling with all the sauce smells and boiled and roast meats and grilled chickens and steaks, the short orders surrendering their tenderness and fragrance in the searing heat, the fragrance being sucked up by exhaust fans, all so the meat finally presented on the plate is just so, soups in silver cups, sauces tartar in silver carafes, and whatever else guests order from the menu, whatever passes by my cash register at the Hotel Paris. Now that the swinging, decorated brass-plate doors to the billiard room open for a moment, I see a player crane over the blinding green velvet, over the blinding billiard balls, filtered light falling from the wrought boxes above, other players, not playing, lean on their cues, or carefully chalk them . . .

"May I join you?" I looked up and there was a guest leaning over me feigning interest.

"If you're going to eat," I said.

"I am, but later. I'd like to invite you to join me in a glass, I'm so lonely and I feel so all alone," said the guest and he was charming and sweet.

I said, "I'm going on my shift soon, I work here, you understand?"

"Could I wait for you, till your shift's over?" the guest persisted.

"Probably not, I'm a wreck after work, my hair stuck together, feet all dusty . . ."

"I beg your pardon," the guest apologized and moved away, trying to walk back to his table with some dignity so none of his friends would know I'd given him the brush-off.

A fine man, to be sure, but I don't go in much for fun and games anymore, the only place I used to really have fun was at home, when Daddy's house was filled with people, back then I was the center of attention too, because I was fifteen going on sixteen, in fact, the mirror told me I was beautiful and people told me too, and even Daddy told me, and I was indeed beautiful, when my sister got married, the best man was the Reich's youngest general, von Norden, half the wedding party was in uniform, including the groom Sepp, wearing those gorgeous uniforms soldiers still wear today walking around East Berlin and Dresden. I used to have such a wonderful figure; I took dance lessons, gymnastics, I wanted to be a dancer like La Jana, the one thing that has stayed with me is that I always stand in the first position of dance, right foot angled, toes first, I was lovely, for that afternoon the young general, while he was pushing me back and forth, out in the garden on the big swing, whenever his hands met mine, I held on to the rope and he would touch my clasped fingers, once the swing went by him our eyes would meet for one moment, as if time held still for one second, I saw how he looked like Marlon Brando, the air filled with sparks then, which flew through me, and then it wasn't just Daddy but I heard it from the general himself I was beautiful, and that night we danced and sparkling happiness filled me, and then he left for the front and after a time they told me he'd been wounded by partisans and then beaten to death like some alley cat somewhere in the Carpathians, but at about that same time my brother Karli came back from the front, in a hospital train; they'd shot him through the chin somewhere near Kiev, it was my birthday and my brother Karli had come back from the front, head in bandages, Karli, the one who'd studied engineering in Prague, the one who'd rowed for Slavia, who used to go out with his Czech buddies to chase the Czech girls, well, Karli lived in the Sudetenland like the rest of the family and was therefore a citizen of the Reich and had to go to the front, from whence he returned with a shot-through chin. And back then, when I was sixteen and celebrating my birthday and our whole house was full of guests and Wulli and Liza were there too, Karli told all present that the best thing that ever happened to him was to live in Prague, and now he not only felt, but was sure the Reich would lose the whole war. Now I sit in the Hotel Paris, looking back at the past, and Karli had been right, even when Mommy and Liza were shouting that Hitler had a secret weapon, that the Reich would prevail, I remember looking at Daddy, but already he was sad, he didn't have much to say anymore, he already knew, Karli was right . . .

I got up, looked around the restaurant at the Hotel Paris, through the white curtains, the people out in the street appeared to stream past as if walking through falling snow; I didn't have to pay, what we spent worked as our hotel allowance; one last time my eyes played over the columns garlanded in plaster, I glanced up at the little chandeliers and the giant chandeliers, went out into the hall, and was back in the kitchen, then I remembered in the hallway I'd glimpsed the salon through an open door, so back I went, I was simply holding the knob to the kitchen door and looking through to the salon, the wedding guests were beginning to loosen up, they stood in small groups, holding champagne in glittering glasses, the bride sat under a mirror, eyes down, smiling, her tiara tipped with a coronet woven through with myrtle and topped off with a white bow, her satin dress was low-cut and clung to her shoulders, and pinned to her breast was a red carnation; I gave a start because the bride looked a lot like me, I'd also come to Prague just to be done up exactly so, like the bride sat here, this is how I'd imagined my own wedding, and at the Hotel Paris too, except that my jazz jewel, my singer-guitarist, the one whose socks and stained underwear I'd scrubbed, whose colored dress shirts and getups I'd ironed, even though he sent me off to Prague, he himself ran away with that other one, the one I knew nothing about, sure I knew that treasure of mine had women, but I didn't know he had just the one, the one he married, while his mammy and I were knocked dead by what her dear little boy, my fiancé, had cooked up for us. My lovely looking louse . . . and me, his Raggedy Ann.

And I let the doorknob go and the door shut and now I entered the kitchen, the heat washed over and closed in around me, at the stoves stood two junior cooks grinning at me like two demons, somersaulting meat from their pans like a pair of jugglers, here and there a spot of grease flamed up, ten people were spread around the various counters, stooped over their machines laboring, in order for guests at the Hotel Paris to feed, in order for them to relish. Eva, the cashier from the morning shift, slid down from her stool behind the cashier's desk, she wore only a white smock and a bra, she showed me how hot she was by tugging on her bra straps and they slapped back to make a sound like two fish hitting water, she was still wet-eyed and all the colors ran together, because she liked to paint not only her lips but her eyebrows in too, in fact, she even wore false eyelashes to the job, she was weeping because she had to have her beloved tomcat put to sleep, and she mourned his loss even more than after her own boyfriend had dumped her, the louse. Eva carried her documents, all her receipts, and while I unloaded my stuff and put on my white smock and white cap and pinned up my hair, Eva passed and we leaned toward each other a bit, touched foreheads, shut our eyes and stayed like that for a stretch, she looked up at me, she was one of my favorites here at work, trusting as a kitten, now she raised those daisy eyes of hers and stumbled off to her locker and I took her spot, while the waiters with their trays waited for me to get their bills ready, the ones already in for their afternoon shift . . . The maître d' Mašek gave me a bow, leg back, as always he was pomaded and groomed like he'd just stepped out of the shower, he was all smiles, because of his daughter Hana, a fourteen-year-old girl, who Mr. Mašek took to the winter stadium in Štvanice every day at four in the morning for practice, his little Hanička was the number one student, wherever Maître d' Mašek did go, there went his little daughter dancing on skates, he had one beautiful goal, that she'd be number one in the Republic, and then all of Europe perhaps. Maître d' Mašek liked me too, he just shrugged his shoulders and cocked his head, as if to ask have I my permit to live in Prague yet, since I needed one to get permanent employment too, he actually kept me here on the sly; I shrugged my shoulders and smiled guiltily, like I didn't have anything yet, he gestured in return, like what can you do, patience, patience. The waiter Borek with the black hair parted straight down the middle, the waiter who didn't drink, didn't play cards, or even chase after women, gorgeous and all as he was, he had a doggie at home, a dachshund bitch, the only thing he thought of while he was at work was his doggie, all he talked about was what that doggie was up to, and just like Maître d' Mašek had his little Hanička by his side, so too Borek had his little dachshund weaving in and out of his legs; after their shifts, they both had goals, beautiful goals, that made them happy, that they looked forward to, that were within reach, while what I had for me at home in Žižkov was Ema, that self-proclaimed second mother of mine, Ema, who wrote her son she was disowning him for what he'd done to me; I begged her to write I wasn't angry with him, that it all had to happen the way it did, now I saw everything stretched out before me, that whole tunnel I was going down, I realize, it was because I didn't know how to adapt, how to live, and because I didn't even care what style of clothes I had on, what style of shoes, somehow I'd become a voluntary Cinderella, demonstrating to everyone, including myself, how wretched I was, that I had no father and mother, that Daddy died, that I was orphaned, I walked about like a tramp, always wearing something ripped, I never cleaned my shoes, it was even an effort to have a bath, to get washed, because in fact I had nothing to look forward to, nothing waiting for me, like Mašek the maître d' had, or like Borek had, like the two junior cooks who kept one eye on the clock because they were so keen for their shifts to end, eager to just untie their aprons and take off their white chef's hats right after work and push their motorbikes out the Hotel Paris yard; they both raced motocross and lived only to ride those CZs of theirs, just like Head Chef Bauman lived for his work in the kitchen, for whatever type of menu he would put together for tomorrow, for how he'd divvy up the work in the kitchen . . . in fact he was the happiest person here, for Bauman, being chef was be-all and end-all, he was tuned in to every tinkle and stink, not even the whirring clatter of the dishwashers bothered him, not even the automatic potato peelers, not even the hoots and chatter of the scullery maids, not even the draft. That's the way of Head Chef Bauman, who'd personally prepare the finest fare for everyone, potato soup, pancakes, dumplings, toast . . . We were all so saturated with the spices and ingredients of the kitchen fancy foods, we preferred to eat poor peasant food, country fare. And Head Chef could handle the lot. One time in spring there was this air show, they brought a ton of wieners out to Ruzyně airport for us, Eva and I stood there in our white smocks and white caps, a tarpaulin over our stall, but every half hour it filled with water, and it was raining noon and afternoon and it was so hot, people didn't come out to the air show. So we took the ton of wieners back again, the management wrote them off, but of course we had Head Chef Bauman, who ordered the waiters to buy twenty small herring barrels, demanded they be washed out, and then ordered the whole kitchen to begin slicing onions, the entire kitchen was in tears before we managed to cut the ton of onions, but Head Chef Bauman wouldn't give an inch, and then personally lined the bottom of every herring barrel with bay leaf and one layer of wieners and one layer of sliced onion, sprinkled through with black pepper and allspice, then he ordered the cooks to boil up a hundred liters of brine and he loaded twenty small herring barrels with the ton of wieners, topped everything in brine and hammered the lids shut and ordered the barrels placed in the fridge and wieners henceforth added to the potato salad. But Borek the waiter took a plate of it one time when he wanted to fix an upset stomach, and he gave everybody else a sample, and from then on they never put the wieners in the salad again, but whenever any employee wanted to fix their stomach, they'd have a serving at cost and just like that the wieners went in under a year . . .

Head Chef liked me, he was the type of character Daddy was, and also the one who had pushed through my staying on, even though I had no place in Prague, he'd been the one to stand up to the personnel screeners for me, when they insisted I could only work once I produced a permit to live in Prague. Just like my daddy, Head Chef weighed 130 kilos, they say the way he liked to spend his vacations was to move his family from Prague District 7 to Prague District 1 for three weeks and put everybody up at the Hotel Paris, so while his family moseyed around Prague, Mr. Bauman was in the kitchen, for he couldn't conceive of liking anywhere better than our very own Hotel Paris. That's also because Mr. Bauman apprenticed under Mr. Brandejs; he came up the hard way, in fact they say Mr. Brandejs used to smack his employees, because he liked them, wanted them to learn, and so from time to time even today Mr. Bauman will prepare a food parcel and take it out to Mr. Brandejs, who's been rehoused out in Klánovice—Mr. Brandejs who owned the Paris once—take it out to him as a small gift from us, because last year, Mr. Brandejs slapped himself on the forehead and let on to Mr. Bauman as to how he had a box freezer rented in Rytířská Street under the Prague market, surely nobody else had claimed the box yet, and back when he shot a deer in the Carpathian woods he put that deer in the box freezer personally, and most likely that deer was down there to this day, frozen solid as a Siberian mammoth. And sure enough, Mr. Bauman discovered that the National Restaurant and Cafeteria outfit kept up the rent on that box freezer, so after proving who he was, Mr. Bauman got the keys off the watchman and took me with him, we brought the cargo van, and when we descended to the cellars, down into the realm of the box freezers, there we found and unlocked Mr. Brandejs's box, and there a stag lay, frozen solid as a rock. Not even a butcher's or coping saw could do the job for Mr. Bauman; only after he'd gone and borrowed a full metal saw from the blacksmith's did we manage to hack through the legs and neck of that buck and haul him up to the van and cart that deer as heavy as a small heifer off to the Hotel Paris. Once we got there, everybody said we ought to defrost him first thing and have a big feast for employees only. But Mr. Bauman started to yell, "Call yourselves chefs? It wouldn't be worth a damn, that deer must be allowed to thaw slowly, like snow off the mountains, nice and easy, tenderized for two months, given a chance to cure, just like pork marinating before smoking."

That was how Mr. Bauman, who loved the Hotel Paris, was, how Maître d' Mašek, who loved his daughter and glowed and swelled at the luckiness, and even how Borek the waiter was, who thought of nothing other than when he'd see his wee doggie again . . . Even the scullery maids in our kitchen always had something to look forward to, their lovers, construction workers, garbage men, boiler men, any man would do, so long as he liked them just a little, and someone waited for them, someone to talk to; I often saw the door open and a man would be standing there, like some hobo, and the maid, in the middle of chopping up her onions, would blush over her poised knife and race out into the hall for a whisper with her man and sometimes even kiss out there, those maids of ours, those battle-axes, once I ran out in the hall and saw one up against the wall, knife in one hand, her other down her man's trousers. I was the only one with nobody, up at home there in Žižkov Ema was waiting on me, that second mother of mine, who'd begun to reproach me for being an ingrate, not showing her more gratitude for taking me in and letting me live with her, and not listening to her the way a daughter should . . .

So that whole kitchen ran hell for leather for hours, I hardly even had time to wipe the sweat off, we were all working together, like twenty marksmen hitting twenty bull's-eyes in a shooting gallery simultaneously, and all the toys and all the machines in the shooting gallery binged at once.

When in on this the doors flew open and there stood the coat-check lady, yelling, "Eliška, you got a letter here!"

And everybody followed the letter as the coat-check lady carried it slowly in, I backed up, a wonder I didn't knock over the cashier stand. "And it's for me?"

The coat-check lady put on her spectacles and read out the address for the whole kitchen triumphantly, the right address, to the Hotel Paris.

"Liebesbrief! Liebesbrief! A love letter! Who could it be writes to you, Eliška?" The waiters teased, even Head Chef Bauman teased, everyone teased and I was red with embarrassment, because of no one believing I would ever get a letter, as if I really were the resident Cinderella, a woman already written off, pretty, certainly, but one who had declared herself a waste, a crank, a killjoy . . . And when everybody was back at work, I opened the letter, was disappointed, it came from my aunt in Vienna . . . but as I read it, I grew afraid, dismayed even, and then I just had to smile at my reaction, for my dismay brought me the clarity, which showed me . . . *Meine liebe Pipsimaus* . . .

Warm regards from Vienna,
I have received heartrending news of you; remember the class of family you come from, your auntie Pišinka, though far from well-to-do, always dresses neatly nonetheless and tastefully and goes about Vienna very elegantly, Pipsimaus, what would your Papa say if he saw you? Look, he would say, if you intend to display yourself as a down-and-out, people will treat you as a down-and-out, see here, young lady, try to display yourself as a pastry from *Paris* and people will treat you like a pastry from *Paris* with whipped cream on top.
   Love from your auntie in Vienna,
   Pišinka

■ □ ■ □ ■

CHAPTER FOUR

ONE DAY I SET OFF DOWNTOWN, STROLLING THE STREETS, WINDOW
shopping on Železná and up in Příkopy Street. But strolling through
Prague's city center I was focused only on dresses and shoes, that was
always my thing, to step out in my red high heels, shoes—coral-red
shoes—as red as the *Salvia splendens* I once had in my garden, as
the flames of love. And first thing, I bought myself two pair of red
high heels, and that mustered my courage to try on an Italian dress
in Celetná Street; I said to them, since it looks so good on, I'm going
to leave it on, parcel up the old outfit . . . And so I strutted in my
red high heels and dark blue dress, and when I caught sight of myself
prancing along in the shop windows, I chucked that bundle of old
tattered clothes into the first alleyway, and felt like a hot-air balloon
casting off bags of sand, but I knew this still wasn't enough, what I
needed now was a new hairdo.

So I went to a salon, and first they gave my little head a wash,
then did my hair, gave me a pageboy, the style worn by basketball
and volleyball players and girls in reform school. And once I left the
salon mirrors and set out into the streets, once I saw for the first time
how other people looked at me, I knew I was beginning to be a little
like that pastry from *Paris* with a whipped-cream topping. And because I'd never understood what to do with my hands, I went into a
department store and bought myself the loveliest umbrella, a powder
blue one with a handle fashioned of faux silk. And then I flounced
along as I used to years ago, when I'd prance alongside Daddy, who

always filled me with confidence, how he carried himself elegantly and lightly, even though he weighed 130 kilos. So for the first time, I was striding out alone, just me, who'd lost the marriage battle, but who all of a sudden had won the battle with herself, so handily in fact I bought myself some lipstick, and some eye shadow, and from then on I couldn't care less if I had a permit to live in Prague or no, I felt like I owned a new identity. Then when I got on the tram and went up to Libeň, I didn't sit there mousily, but threw my leg across my knee, leaned on my little blue umbrella, wiggled my red shoe back and forth, and that red color and my new Italian dress gave me fortitude, so much fortitude I could look people in the eye, I even smiled and nodded and returned people's glances, the people out on the street looked beautiful to me, every building the tram whizzed by, every building out there in the sunlight looked a marvel. And as the tram went by several playgrounds, all the children appeared like jewels scattered there to me. And when the tram crossed Libeň Bridge, I stood, leaned against the window, and gazed out at all there was to see across the river. The Bulovka district, the hospital, and all the huge buildings strewing the hillsides reminded me of photos of Tibet I had seen in magazines, all the beautiful palaces up there in Bulovka, they were scattered like dominoes . . . And then the tram swung onto the Libeň main street, I stared in every shop window, one after the other, and when I wanted off near the theater, around the corner from Na Hrázi, I felt like I was back in Břeclav, sixteen years old again, that's how beautiful this Main Street struck me. So I read out the pub names, Automat World, then the Hawk, then Down by Green Tree, Libuše's, the Old Bass, the Beggar's, Charles IV's, and then the Coat of Arms, Ferkel's, and finally, Bistro by the Smithy. I got off the tram then, charmed by a little pastry shop in Bulovka, a pastry shop in a squat building; I caught another tram then, at the stop there, and continued down the hill, I couldn't get enough of Main in Libeň, but what moved me most was the Red Cupola, a clutch of little houses and ramshackle sheds and a little factory and everything drowned in green bush and tree, and jutting out from the hill flank a run-down old country demesne. And I continued on downhill by tram, and I knew I looked good with my new shoes, new dress, new umbrella, just like when Daddy used to buy me things brand new for Easter . . .

32

And when I made my way down into Libeň, it reminded me again of Hodonín, where I lived till I was sixteen. Libeň was quite like a town in the country actually, much different from Žižkov, where I now lived. From the tram here I was able to see parks and trees and the Rokytka River, while up in Žižkov everything was only miles of stone and even the names on Žižkov streets are horror-filled for me, Advent Mass and Reformatory and Barracks and Penitentiary . . . Charnel Square, Tomáš Štítný Street, Milič of Kroměříž, Roháč of Dubé, Jewish Oven Way, and Jesenius Street, a street stinking of tanning horse hide. I was struck by the utter beauty of Libeň and by how smartly dressed young women there were. To get a better view I needed to lean against the tram window on my way up the hill, and was struck again at how every young woman on Main Street was decked out exactly as I was in a nice dress, fine shoes, I saw that for these women Main Street wasn't just a good place to shop, but a spot to be seen, not only by each other but by everyone else, in fact, they played it like a piece of theater, touching each other with their lacquered nails and talking and laughing . . . never losing sight of the impression they made on the other women, and on the men too. And I could appreciate the whole thing, even the way the women knew how to stand in the first position of dance, same way I used to, same way I stood right now, even though standing in a tram . . .

I stepped off the tram into the sunlight, walked past the theater, then past the shop windows of the fashion boutiques, in spite of myself I stopped before a window of wedding gowns and tiaras and coronets and wedding veils and I blushed and looked to see if anyone was watching. The thing is, it was *I* who'd been sent here not three months before by my fiancé to do the preparations for our wedding, and so whichever way I turned, whatever I regarded mocked me, sneered at me, because, goddamn it, that fiancé of mine, that jewel of mine, the sole reason he'd brought me to Prague was so I'd be stung with it, setting up a wedding, my wedding, while he loped off to marry another, well out of the way, for the jerk well knew that before I'd ever try suicide, I'd murder him with a kitchen knife, that jewel of mine, soon as he told me he didn't want me anymore, he'd found another . . . I'd slice him slowly with the kitchen knife . . . And now, in-house weddings, weddings in Hotel Paris, shop windows choked with wedding gowns and tiaras and coronets and veils. I went red, feeling somebody'd sprung this wedding froufrou on me like a trap, like in a horror or drastic detective novel. God!

And I turned down Na Hrázi Street, and here felt fine, here in this street, though I'd been here twice already, the street curved away into the distance, I strolled at my ease, on the right-hand side a tall building rose, I could tell instantly it was a small furniture-making factory, or to do with wood, I heard the agreeable sound of circular and band saws, saw wire windows go four floors up, scent of sawdust and wet wood everywhere, I could see into the works yard and that improved how I felt, seeing the workers stand the window frames in stacks to prevent them warping, I could see them lay boards on little support blocks, I felt as I did back in our own little veneer factory; Daddy used to travel the world, the Carpathians, the Andes, the Alps, and Lebanon too, buying all the rarest woods, all he carried was his checkbook and a little hammer, Daddy's monogram, his initials on one end, he'd tap the hammer head to inset his seal on the felled log, to demonstrate the tree was his, it had Daddy's mark, Daddy, who would at times be gone for two, even three months on end, but who always brought a little present and a kiss for me when he returned, because he loved me. And I fell in love with Na Hrázi Street, because of what I saw, even though they made no specialty plywood, nor the line of furniture they make in the UP Co., but it was just how they flat-piled boards and doors and window frames, setting them to not warp . . . and then the noise and wood scent . . .

And as I strolled along, daydreaming away, my red high heels flashing left and right under my blue dress, my little umbrella swaying rhythmically, somebody called to me, "Beautiful hafternoon, isn't it?"

What was that, what was that? I gave a start, for there was no mistaking what she'd said.

"Beautiful hafternoon," said a woman on the second floor, the woman was horribly cross-eyed; I nearly passed out, I wanted to faint, see, because Ema, that second mother of mine, said hafternoon too, laying the emphasis on the "h," in the same beautiful way she'd say waygon instead of wagon, and balgony instead of balcony, and shoe gream instead of shoe cream . . . But I was rescued by two little girls exiting the building, the building where the cross-eyed blonde sat leaning out her second-floor window, through the narrow doorway flew the girls, both trying to squeeze past at once, and when they'd fought their way through, they stood there choking, screaming with laughter, each trying to whisper some anecdote or dirty little story into the other's ear, but whatever it was made them both squirm, they covered their ears, didn't want to hear it, they squealed and screamed with laughter and stomped on the ground and alerted the whole street to them peeing their pants were they to let on to each other what their secret was, they beat on each other with their little fists . . . I looked up and there over the window was a battered but still readable sign, BRUSH AND PAINT SUPPLY. And I continued on down this street I found so cheerful and pleasing, mainly because here I was, all alone, done up like I'd just stepped out of a fashion magazine, and hoping, just like I used to back when I was sixteen, that something extraordinary would come my way.

And right at the corner of the street named Ludmila was a fenced-in garden, it looked to have been a garden restaurant at one time, six old chestnut trees, and next to the wall a tumbledown old ninepin alley, and then a house, which bore the name Hausmann's. There was a low wall there, grainy, glittering in sunlight. Nobody around. But I had to laugh when a young gypsy wearing a woman's green dress sprang up on the other side of the street, he carried a small saucer and set it on the wall in the sun and began to eat greedily, and when he noticed me he began to lament.

"Ma'am, the missus wants Helenka to go off to work right away and start making money, but what I want, and Helenka too, is for her to learn how to become a hairdresser! Yes, ma'am," the gypsy said, weeping into his little saucer.

I stopped, leaned against my little umbrella, which gave me confidence, I stood there, one red shoe arched out in the first dance position.

At that the gypsy collected himself, ran over to the window he'd jumped out of a short time earlier, and started yelling in the window and then pointing his fork at me. "Yessir, there you heard it, the lady agrees. Helenka oughta go to hairdressing school!" But before the gypsy could continue, a curtain swept back and a gypsy woman leapt out of the window into the street, she looked much older than the gypsy, but likely was younger, I knew every gypsy from our street in Žižkov. The gypsy woman felled the man with a swift blow and he dropped to the ground in front of me in that woman's green dress, he had a moustache and he lay there on his back, holding up his fork in his own defense, and with a chuckle, the gypsy woman told me Lajos was a ne'er-do-well prick . . . And I could see half her front teeth were missing. I stepped over the gypsy, shrugged, and kept on walking, I couldn't care less whether or not Helenka was going to become a hairdresser today, for today was one beautiful hafternoon; I crossed a small square and then off in the distance the gas lamp was already visible in front of the beige building, I passed by a shuttered storefront with a sign which read CEMETERY URNS AND LANTERNS . . . and then there I was beside the gas lamp, standing and blushing with embarrassment, what would the doctor think, if he was even at home, that is, what would he think knowing I'd actually set out simply to see him, to see if he was at home and what might he be doing? And there and then I wanted to bolt back to the tram stop and jump on the first tram out, away from that building, somewhere far away, I wanted to run, but once I had taken that couple of steps I looked around at my red high heels, and once I saw then that even my blue umbrella was bolting, I felt mortified and went on repeating to myself, You better, you better, and resolutely I turned back and opened the door. And I stood there then in the shadows and before me stretched that wet hallway, but the hallway led to the courtyard, and out there in the courtyard a full golden sunlight shone down, it overran the ivy-covered walls, and every tiny leaf of ivy was lit up as if slathered in butter, and the door frame, the frame of a rare painting, so beautiful was the prospect in the courtyard of that building. And I walked in, and sure enough, there was the window to the neat woman's flat, and there, the stairs leading up to the small courtyard. And I stepped into the courtyard and gazed around, and yes, the two-story structure *is* there and here is that welcoming window.

"Good day, good day, good hafternoon!"

A man's voice coming off the roof of the little shed filled the courtyard and I heard the tap of a typewriter, I turned around and there in afternoon sunlight sat the doctor in a low chair, in front of him a typewriter was on a stool and knees splayed he was hammering furiously at the portable typewriter, which jammed occasionally, but the doctor's fingers would poke in and the typewriter would write on, the return bar shifting it a line ahead, the doctor turned out a page and set it on a pile of finished pages and weighted it down with a stone, he fed the typewriter another page and went on furiously with his writing.

"I'll just finish, and I'll be up and out of my heaven right away to join you," the doctor called down happily and kept on writing and talking in between writing. "See if I don't write this now, then I'll never get it down, for when a beautiful thought comes knocking, best be quick and open the door to your soul, for she never comes in alone."

And he went on writing and I watched that man, could see and hear the writing, keys banging away, sounding the same as when we'd throw a handful of spoons in the hotel dishwasher, he was sunlit, cap pulled down over his eyes to shield from the glare and in the courtyard I stood in my new dress and leaned on my umbrella and nudged my right red high heel out, it was nice to see someone the first time working on a typewriter, hooking his thought midstream, and I saw the stool the typewriter sat on as well as the stool the doctor sat on each had one leg sawed down to take in the slant on the shed roof, over which the tall wall of the machine shop loomed, the wall that spanned all the way over to the building with the asparagus in the window.

And now the doctor finished up the writing, pulled out the page, and put it on the rest of those blindingly white papers, he doffed his cap, then jammed it back on his head and looked at me, and I raised my eyes, I saw him check me out, check my hairdo, saw him see my beautiful dress, and I lifted my foot to let him see my coral-red high heels.

I saw him looking at me with pleasure, I knew I was being seen the way I wished everyone to see me, but him mainly, the man I'd come for, I wanted him to see me as I ought to be seen, quite different from the first time I'd been, to see me as that Parisian pastry topped with the whipped cream . . . He noticed me and nodded approvingly and I blushed and turned full circle, raised my arms up as though I wished to fly, turned as models do on a catwalk, and my head began to spin . . .

And the doctor straightened, then handed me his pages of writing and asked me to set them over on a small table, the type of table we used to set up back there in Moravia where the town ended and the fields began, where I would place a crucifix and a vase full of peonies and wildflowers, and the priest and procession would pass and stop at the small table to pray for a bountiful harvest. Then the doctor handed me that typewriter, it was tiny and all the keys folded in, like a sacramental tome, and when I glanced at the pages, I noted the machine's German make, Perkeo, a deco typewriter without Czech diacritics, and the doctor's text was loaded with typos, and little wonder, I told myself, when in a few short minutes the doctor had hammered out everything pouring through that head of his . . . And the doctor jumped down the little wall at an angle to the stairs and stood next to me explaining his writing in the courtyard; he took the little table and set it by the wall, near the doorway that led up to Liza's, and with great pride he explained, "Soon as it's sunny, I can't write inside, I've got to get out, I write here all morning and then, afternoons when the sun moves, me and my table move, see, at one o'clock I follow the sun over to here."

He picked up the little table and moved it the few meters over.

"And so I hammer away at my atomic Perkeo *schreibmachine* until the sun slips in behind the laundry room, and then I take my table over to here, till I'm halfway in shade and then the shade cuts my head off, and then the shade keeps advancing till I have to go up onto the little roof, where it stays sunny until sunset . . . but as you can see, the roof slopes, have you any idea how many times I've had to cut the stool and chair legs? You'll never guess! Far too many! The first time I cut too much leg, so when I set my stool up there the angle was worse, so bad my *schreibmachine* would have slid into the courtyard, then I angled the legs in the opposite direction, so far over that the *schreibmachine* slid onto my crotch, and twice I cut the legs on the chair, too, I botched it so badly I had to chop it up and get another one, till finally I had the angle right on both my little chair and my big stool, which, as you have seen for yourself, holds my atomic Perkeo *schreibmachine* perfectly level."

And then what I hoped to happen, happened, a window flew open up on the balcony and out leaned Liza to fasten the window cleats, and once she saw me, she gave a start, but then laughed, I could tell it was a sour laugh, for she'd been taken aback at how good I looked.

"Pipsi, no way, you look incredible, come on, show yourself, no way!"

And she couldn't bear it and vanished from the window, then I heard her shoes clack down the stairwell, then she was at the hallway door, trying to get it open, but there was a pile of rubble still there, so she had to knee the door full force three times to make it open, then she ran into the yard and raised my arms and spun me like a mannequin, delight in her voice, but I was well aware of what I sensed in that voice, envy not just for my dress and my little umbrella but for the fact that I had changed, wasn't on my knees, didn't need help from anybody anymore, because I had helped myself.

The doctor said, "Over to my place again—Miss Pipsi, yes, come on?"

Liza said, "Pipsi, come up for a little coffee, we have so much catching up to do."

"Liza, I'm going over to the doctor's place first," and I started off, carrying that Perkeo typewriter, and Liza turned around, behind me I could hear her angrily closing the door over and over, then I heard her angrily slam the window shut . . .

The doctor's room abutted on the wall of the machine shop, from which a rumbling sound arose, then the high whine of a saw, a whine that shook the doctor's room, like a gigantic dental drill drilling into a molar the size of the doctor's whole apartment. The doctor lit a match and after a time the stove began to roar. The doctor added chopped-up boards and planks to the fire and bits of wood he'd scavenged up at some demolition site. I stood looking at the beautiful asparagus interwoven with ivy, asparagus rising to the ceiling while ivy fell to just below the windows. The angled roof of the shed let in a wedge of blue sky not much larger or different in color from the blue of our state flag. A stem crept up the shed wall and then ran directly across on a wire, cascading shoots and tendrils of wild ivy. Hung from a nail on the shed was a death mask, tied up with wire like a broken earthenware pot, it took very little to recognize it as the doctor's face, the death mask of a soul girdled by tendrils of wild ivy. The doctor gave a start.

"For God's sake, please, sit down."

He offered me a chair, I sat down, I kept leaning against my little umbrella, I crossed my legs and swung my little red Italian high heels to and fro, the high heels I bought today simply because I wished to begin living like a Parisian pastry with whipped-cream topping. I could see the doctor watching my knees, he blushed faintly and swept a hand across his brow.

Then he got up and pointed at the wall, listening. The sound behind the wall grew louder, some sort of giant machine went into high gear, then the sound stopped, and a huge blast rang out, shaking the building foundations, like a blast underground in a coal mine, the stove shuddered and the chimney pipes along the walls rattled and outside the remaining plaster ripped away, several bricks rained down, a cloud of smoke went up in the courtyard, and a pile of mortar and brick went rolling over the slanted roof into the next.

"Beautiful," I said.

"Isn't it though," he said, "and I'm lucky enough to live in such a beautiful building."

A woman came teetering and stumbling across the courtyard, carrying a bail of boards and planks tied into a tarp on her back. When she had waded through the rubble, she turned, undid the knotted bail, and let the load drop to the ground behind her. Now a young gypsy woman appeared at the window, smoothing down her hair, sweating, she extracted a bobby pin from her locks, set it between her lips, and stepped into the room.

"And the gentleman has a lady visitor, good evening," she said, bowing, "there's the gentleman's lumber, yes, for his letting us sleep here, but . . ."

The doctor searched his pockets, then opened the wardrobe and went through the jacket and pants' pockets, then he wrung his hands, blushed, and said, "Loan me twenty crowns." I opened my purse, gave him two tens, which he took and presented to the gypsy woman, who bowed for him, took the bobby pin from her mouth, wiped a hand across her wet brow, and pinned up her hair.

Then to the gypsy the doctor said, "Look, here you go, and when your man starts to act up again, you take your girl and you know where you can come sleep, understand?"

"Oh, the gentleman is kind," the gypsy woman said, eyeing me, and then she repeated it, nodded her head, "Yes, the gentleman is kind." And she went out, collected the tarp from beneath the planks and boards and drew it in her wake, sidling away with a nomadic dance step across the rubble-cluttered courtyard.

"She doesn't have it easy," said the doctor. "Her husband's a drunk, a Czech, he beats her sometimes, so she has to come here, to my place, to sleep, her little girl sleeps in a wardrobe drawer. Well, that's how it goes, but might I invite you for a glass of beer so we may progress to more cheery thoughts?"

The doctor laughed and stroked his face, as if he felt sorry for himself.

■ □ ■ □ ■

CHAPTER FIVE

ACH, HOW GORGEOUS THE COUNTRY *SCHWEINFESTS* ARE, *SCHWEINFESTS* IN the backyard, when stoves are brought outdoors and the aromas all head for the open sky, while the pigs' heads bubble in pots and are then dumped onto butcher blocks in the washhouses, for the doors and windows are thrown open, and all the reeks of a slaughter roar up to the heavens. Still in the Prague of that time, at even the finer hotels, it was the vogue to offer guests a *Schweinfest* once a month. And every guest could barely wait to get a plate of choice hog's head and then white sausage! And so, even at the Hotel Paris we had our first *Schweinfest,* from morning on we sweated in the kitchen and inside two cauldrons pigs' heads boiled away, as steam from the *Schweinfest* rose to the ceiling and exhaust fans couldn't keep pace with the vapor, slowly but inevitably the kitchen turned into a wet hell, steam churned a trail over my way, I sat on my small stool already marking down the first plates of jowl and ear and liver, dollops of horseradish and mustard, it wasn't sweat I felt running down my temples and trickling from my hair, even that running down my back wasn't sweat but steam condensed from the *Schweinfest,* even the waiters sweated it out, and even their tuxedos were soon glistening with the grease. And while guests in the restaurant proper were delighted—some regulars so happy indeed they sent glasses of pilsner to the kitchen, where two cooks were at the table chopping up boiled meat, adding spices, spice aroma mixed with the pungent odor of the *Schweinfest* lifting off their fingers—and while assistant chefs readied large intestines for blood pudding and boiled barley blended with pig blood, everyone at work in the kitchen smelled like they'd been tipped one after the other into a vat of soup. And then the cooks were cussing and swearing over the *Schweinfest,* battling with the sausage filler, because they'd never worked a *Schweinfest* like this before, those two young cooks of ours were getting desperate, outside it was warm, and inside the kitchen, not just our underwear was sticking to us, but our clothing was sticking to our underwear, and so while the sausages boiled away in the pots, we glared at each other spitefully and cursed the very establishment that had come up with the idea of having a *Schweinfest* . . .

And into the kitchen came a huge bouquet of flowers, roses, and I gave a start, because the flowers were coming toward me, and suddenly the roses moved aside and none other than the doctor stood there, in his fedora and linen apron, and the torn shirt, presenting me with the bouquet, and everyone in the kitchen stared at him as though he were an apparition, as though he had just dropped out of the exhaust fans. I couldn't utter a word and somehow my arms had gone numb, not because here stood the man from Na Hrázi Street in Libeň, but because I was embarrassed by the sweat commingled with grease dripping off my face and the reek of *Schweinfest,* so the doctor thrust that bouquet my way and now all of me was buried in roses.

"Help me out," groaned the doctor, "take the bouquet, I had this idea it might make you happy."

And so the cooks frozen behind the stoves began to move again, the fact this man had appeared in the kitchen had paralyzed them also, like the magic wand out of *Sleeping Beauty,* but now the cooks resumed stirring their pots of sausage and blood pudding, afraid of overcooking the sausages. And when the doctor heard them, he said, "May I?"

And they all simply stared at him, none of them with the nerve to throw him out, so surprised they'd been by the man in the fedora and linen apron, who now stepped up to the cauldrons, raised his hand, and said, "Look now, sausages have come to the top, and you know they're ready when you can twist the spits at each end, like winding a clock, that's when they're done!"

And he nabbed one of the sausages that had bubbled up and said happily, "At any moment now, the sausages overcook—they burst and it's all over!"

And then the doctor in the trampled shoes came to me and said with downcast eyes, "Tomorrow's Saturday, will you be coming to Libeň again? We'll go swimming . . . up by the weir, yes?"

So he stood there and blushed, and the young cooks were ladling the sausages into buckets, from which sprang the *Schweinfest* stench, and grease dripped down from the ceiling and the steam ran down all the walls and the doctor burbled on, "In some way I went over it in my mind yesterday, I have these enormous hangovers where I think small. Like I have now . . . Five times I paced around the Hotel Paris with these flowers, five times I came in and went out again . . . and now I finally made up my mind and made it all the way in."

And there he stood, the waiters standing in line with their plates of sausage and horseradish, I wrote in all their bills very rapidly, and one of the cooks came over and took the doctor by one torn sleeve and inquired, "When's the blood pudding going to be ready, then, when's the headcheese?"

And the doctor picked up a long wooden skewer from the cutting board, sharpened it with a butcher's knife, and then he and the cook strode over to the cauldrons where the blood pudding and headcheese were boiling, the doctor leaned over and pricked the blood pudding and advised the cook, "As long as blood's still coming out, leave them, but when the chocolate comes running out, then it's all done."

And he handed the cook the skewer, bowed to the kitchen crew, blushed, and apologized, "Please excuse me."

And out the kitchen he ran, and I sat buried in roses there, but embarrassed still, because the grease off our first *Schweinfest* was running between my breasts and soaking into my bra, I could even feel sweat commingled with grease running down my thighs, I could feel my underwear stick to the white smock, was horrified that if I stood the sweat would pass right through the smock and there'd be a puddle on the chair. I was feeling this while keeping my grip on the bouquet of roses.

Borek came over and set the flowers in a vase, then put the vase on my little table and told me, "That gentleman is in love with you, it's obvious at first glance."

And I went even redder, I felt if I pulled on the elastic band of my underwear right now that my sweat-soaked undies would slap back and stick to my skin. And I went redder still when the doors flew open and there stood our two delighted regulars, crying, "We've never eaten better sausage in Prague, a keg of pilsner for a kitchen like this!"

And the doors closed and the cooks doled out the sausage and blood pudding, the bartender came in bearing an armload of brimming glasses, and Head Chef Bauman rose from his table, placed a greasy hand on mine, and said with a smile, "So Eliška, my little bride, it looks like you won't need a permit to live in Prague anymore, and you'll be in permanent employ here with us, I can see it all now, that saddle of venison we carted over here together, when the time comes I'm going to do that saddle as a cold roast for your wedding. I'm going to leave that venison in the freezer and personally bring it over."

He looked at me as I nodded my head like a bobblehead Chinese doll, tears in my eyes, the waiters in a row with their plates of horseradish and blood pudding fresh out of the pots, these waiters were impatient, they wanted nothing more than to be back in the fresh air of the restaurant. Head Chef wiped his face with a napkin and returned to his tables, because it was time he began slicing for his specialties, because he wanted no more to do with this *Schweinfest,* the very idea of this in-house *Schweinfest* happening in such a famous hotel made him ill . . .

And that night I came home late, because the management decided after catering for that size of a *Schweinfest* anyone who had no bathroom at home had the right to take their turn at bathing in one of the empty hotel rooms. Once I was in the tub and lathered, I was horrified at the amount of dirt that came off, and when I stepped out of the tub, it had a layer of grease over it, and I only felt better once all the water had drained off and I rinsed the tub down twice. Standing there over the tub I recalled how practically no one in the kitchen could swallow a morsel, myself included, we were so saturated with that horrible smell, the only thing we could do to keep from throwing up was drink beer . . . So I went home with my bouquet of roses, hair still wet after my bath; Ema, that second mother of mine, she didn't have to wait up for me, but the only reason she did, and the only reason she'd kept the sauerbraten she'd brought from her Two Cats restaurant warm was so she could sit there eyeing me reproachfully, as I set the roses in a big vase, I just waited for her to start in lamenting about how I should be more grateful, and so I rearranged the roses, I delighted in them and was in bliss, while an irascible Ema set plates on the table, she didn't bother to ask if I was hungry, or even if I felt like eating, she served up the dumplings and ladled out gravy, added meat, and sat down and started to eat.

"Where've you been for so long? Twice I had to heat it up."

"Mother, I don't feel like it today, I can't eat."

"What? Ach, what's happening to you Eliška? I should heat it up again? And besides . . . people from the town council were here, asking when I'll register you, you *are* still living here on the sly, working at the hotel on the sly, not even a change or transfer of address filed from your previous residence; they're putting you on notice, you'll have to return to your last place of residence and employment, probably, because I can't register for you here, I'm living on the sly here myself, on a sublet . . . and you're out shopping and spending money on shoes and clothes and now you come in late with a bouquet of roses."

"Mother," I said, "you know yourself how it is with me, I'm a mess, all right, but Mother, somehow I've recovered, I want to live again, it's as though I've been sick for all these years."

"Good, so know what, Eliška? Tomorrow we'll take a steamboat ride, what do you say?"

"But, Mother, that won't work . . . I promised someone I'd go swimming with him."

"But you can't do that. Were you not about to get married? Are you over it so fast?" Mother cried at me and got up angrily, carrying her plate over to the sink and laying my plate of dumplings under the bouquet of roses.

I got up, the sauerbraten's smell wafting up through the rose bouquet incensed me, and I got up so fast I bumped against a chair, I moved the plate away and said, "What marriage? That shameless groom of mine ran off with another, he knocked me so low, you yourself know, I didn't want to live, I wanted to leave this world."

Mother put her head in her hands and said, "He left you, but you'll see, he'll be back before the month is up, I know what he's like, you'll see, he'll be back to us."

I sat down on the bed, then I stretched out on the blankets, my feet ached, I gazed at the ceiling and repeated, "He'll be back to us? What do you mean, *us*?"

"Well, to you as a groom, of course, and to me as a son."

"But, Mother, I don't want him to be back with *us* again . . . Why *us*? Let him be back, I've got nothing against it, back to you though, to me, never again."

Mother tore open a drawer, yanked out an envelope, and stood shaking a letter over me triumphantly, "So here *is* his letter. It says he's thinking about you, hoping you can forgive him, here it is, in black and white!"

"Not interested anymore, Mother."

"So you don't even want to read it?"

"Mother, I've already been put through the wringer by that jewel of yours, that jerk of mine, it's too late for anything now." I sat up on the blankets, groaning at the ache in my feet, and continued, "Mother, I know I was in love with your Jirka, I know how beautifully he played guitar—the guitar's my favorite instrument, Mother—Jirka had an electric banjo, a silver-and-blue tux, lovely hair, but what good did it do me when I was his washerwoman and servant? He had to be a big shot, always impeccable, while I was perched at home to do his washing and always be in wait for him, sometimes two days before he came back from those women, but because I loved him, I forgave him everything, and when I went down to see him at the place he was playing, his two tramps sitting there, all done up, him gazing at them like they were his muses or something, like those two sluts were the only ones he was playing for, they sent him up cognacs while I sipped grenadine, and when the set ended, those sluts fell all over themselves, they clapped so hard, and he did a bow and I just sat there in a corner, sipping my grenadine, and then went home while he went with those two draculettes, off to some other bar, since they were the ones to pick up the tab, and then he'd come back penniless, while I'd be the one handing him money for the next day."

"How can you talk like this?" Mother said, covering her ears.

"How? My aunt in Vienna, Daddy's sister, wrote to me, she told me not to forget what kind of family I come from, not to present myself as a tramp, but to present myself like a Parisian pastry with whipped cream on top . . . and that letter set me on my feet, while that pap your little son writes you . . ."

Mother yelled, "What he writes *us,* read, it says, 'Dear Mommy and Eliška!'" She wagged the letter and pointed at the words, but I turned the other way from her and said, "Daddy, if he rose from the grave, if he caught sight of me like this, would have to thrash me with his cane, if he saw how I allowed myself to be humbled, and for what? Just for love, just because I loved Jirka . . . Even though we lost everything, I'm still the one who lived in a house of thirteen rooms and had a nanny, and Daddy had a Studebaker and a chauffeur, and Mommy, two maids. And with his logs and his wood, Papa was king of middle Europe and a sought-after adviser not just in Brno, but in Vienna and Budapest and Lviv, and we had a factory."

"Had, had, but for God's sake, Eliška, the Germans lost the war, so you lost everything. You even lost the war," cried my second mother.

"I lost nothing. How was I supposed to do anything? When the war ended I was sixteen, I didn't lose a war, but it feels like I did battle regardless, lost everything and the one thing left is a thing called honor, something I forgot, but have found again, now."

I rose straightening and rearranging the bouquet of roses . . .

■ □ ■ □ ■

CHAPTER SIX

I ENTERED THE BUILDING ON NA HRÁZI STREET, THE HALLWAY STANK of wet walls, I shivered from the cold, but when I was coming through the tunnel, out in the courtyard the sun shone. And sitting outside her flat in the sunshine was the neat lady, the floor tiles glittering spotlessly, water glinting, and the neat lady sat out there in her violet panties and bra, sat on a chair with an issue of *Saturday Ahoy* in her lap. She was turned, her massive back to the sun.

"The doctor's home," she said, pushing her glasses up the bridge of her nose.

"Thank you," I said, and I could not prevent myself from peeking into her flat, on the other side of the window the artificial flowers glowed in sunlight, the bed under the window was meticulously made, decorated with plush teddy bears, a doll, little embroidery blankets. I went up to the courtyard with the sun and there on a chair sat the gypsy lady, the one I had recently loaned twenty crowns, she was smoking and the doctor stood beside her, leaned over a sink and scrubbing a pot with a wire brush, last pot, other pots and plates laid out to dry in the sun upside down, dripping water, and the doctor continued to scrub furiously.

"Hello," I said, "well, here I am."

"Hello, madame." The gypsy lady blew out smoke, one leg crossing over her dirty multicolored skirt.

"Hello," the doctor said, and he didn't raise his eyes, and on he went, furiously scrubbing the bottom of the pot.

And I stood there in the courtyard in my new dress, the one I'd bought in the House of Fashions, a linen dress which instead of buttons had little green dice, I stood there leaning on my blue umbrella and in my other hand I held a mesh bag with my bathing suit and a packet of schnitzels and bread. And the doctor kept on cursing and scrubbing the pot, "Damn this work! And my head splitting like a four-year-old cabbage!"

Then he straightened, and when he looked at me, I could see he was tired and he'd been drinking heavily the night previous, he had circles under his eyes and his hands shook so much the pot he held chattered in them. Then he set the pot down and went into the kitchen, into his room, and came back with a chair which he placed in the sun for me, and the gypsy woman went on in her alto voice with the story she'd been recounting for the doctor before I had arrived, "Yes, sir, that type of gypsy wedding ends with the bride and groom on their knees in the middle of the room, and gypsies, wedding party, they lay hold on their open bottles of red wine and they sing gypsy wedding songs, and music, violins and dulcimers play and the gypsies tip red wine slowly over your kneeling bride and groom, and wine runs over the floor, and down the wine runs over the bride and groom, yes, sir, that's gypsy tradition, whenever there's a house wedding."

I watched the gypsy woman and could see how proud she was of what she was unfolding, the slow way she described those gypsy weddings, although I could see the only reason the doctor kept on at the pot was to gain more time for his recovery, it was ten thirty, the time a hangover is at its peak, and it was pretty obvious his head ached, exactly as he said, like an overblown four-year-old cabbage. And the gypsy woman went on in her elated voice.

"Or this thing I saw, swear to God, I did. We had this funeral in Sokolov, when our baron passed on. Gypsies came from all parts, as far away as Vienna and Budapest even, Slovakia and Moravia, we pushed all the tables together, in this dilapidated villa, pushed the tables all together in the main hall, we sat the baron down at the head and then started in singing our gypsy funeral dirges and drinking, and with every new round we'd give the dead baron's mouth a shot of booze, then went on with the songs, and it was drawing on dark already, and the baron kept on getting these stiff shots, the drink the gypsies gave him from their glasses, and all night through, and into the next day, the gypsies took their turns honor-guarding our dead baron, and through into the second and third day, the rounds of booze kept on coming, and our baron taking shots till our baron was liquored to the gills . . . Yup, then and then only, did we bury him."

So spoke the gypsy woman, and solemn she was and looking off into the distance, as though transcribing everything she spoke of, and all of a sudden she was beautiful and her long eyelashes stood still, staring off into the past, to Sokolov, to the dilapidated villa where the gypsies bade their dead baron a fond farewell.

And the doctor persisted in scrubbing his pot meticulously, too meticulously in fact, while I, who had been almost ready to get up and leave some time ago, simply sat in the sun there, my legs crossed, propped on my umbrella, then I got up and took the string bag, the blue string bag, which held my bathing suit and the Viennese schnitzels, and set it in the shade out of the sun. And at that instant the doctor looked my way gratefully; by some means recognition that I was making sure the food wouldn't go soggy in the sun drove him over his hangover. And one time more he plunged the pot into the tepid water, rinsed it, and when he looked into the bottom, there was still a skim of encrusted meat. And his sleeve slid, almost into the grimy water. I put down my umbrella and went over and stood right next to the doctor, he held his arm out, and I rolled his sleeve, touched his arm, rolled his sleeve up, and for the first time felt the muscles in his arms, I took my time and rolled up that shirtsleeve in slow motion and made my hands greasy.

And the gypsy woman looked on into the distance, went on smoking and telling us everything she saw, "Sir, once All Saints' Day's here, I'll take you and me to the two barons' graves, up to Olšany, when gypsies come again from miles around, and for two days we sit there, squat on the ground and sing our dirges, and every gypsy as visits those graves brings some kind of gift . . . And so by the first night of All Saints', the graves are already buried in flowers, thousands of carnations in vases, dozens of gift baskets, hundred-crown notes strewn about, and five hundreds, yes, five hundreds even, and the barons' graves are as lovely as the Pramen deli shop windows, there's Viennese Meinl chocolate and Hungarian salami . . . me, I'm saving up toward a little gift basket for our baron, and that's why I'm back here now, because that Czech of mine drank the deposit dry, and so I'm come to ask your gentleman here to lend me a little pot of yesterday's leftovers, give me a little goose fat." The gypsy woman broke off speaking because I stood at the sink, no longer looking at her, but off to the Olšany cemetery, to the two barons in their graves, graves buried in banknotes and gift baskets and carnations by the thousands.

And even the doctor stood enchanted, keeping his hold on the pot, entranced by the young gypsy woman's story, whose soul, once she noted the effect, came back into the courtyard to remind us of the real reason for her coming. Now she rose heavily up out of the chair, she had torn white tennis shoes and tanned brown legs caked in dirt. When she saw me look at her legs, she shrugged and laughed, and I saw a number of her teeth knocked out.

"And he beats up on me too, heheeee!" she shouted and stuck a finger into her gums and splayed her teeth at me, and even the few she had left were already blackened.

And from downstairs the sound of water filling a bucket arrived, a chair scraped along the ground, and when the sound rose to the edge of the bucket, you could hear water topple into a second empty bucket, and again the rising sound of tap water angrily rushing and then a loud powerful splash and then the sound of a wire brush and the neat woman grumbling, washing down the tiled hallway beneath her window, "I'm a neat woman, I can't bear dirt!"

"Miss Pipsi," the doctor said, "if you will be so kind, over there on the window is a big pot, and beside it half a tub of goose fat, bring it here. I believe I'm going to have to throw out this pot, goulash is so burnt into it, damn! If at least my head didn't hurt like a three-year-old cabbage!"

And I stepped from the hot afternoon sun and into the shade, went in through the door, the stove not on, shivered at the cold, grabbed his pot and his goose fat, and sprinted back into the courtyard as fast as I could, and when I strode out of the shade, I felt better again in the sunshine.

"But, man, is your place fresh!" I said.

"Tell me about it," the doctor growled, "my place you need to heat the most in July and August, who'm I kidding? Practically year round!"

And the gypsy woman reached out her hands, I handed the pot over to her, for a minute our fingers touched and we looked into one another's eyes and smiled. I saw this gypsy woman loved the doctor, saw they slept together, but this gypsy woman loved the doctor differently, loved him because of always having somewhere to turn when in need, a place to sleep first of all, and now, as I could see, a place to get a bite to eat, where she could cadge some money for cigarettes when she didn't have enough and for her little daughter, the one who slept in a dresser drawer at the doctor's . . . And the gypsy woman set off through the yard. I pulled a rag down off the clothesline stretched between the washhouse and an old hand pump, and from downstairs came the noise of the neat lady bellowing at the gypsy woman, "Out of my way, you black mouth!"

And the splash from a bucket rang out, then the slap of tennis shoes, the gypsy woman pumping water from her tennis shoes, yelling filthy gypsy obscenities, her voice sounding off the wet hallway; I was rinsing plates in the sink, stacking them one on top of the other, the doctor went into his room and brought a wet carpet out into the sun, he draped it over the carpet stand, then dunked his scrub brush, that same scrub brush he'd been scrubbing the floor with the first time I'd been round, and he cleaned the sodden carpet and said to me, "Is it likely, you tell me, is it even any way likely the poet Bondy would pull a stunt like this? Tell me what you would do to that poet, if you wined and dined him like I did, downing beer all afternoon long, even over at Vaništa's, bringing back two pitchers as a nightcap, to toast our in-house wedding, tell me, as a lady, what you would say if you woke up in the middle of the night to the sound of water running out there . . . I had a sense of what it was, but foolishly stuck to the hope it was just the tap, but I turned the light on and my fears were fulfilled, Bondy seated on the edge of the bed peeing onto this carpet here, there you have him, the poet who translated Christian Morgenstern, what would you have to say if you caught sight of that?"

I stood up, picked out the dried plates and cutlery, and said, "I'd tell him, 'I'll kill you!'"

"Now there you see," said the doctor, whisking water off a pot, "that's what you would say, because you have a kindly disposition, but I'm a criminal, with an ex-con's disposition, so I didn't kill him, to kill a poet's a sin, but I did say, 'Okay, Bondy, my boy, an eye for an eye then, *lex talionis*,' and unzipped my fly and peed in his shoes, because Bondy has always had a shine for his little shoes. But apart from that, madame, we had a delightful night last night, there was a wedding going in Ludmila Street, so we determined we'd have our own little wedding too, and Páša came, crafty little bugger I've known for years, the drink's our bond, one time it got so bad we drank our way not only through our paychecks but on into our advances, we were afraid to go out anywhere because we owed everybody money everywhere, to this day I still owe my landlady half a year's back rent, so Páša and I etched a solemn oath with a nail, first day of spring we would take the cure at Skála's, but then gave up on it, and Šally came down too, the stage manager from Teplice, a German Communist from Sudetenland, one who loves the theater above his own family, that's why his dancer missus from the Alhambra nightclub ran off with the kids, and then we brought in this groom for a bit, one of the regulars there at Vaništa's, because the poet Bondy couldn't bring himself to believe the tales about the groom's face being as badly darned up as a pair of battered socks . . . and so he comes over to see us, and Bondy's delighted, in fits of laughter, throwing up his arms and beating his little fists on the walls, and then he ran out into the courtyard, and as Mrs. Slavíčková upstairs was toting her milk by in the dark, he slammed into her and the milk flew, and to top it all off Bondy shouted, 'You old bat, can't you watch where you're going when you have a great Czech poet out here in your courtyard dancing?' You see, when that groom was a young boy he was carving a little boat out of a slab of bark, and as he admired his handiwork, a swarm of wasps came at him, and Vaníček, that's the groom's name, started fencing with his jackknife to prevent his face from being stung, but as he defended himself, he botched his swordplay and ten times crisscrossed his own face, and now it looks like somebody juiced his face like a lemon . . . There you have him, Vaníček, our Libeň dandy, Jirka, soon as you say the name, a particular picture comes to mind . . . of a little dandy, always the clean shirt, beautiful tie, jacket, all kinds of little pullovers, that's Jirka! And he always has new shoes with these raised heels and fancy laces, in sum, the man about town who spends more than he rakes in, but the man about town nonetheless, Jirka, whom girls chase after like a chicken after spit."

The doctor paused and then went on cleansing the wet carpet with the yellow brush until suddenly he stopped, felt the back of his head, and to his delight, "My headache's started to go, still hurts, but only like a two-year-old cabbage now."

And upstairs, above the doctor's flat, up where the balcony spread along the second floor, someone started closing windows angrily, grumbling to herself, and then a door opened and a woman came out, her two kids in tow, all dressed in their Sunday best, the woman locked the door up angrily, then three pairs of shoes descended the staircase, the iron gate to the circular stair swung open, and the woman took it by the handle and slammed the gate so hard the whole edifice shook, then she shoved her teenage son and daughter ahead, her daughter's hair still wet and neatly combed, her son's parted perfectly down the middle, both kids smiled for the doctor, while above and behind their mother's angry eyes glared. The kids wanted to give the doctor a hello, but the lady gripped them by the shoulders, and with her nails pressured them into not bowing. And so three pairs of shoes sped on down the stairs, to the woman's shouts, "That's the last straw, Mrs. Beranová! This is no apartment house, it's a drinking den! Did you get any sleep at all last night!"

"I didn't," neat lady Beranová said, "but so what?"

"How are we supposed to sleep with our windows open when a mess of drunks are down there screaming like baboons? How do they laugh on and on? How come they don't tire out? Lunatics!"

And Mrs. Beranová's cheerful voice came back, "Lunatics, true, but tire? I get tired out, you get tired, your husband tires, everything's tired, the only ones not tired are the drunkards. Because they're busy entertaining."

I listened and my heart beat for the doctor, who was pale and rubbing his forehead and saying cheerfully, "If I had any character, I'd go hurl myself under a train, or into the Vltava, but since I'm a person lacking in any character whatsoever, what do I do? Life goes on."

I listened and my heart no longer beat for the doctor, but that jerk of mine, Jirka, turned up, he was a Jirka too, the doctor had described his nature to a tee, without knowing, when he'd told me of the groom from Ludmila Street, the fellow who'd been there the night before with his clean shirts and fancy neckties, just like that jewel of mine, always the new shoes with the built-up heels, Jirka, who spent more than he ever made, little Jirka, mommy's little boy, who made off with some slut who drank my pond full of tears dry, Jirka, who shipped me to Prague so his mommy and I could prep our little party while he high-lifed it somewhere in Vienna with somebody else.

"You know," continued the doctor. "Youth is a mindless happiness, but one day, while I'm still alive, I'll settle down enough to abide my own death. You know, Pipsi, you know what my life is? I'm so glad to be alive, alive in this world, whatever beautiful thing I see, I'm married to instantly, not just people I'm in love with, but things, work, ach, how I've loved everything I've done, loved being an insurance man, loved being a dispatcher, loved being at work up in the Poldinka mills . . . Ach! Every beam that came out of the mill, every blessed one had the stamp of a beautiful woman's head in steel, a ringleted head seared with stars, do you know, Poldinka was the name of the Jewish girl the factory owner loved so strongly he had the image of her little head stamped into the steel, and still today that beloved face goes out into the world aboard every beam . . . Do you know you have the same profile as Poldinka? And when you visit me on the job, just see how proudly I bale the paper and load the bales, how happy I am being wherever I happen to be. Because life is not at all a valley of tears, but a wedding and a feast, that's why I hold weddings in this building here and why I'm fond of gypsies, why I make some squeamish, too . . . But you wait till you see Ludva tonight, last night he was here too, ach, that butcher! One handsome person, a muscleman, a Marlon Brando look-alike, blond hair and blue eyes and muscles out to here! That guy, when we worked up in Kladno, at Poldinka Mill, we'd load the scrap into bins in the scrap yard, and Ludva would cut the axles off of cars using a welding torch and toss the half-ton of scrap right into the bins, and we're still mates, for wherever Ludva goes he turns women's heads, they'll even get off the tram and follow where he goes, that's how gorgeous that Marlon dressed up as Ludva is . . . and yesterday Bondy sat here eyeballing and listening and drinking his copious quantities of beer and stroke, stroking his beard and yelling, 'Doctor, by God, all this stuff around you, write, man, I could murder you! You're a magnet for stories, ready-made!' And I don't even know what it is about me, but I attract kids most, courtyard here used to be full of them, and since the building's owned by Mrs. Fialová, all the males here get called Fiala, it's not just me kids call Mr. Fiala, they even call Wulli that. But only out in the street nowadays, as soon as I'd get home, they'd come right in, the courtyard here and my place packed . . . always with kids . . . Up until the projectionist at the Metro's case, cutting up that little boy, in the projection booth, slow and sadistic with a pair of scissors, as soon as the news spread through Prague, I was here sitting typing on my atomic Perkeo *schreibmachine,* kids playing away here in the courtyard and me writing happily on, when two women flew up the stairs, beat the kids over the heads, and screamed at me, struggling with the kids and kicking them downstairs, telling them they're never to come back here, that if they do, they will beat them so hard they'll vomit, and I sat there and went on writing, I had an idea and knew if I missed getting it down pat I'd lose it for good, so they went on screaming at me and waving their arms, their eyes rolling back into their heads, 'Our brats'll end up like that little boy in the Metro Theater!' And I went on writing and hammering at the typewriter, and it wasn't until I'd finished writing and the women and the children had gone that I played back all the guff those women had poured into my skull, and was horrified by their very thinking that I, who loves children so dearly, could be capable of cutting them up, like that sadist at the Metro."

And now neat lady Mrs. Beranová stepped into the courtyard, dragging a chair behind her and her copy of *Saturday Ahoy,* her glasses on the tip of her nose, and still in her violet panties and bra, she drew up her chair and said, "Shade's starting in downstairs . . . you and me we are the one nature, Doctor, we must follow the sun. But! Nobody's here, they're all gone, so look here, a pot of chicken à la pheasant's at my place for you, a little treat for you, two helpings, if the lady feels like some . . . but I can see!" She nodded at my mesh bag, at parceled schnitzels and bread. "You're probably off to the river too, eh?"

■ □ ■ □ ■

CHAPTER SEVEN

THE DOCTOR AND I STEPPED OUT ONTO NA HRÁZI STREET, I WALKED by his side, balancing on my little umbrella; the doctor wore gray pants and a blue T-shirt, people greeted the doctor, and he returned their greetings enthusiastically, I felt how each greeting was a pleasure for him, at times he'd say hello to people he didn't know, they'd stop, look back, then continue on, we got to the main street, streetcars went by in their red stripes, stopped, people got on and off, for the first time I noticed people dressed in their finery, old folks strolled past Cafeteria World, in their Sunday best as well, strolled through the square past the mansion, sat on benches, packed benches among flowers, the doctor walked right by my side, took my elbow, in fact, for a time, and so we walked along, attracting attention together, eyes by the dozen on us, unable to tear themselves away, from my cotton dress to my red high heels, to my little umbrella, those eyes followed, I could feel them watch my every step, and then another set of eyes, as the stream of pedestrians gathered in an old alley of chestnut trees, under the branches. The square spanned the River Rokytka, which rippled and ran by the shady chestnut alley, here the principal promenade of Sunday-afternoon strollers flowed past, colorful prams pushed by young mothers, bright-colored clothing, all to form a river flowing with clothing and faces, and movement; I felt myself blush a little, the doctor led me lightly by the elbow and thus we set course for the colorful mass of people, all out for a prelunch stroll, in the river lay wire baskets and pots and even an old stove, very like the doctor's in his room; in that manner we reached where the Rokytka emptied into a dead branch of the Vltava, on the other side of the river, over a small factory, a sign shone in the sun, MANUFACTURERS OF PATENT WASHTUBS. There, where the little river purled, then quieted into the old branch of the Vltava, sat fishermen by the dozen, watching their lines, people stood at the river's railings, merely watching the floats and fishing lines, and you could see on the other side of the alley now a field of children, and benches with mothers and grannies and nannies, all sitting with their faces to the sun, stock-still, and from the field a path wound uphill through shrubs and trees blossoming, above which towered giant planes and poplars, the jut of a red chimney, and at the top of the path long tables and benches filled with oldsters in Sunday best playing cards, you could hear the cards slap, the players' laughter . . . Both hills were awash in people going up or down, people obscured partially or lost behind the bushes and trees, it was like attending a grand theater, seeing a color film, I never imagined people were still able to keep Sunday . . .

And I walked and I was happy, not for the doctor being there beside me, but for my taking a good look about me for the first time, and I saw how the people lived, people perhaps the same way off as me, who had businesses and restaurants and factories, who owned property, but by some means came to terms with it and kept Sunday as though nothing had ever happened, but I saw even though most young men and women probably worked similar jobs to mine, they all had their one goal, one place to go, and they kept these Sundays as a gift, a little something, and I wanted nothing else right then except to go out walking every Sunday, out swimming; under his arm the doctor carried an inflatable mattress, I carried my bathing suit and didn't know where we would swim, everything ahead was a surprise . . . At that hour in the morning, as we walked, we said nothing, we simply looked about us, the doctor, happy I saw the same things as he, and I, glad this person I walked with, who buried me in flowers at work, had quickened in me an interest for something besides that torture with my fiancé, in fact, whenever I gave him a thought, I was glad he left me and married another, this day and this morning made it good, because as I walked, I saw into people's lives through their eyes, and perhaps, for the first time in my life, even noted the scenery, the Vltava's dead branch dotted with little boats on the far shore, for the first time I looked beyond *me,* I admired the old trunks on the trees, raised my head and gazed through branches into the sky, couldn't hold back, and I touched the old bark on the tree's trunk, I put my arm up to rub my fingers against the leaves . . . I saluted the lot, and as soon as I looked into the doctor's eyes, I saw his face light up, in some way he grew younger on all I was seeing for the first time, and nodded and let go a profound sigh . . .

So we reached the alley's end, people in their finery already on their way back to Sunday lunches, the Vltava offshoot emptied into the main river flow, along which sailed a holiday steamboat, leaving a plume of light smoke and the muffled music of a brass band in its wake, the whole boat brimmed with holidaymakers, in fact you could barely make out the steamboat itself, it was a cluster of faces and colored T-shirts, a cluster of folk sailing off Roztoky way. And the doctor went down to the path which skirted the river, there the view opened into a wide valley drowned in greenery, there were red-chalet and cottage rooftops protruding, and on the far side rose a long green hill, so steep the crisscross of trails leading to the top stood out, the hill so steep you could see buildings and cottages, gardens with people at work, and atop the hill a fine mansion with a small tower, and a stone wall wrapped around, and straight off the wall ran a cliff into the Vltava valley, and below the cliff, house and villa turrets jutted. And in that valley, where I had never been before, I walked by small houses and plots of land, the plots were vegetable gardens leading down to the river, everywhere women in aprons watered their vegetables, or tended their gardens, every house was open, you could see stoves, couches, the houses ending in a path lined with tall aspens, though windless, the aspen leaves shivered and made sweet music, the sun shone and elsewhere a bell tolled noon, across the alley, which turned into a dirt track . . . gardens, overgrown with fruit trees, stretching on up to Bulovka, and here and there, amidst the greenery, a colored shirt flashes, a shirtsleeve, now and then a flowerbed stooped over by a figure, I even caught a watering can, a watering can ascending, water poured from its font spraying rain . . . I was surprised to have it in me, I saw so many beautiful things, people, trees, I'd never noticed before, it's not like I never had the time, but these Sundays I always passed in a daze, engrossed in my own problems, as a matter of fact, even as a little girl I'd never remarked how beautiful the trees were, how fine the leaves and bushes were, how beautiful flowerbeds were, truly, I'd never noticed, till then, how beautiful vegetables were, vegetables watered by fat ladies dressed in just their enormous aprons, aprons nobody put on anymore. Actually, a whole transformation was brought about by the person striding next to me like my nanny, my tutor, no need for the person to explain, or lecture, in fact it suited me fine and dandy, I was stubborn, took after my mother, let him try preaching to me, I wouldn't have looked at a thing on purpose, or noticed, I would have sulked, teared up, stared at the ground . . . But he just walked beside me, gazing around, and I looked where he looked, saw almost what he did, didn't check my watch, I almost wished time would quit, so I might have walked in that space we had entered together, forever.

"Thank you," said I.

"Hihihi, don't thank me, but all you see . . . first it's all there," he tapped his hand to his forehead, and then, to his eyes, "here. Pelc Tyrolka," he said and pointed to a two-story building, ten arched windows, a pink construction amidst the greenery. "Where I used to go dancing, a dance hall's there on the second floor, downstairs a little restaurant, outside three red tables with white tablecloths, the Pelc Tyrolka, for lovers."

"But we're not going there," I said.

"Still time for it, but over yonder is Kuchyňka's, a garden restaurant that admitted kids too, Jugendstil, a piece of Grinzing, a memory of old Austria, a smidgeon of Vienna, but all deserted, no people, for our eyes only, eyes that appreciate what's been discarded as old rubbish. Nobody guards, there's no security for the place, we can go up and take a walk around," said the doctor and smiled. Then he walked ahead of me, crossed the road, and on an overgrown sidewalk leading up to Kuchyňka's, through trees you could see the rambling two-story restaurant, before which stood trees in four rows at the end of the overgrown path. In the center popped up a bandstand, small pinnacle askance, a music bandstand, crammed with broken benches and busted rusting folding chairs, the bandstand columns were wrought into ornamental garlands and were crumbling, as was the peeling tar-paper roof. There, among the dozens of old trees stood the bandstand, but by the path side were two children's gazebos, leaf covered, children's gazebos with small shattered roofs and points, children's gazebos with see-through latticework walls, the doctor tiptoed into one gazebo, brushed some leaves off a table, rubbed his hands together, "This is where we shall eat."

And he took the string bag from me, unwrapped the food, took out a schnitzel, and began hungrily to eat, I had some too, but I didn't feel like it, since this was the design of a villa we once had in Losiny, a villa top-decorated with the same small turrets, our Losiny villa took its design from the villas of Salzburg, *fachwerk* walls, but roof and column adorned with identical wood garlands, in one corner of the garden there was even the same model of children's gazebo, a children's arbor, where as kids we breakfasted and had snacks in the afternoons, where we would play, where we would wonder at our beautiful gazebo, it was just for us, for the children, our gazebo garlanded in initials and vine leaves carved out of wood, decked out precisely, like a building on Paris Street. The doctor wiped his mouth with a handkerchief.

"Could hold three hundred people, this garden restaurant, but we're into an epoch that doesn't like this level of beauty, inside there over at Pelc Tyrolka they had tables made of linden and huge benches against the walls, and heavy wood chairs, but last year they ripped them all out, and instead put in cold plastic tables and plastic chairs, for now the era's different, and beautiful that we two are here to take this beauty in, no dragons, no guardian angels to watch over. I mean to say, it's as though a board broke and we are caught in the splinters of the break, the splinters pierce us, stick in our bodies—so all the while we have a view of the calamity . . . Don't regret a thing anymore, anything you once had, everything Liza let me know about, all gone, lost, and all you can do is look on it with pride, you can look down at your fall, but you must always look up, that fall you must smile at, only then can you escape and free yourself and be as happy as I, who when he sees this former garden restaurant, bleeds, and so my blood, my tears for old Austria, turn into laughter, look in my eyes, I'm proud to have eyes like a Hasidic Jew, wide-set like the rabbi's son from Belz, so what *is* my crime? That we drink beer, my friend with the Jewish name Egon and Bondy, that he peed on my rug? All of us up in Na Hrázi Street who make the in-house weddings, we're all actually children who've been expelled from these pavilions, these arbors, gazebos . . . you actually belong to us, because you are a child too, a child who has ceased crying . . . But that sun-drenched hillside, those people scattered about the hillsides and gardens sunning themselves, you see they are as precious gems, look at everything about you as if you were peering into a jeweler's case, and then you can always lift up your eyes just like Bondy, imaginary son of a rabbi from Galicia, who sees into the essence of all tragic and poetic and therefore beautiful and murdered things, just like the painter Chagall."

And he blushed, out of breath from what he was saying, he was talking loud, as though what he uttered was for the benefit of everyone on the hillsides, everyone walking by the river, everyone playing tennis down there on the eight courts, all the people in Prague, not solely all people on Czech land, but in Vienna and Brno and Jihlava . . . all the people, all over Central Europe.

And he wrapped up the rest of the food, put it quickly in the bag, he took my umbrella, jammed the mattress firmly under his arm, put out his hand and I took it, hand in hand we ran down the overgrown path, ran as though we'd stolen something, as though we'd set light to the bandstands and gazebos and arbors, we ran until we halted at the bridge, by the tennis courts, where the doctor released my hand, he was breathing hard, I was breathing hard, blood rushing to my head, I couldn't catch my breath, the tennis players on all the courts stopped their games, they had watched us run down, already seen us from up top, and now once they saw us begin to smile, saw us burble into laughter, they relaxed and returned with a greater focus on their volleys and services and lobs, to disputes over iffy shots . . . We walked past players sweating, players in white shorts, players half-naked in their wire tennis cages like birds in an aviary at the zoo, they poured with sweat, the noon sun blazing down on them, but they were happy every one, even the ones losing, and the ones cursing over a bad ball . . .

■ □ ■ □ ■

CHAPTER EIGHT

WE FOLLOWED A NARROW PATH ALONG THE VLTAVA TOWARD THE sound of rushing water, somewhere ahead was a weir, water rumbled and fell relentlessly, the river gathered speed, we walked along the riverbank into the sun, over on the far side poplar and alder soared. "Go on ahead, will you?" the doctor asked, "I have to step aside for a second," and he blushed, for this must have been about the fifth time he asked me to go ahead. When he caught up to me, he was breathing hard; here and there a small stair led down to the river, the doctor bolted down each and squatted on the last step, scooping water to wash his face and neck, only to come back up each time, completely soaked.

Along the bank we walked toward a hillock, which had a vineyard laid out over it, above the vineyard stood a chapel, and behind, a pine grove, and where the vineyard commenced was an enormous orchard, over which hovered the rooftops of a large castle.

"Now then," the doctor told me, "that's the Château Troja; Prince Šternberk lived there, a German but also a fine Czech. Palacký, the father of the nation, and other patriots went to him to make their own Czech better."

I walked along beside the river, which mirrored sky and white storm cloud, the trees from the far shore mirrored in the swift rush of surface water, their reflections streaming as if over rain-swept metal shutters, now the doctor seemed to wilt somewhat, age, a hangover, most likely, the results of the in-house wedding he put on the night before with his friends, finally catching up with him. That élan, which accompanied him as far as the river, now deserted him, he told me about himself, but actually sounded more as though he were harping on about it.

"Never have I been the harlequin, never have I been able to lure anyone's girl away, I've always been the Pierrot, who had all his beautiful women taken, harlequins stole them away from me. That was me as a young lad, a sad young gent, not disposed to fight over love, because I always gave ruin and bad luck and death pride of place, that was my poetic as a lad, as a young man, as a loner . . . and now at this end it's no better, I'm still the sad clown, still the Pierrot . . . That's why I do this stupid drinking, I don't even like it, I drink because I want to amount to something in the circle too, I want to be a number one . . . *aber die Enden* . . . Now I'm in the dumps, now I really do feel, if there were one going by, like jumping under a train. Here, in front of you, in front of myself, I'm mortified . . . I know, a couple of beers and I'm back in business, risen from the dead . . . but what's to be done?"

He ran down the steps again to the river and scooped handfuls of water and lashed them onto his face, but even that didn't do, he tugged off his shirt with his wet hands and splashed his chest all over with water, and when he came back up, he held the wet shirt in his wet hands and let water run down his waist and splatter and wet his pants. He walked up ahead of me, and I had to tote the inflatable mattress, I was dismayed by this abrupt alteration in the doctor, all of a sudden sorry I'd left for the river with him, all of a sudden to me this person seemed repugnant, this person who bolted down the steps to the water again and again and started slapping water onto his face, over his heart, but even that wouldn't do for him, he bent double, angled his hands to lean on the last step and dunked his head under the cool water. When he came back, he breathed a sigh of relief, shook himself off, worked his shoulders, I looked about me and took comfort in the fact we were nearing the weir, you could see clouds of exploded water droplets rise from the depths of the tumbling current over there, and a metal footbridge that spanned the river—a person walking across the bridge stopped midway.

"That's the dam keeper, what I'd like to be, a dam keeper," said the doctor. "Two elements I love in this world, water and fire. But we're by the water! You see, there in Nymburk, I grew up close to the water, I had to cross a bridge to get to grade 1 in the city, I came home over a bridge, school didn't interest me, I was just marking time, since I was six my life is just water and more water, streams and rivers, ponds, but flowing water, mainly, and when the weather changes, the water changes too, the face of the water changes according to the weather and with the weather I change too, perhaps . . . Whenever it rains, I'm as morose as the sky, when I was a kid I would go fishing, fish would bite any time it rained, I would go to fish because even now that I'm older I love fish . . . Only when I grew up, I gave up catching fish since I had to have a license . . . The Labe flowed around the back of the brewery, for fifteen years I caught fish, loved a swim in the river of my childhood, as soon as late spring came I'd swim, I swam right through the summer holidays. I loved to swim on nights when there was a moon . . . There by my river I learned to be quiet and not talk . . . I gazed at that river as at a beautiful girl, lovingly, and this river I love too, this is where I'm at my happiest . . . this place here named Šprlata . . . is the loveliest stretch of the Vltava." Now the doctor was bellowing, because we stood next to where the footbridge ran over from the other shore, and there on pillars and beams astride the full swell of the river was the weir, made of tightly lashed oak logs, five-meter-long logs projecting vertically from the footbridge, cleated top and bottom by solid steel mounts, clipped like a pen into a breast pocket those logs were . . . And the whole river crossed those logs and through the fissures between, it thundered down from on high to crash and churn and clouds of water droplets flew along its length, and wind bore the spray downriver to where the current rounded a small island girt in perpetually wet willows and thick grasses.

And where we stood, approximately level with the main current, was a raft sluice, the water curling in a sloping stream over slippery logs embossed with seaweed, moss, and trailing grass, a hundred-meter-long sluice, filled over with a silvery curl of water . . . And the doctor stood hard by the sluice, staring into the water flow, stripped to the waist, drenched in sunlight he stood there and immediately I felt for him, I saw he understood how to be alone, in fact, liked being alone, I saw nothing foreign to the doctor in solitude, it was part and parcel of his nature, in the last few days I'd only glimpsed it, but already I felt I knew him from long before, the point is, the doctor put on no airs with me, to be honest, he wished me to take away the worst possible impression, he made no pretense, but also hid nothing, as he stood there at the lip of the sluice ruminating on the water, I could see he was tanned, liked being in the sun, and like all Praguers, if he didn't get a tan by summer, he'd likely be depressed and develop a complex . . . And hence I watched him, watched that man mull so intently over the water he appeared to blend with it, surely had I called out to him, he would have suffered a horrible jolt . . . I averted my eyes and again took in the river tumbling over and around those logs, tons and tons of water thundering onto rocks and boulders along the river bottom, I could not take my eyes off the fog and fume of water, shot through with sunlight, and at the right angle, just along the rim, the water cloud emitted rainbows, through which you could faintly discern linden and tall poplar on the opposite bank, white pickets and white hurdles too, because somewhere on the far side was a racecourse . . . and even here I saw fishermen on the riverbanks, some stood casting their lures into the distance, a glint of the lure in the sun, for an instant paused above the river and then the glitter of fishing line too, and in a split second the tackle hit the water, and the fisherman reeled in, his line pulled taut as a bowstring . . .

The doctor pulled his shoes off now and stood relishing the hot, sun-warmed granite cobbles, he strode with a dancer's step, setting his feet down in such a way as to not step on the joins between the stones. I followed him, kept turning to follow the river, now able to see that whole wall of water falling, a little frightened by it to be honest, my heart proceeding to pound at what I witnessed there at the weir . . . The doctor descended cautiously to the river, to where the sluice stopped, where the slanted water joined the current close to a small clearing of green grass . . .

The doctor called, I could see his lips moving, but couldn't hear a thing. Again he called, but I couldn't hear, the thundering waterfall drowned out his voice. I made an inquiring gesture, raised both hands so the inflatable mattress was let drop. The doctor sprinted back up the bank, plucked up the mattress, and screamed in my ear, "Water, darling water!"

I nodded, he offered me his hand and led me warily down to the small clearing, around which the water, the darling water, flowed and eddied. I sat down, the doctor took the mattress and began to inflate it patiently, he almost ran out of breath, he plugged the mouthpiece and handed me the mattress, now I started blowing, while the doctor felt the mattress and nodded with satisfaction. Then he stoppered it, I got out my bathing suit, the doctor took off his pants, he already had his swim trunks on underneath, black cotton swim trunks, and he took the mattress down to the river's edge, then moved further off, up to the top of the sluice. I changed into my bathing suit and just sat there a while, dipped my foot in, then felt for the sandy bottom, the water was alive, the darling water tugging, I stood up, then waded carefully in, water up to my knees, my waist, I splashed my chest lightly, then took a few steps more and water was up to my chest, I dove in and started to swim, the water carried me, lucky, I was one for water, too, knew how to swim, my only sport, I took one, two strokes and made it back to shore, probed for the sandy bottom, stood and washed my face in the sweet-scented water, then looked toward the sluice, the doctor readying the inflatable, he lay down on it, and the running water bore him down over the sluice, the red-and-blue mattress tore along the falling waves, and the doctor raised his arm, I raised my arm and waved, then froze, because the mattress was picking up the speed of falling water and hurtling, about to burst through a set of rapids and finally emerge from a flurry of water, right in front of me. The doctor stuck out a leg and got up, standing in the water to his waist, he turned to me and laughed and then he shouted, "That's what it's all about!"

"What's that?" I put a hand up to my ear.

"That's what it's all about!"

"Yes," I nodded, but couldn't understand him, I turned around and got back into the current again, which carried me, I let the current carry me away, along the shoreline walked people in fine shirts, children frolicking ahead of them, watching me, I smiled their way, those figures so close I could almost touch them, I floated with the current until the water took me into a calm, I felt around for the bottom, stood up, turned about.

The doctor had his eyes on me, he hoisted both arms and laughed and was delighted at how he saw me, he'd guessed right off I was at ease with water, as a child I used to swim the river too and wasn't afraid of the current, I could revel in the river pull, give myself over without resisting, for I knew even a river loves those willing to trust in its flow. I clambered out of the water, the current wafting lightly around me, and then I went up along the narrow banks to the top, walked back, and could see the doctor look me over, seeing me practically naked, because my bathing suit clung to my body, I walked toward those eyes examining me, knowingly, and when I stepped off the riverbank and onto the petite clearing of green grass, I saw the doctor toss the mattress ashore and come toward me, he offered me his hand and I sat, my legs tucked up to my chest.

"You have lovely lungs," he said. "Me now, I have beautiful legs," he added proudly.

"What?" I said, surprised.

"I *have* beautiful legs, take a look, a bit crooked, but from soccer, but that's all I'm proud of, other than my beautiful shoulders, my even more beautiful legs." He said this and extended his legs, trying to make the knees meet, but he had a gap between them, and I really must admit, he did have nice, muscular legs, a soccer player's tanned legs, one who'd given up the game not that long ago.

"Bowlegs," I said quietly.

"Because of soccer, I played passionately for ten years, but you have to admit, bowlegs look good on me," he said, chuckling.

"And how," I said, laughing, and then bucked up the courage to say, "I suffered a lot on account of my big lungs, as you call them, at sixteen I had to wear a size nine bra already, you see, back then I was ashamed of them, I never did know how to carry myself like the film stars do today . . . Too bad the Mae West look wasn't in back then, or even the current Marilyn Monroe."

"But I like you exactly as you are," he said, "really, your legs have a little kink too, but all ballerinas' legs have, because *you* always stand in dance position number one, right foot angled out a fraction."

I glanced at his hands, at his fingers, and said, "How is it your hands are so weathered, your fingers so grubby? . . . You can't say those are a doctor's hands."

"They're not, but that's because even as a boy I liked garden work, liked working with my uncle Pepin, shoveling barley malt, why I quit playing the piano, six years I took piano lessons, but these stubby fingers I have . . . and then work in Kladno, four years of nothing but spade work, and my job now, you'll see how tough when you come visit me in Spálená Street . . . but my hands and fingers I'm proud of, often I will go over my palms in wonderment, pore over them, and read everything that's passed through them. Truthfully, I've never known how to do anything else, I had a mind to be a soccer player, but at a game they cracked my collarbone and broke my arm at the elbow, I could have been numero uno at soccer—at piano too, I only got as far as a few Chopin nocturnes, I preferred playing Johann Strauss waltzes at the restaurant under the bridge, but had to give up even that, even as a pianist I would never have cut it . . . During the war, I was a dispatcher, but gave up on that too, then a salesman for the Karel Henry Klofanda Company, before that an insurance rep for the Živnostenská Fund, but had to give that up too, because I never would have gone anywhere in any one of those jobs, so the sole time I was number one was working a shovel up in Kladno, foremen there held me up as a shining example, and when praise was piled on like that, I felt they were rubbing up my chest with lard, up in Kladno I stopped being the Pierrot a little, a *pagliaccio,* a clown, still in my own eyes, but thanks to how others saw me I could look the others in the eye at least, and from then on, in fact, look myself in the eye even and I discovered I'm actually a fairly nice, if not timid, person . . . a Pierrot whom people think a harlequin."

"Honestly," I brightened up at that, "I like cards, rummy, canasta, you are somewhat—can I tell you?—like that card . . . the joker!"

"What?" He gave a start.

"The Jolly Joker," I corrected myself.

"A petty clown?" he said, disappointed.

"No, the Jolly Joker is the card that brings players luck, every canasta player wants a Jolly Joker, because . . . because Jolly Joker, though dressed as a clown, is a card valued more than the tens and kings and queens and all jacks put together, worth more than aces, it beats all . . . he has his smile, but trumps the rest, because Jolly Joker is number one."

"With you, am I number one?"

"Yes, because I had no desire to be in this world anymore, and when at my lowest, I entered that courtyard of yours, and you were there in the glow of the droplight scrubbing your floor with the wire brush . . . then for that impression, if nothing else, you're number one."

I averted my eyes.

Then we just sat beside one another, did not look at one another further, we returned to following the roar and tumble of the river, the constant thunder of falling water, and the rising spray of water forming clouds of mist the wind gathered and carried downstream to spray islets of shrubs and birches. I took the mattress, carried it down to the shoreline, walked up to the sluice top, where the water flowed into a slough three meters wide, I hesitated momentarily, looked down at where the doctor watched, never would have climbed onto that mattress, except the doctor's eyes drove me to overcome my fear, I set the mattress in several meters upstream, where smooth water sucked over the lip of the sluice, and then swung myself out of the water and onto the red-and-blue-striped mattress, and the current drew me onto the sloped water, the sharp, quick water rushed over sleek beams, several times the mattress scraped along slick board and beam, but so strong was the current that I shot the rapids quickly, then some smooth but fast-flowing water, until finally the mattress traversed a last set of curling wavelets at the bottom . . . and the mattress floated into a still, little inlet and slowed, I opened my eyes, as I'd opened my eyes at the hospital, when they pumped a fistful of sleeping pills out of me, pills that would have taken me over to the other side, into death . . . I lay on my back like that for a while, one arm flung over my eyes, the doctor pulled the mattress to him, I simply lay there in my bathing suit, the doctor leaned over, to look at me, study me, then take me lightly by the arm and gaze into my face, my eyes . . .

Then side by side we just lay there, sun shining pleasantly, I grew tired and fell asleep, but before I slept, I could hear people strolling along the path above us, I heard voices, laughter, children chattering, the mothers' voices—reproachful—and the fall of the river rumbling over logs and the rush through the sluice lulled me to sleep, I could feel the doctor lying at my side, our legs touching, and fell fast asleep . . .

When I woke, the sun was already in the tops of the poplar trees on the other side of the river, the doctor, already dressed, seated by the sluice, legs bent, arms around his knees, he simply sat there, chewed a blade of grass, listened, and gazed into the fall of the waters and water droplets swirling, into the nimbus of mist, which flew above the fomented surface and sprayed the isles of sallow and willow . . . I shivered with cold and sat up, I wasn't used to an afternoon sleep, I started to get a headache . . .

CHAPTER NINE

AT DUSK, WHEN THE STREET LAMPS WERE ALREADY COMING ON, WE walked back along the river, black as ink, white gulls still flittered about over on the far shore, Holešovice mirrored in the water, cottage rows, window frames filled with yellow lights, we passed a pair of lovers, quiet, walking hand in hand toward the area we'd just come from, the willow shrubs, perhaps headed for where we'd spent all afternoon, to hear the rumbling fall of rushing water. When we passed the tennis courts, tennis players in their whites were still dodging about in deep twilight, white sweaters and white shorts aglow in evening dusk, legs and faces so tanned, it appeared the white sweaters and shorts dove around of their own accord. The doctor walked beside me, the surface water's glinting and mirrored lights cast their reflections over us, the doctor relaxed now, walked along swingingly, his knee every so often would brush against me, occasionally we even bumped into one another and laughed quietly, the path along the river beamed and footsteps could be heard crunching on the sand. The doctor spoke low, more to himself than to me.

"My youth, you see, and all my growing up years were beautiful, but beautiful only to me, because to my parents I was a pox . . . Primary school to high school, nothing but suffering for my mother, every day she'd wake and groan, 'What's to become of you, boy! What in the world's to become of you!' You must understand, now when I travel back in memory, I break into a sweat, because really, Mother had it right, What *is* to become of me? Thing is, even as a kid I was always away, even when not at home, wherever I was, I was out of it. You see, I failed twice. Wanted to train as a mason, but Dad said, 'Not likely, you can go ahead and fail every grade, but you must get your high school diploma, then apprentice as a mason.' In primary, from third grade on, I was already getting C's and always B for conduct—understand, timid me, B for conduct—my photos from then are fearful . . . Gloomy, glowering photos of me with my mom. Pulling away and glowering, I didn't know why, but somehow nothing at home seemed to agree with me, school didn't agree with me, only thing that did was being alone, fishing, lying in the hay in brewery stables, buried, listening in the hay . . . listening to what all those years? As a student, I loved to borrow Dad's overcoat and walk the river in the rain, run for a while, from myself, through the fields and forests, run till I made the creek, lined with alders, through trunks and underbrush that creek bubbled and flowed, and I'd stand, lean against a tree, and what I was scared of, scared to even think of, caught me, Mother's oft-repeated line when I'd take those hundreds of report cards home, always the same, and once Mother spied those C's and D's and even B's and C's for conduct, a thousand times over she'd pour in my ears, right into my soul, 'What's to become of you?' So I stayed on the run, but when I stopped, too tired to go further, that reproachful line would overtake me, 'What's to become of you?' And so I took a law degree, just a coincidence I picked law, never liked law, I studied it and didn't know why, perhaps I studied law, and studied it well, for Mother to be happy, for her to finally stop saying, 'What's to become of you?' "

We crossed a road, slopes dotted with the villas and cottages' lighted windows, every hill adorned with the streetlamps' gleam, zigzag those lights went to the tip-top, up to where one lamp blazed like the evening star against the sky, tree branches and bushes shielded some lights and wherever I looked, those lights in the darkness all appeared filled with love, all evening long, along with stars, flickering, as though that whole evening and landscape had fallen in love, people came out from the dark, illuminated for a while, then disappeared under the trees again, only to reappear farther down. The doctor continued on, musingly.

"The most beautiful thing about being drunk is not the elation, not getting high, not the hoot and the holler and the ideas that come, but getting drunk's most valuable asset is the day after, the hangover, the guilty conscience, turmoil, what kicks a person when he's down, like you catching me washing dishes this morning, when I was my own mother, telling myself again, as after every hangover, 'What's to become of you?' And that's a hangover's power, a person wishing to start afresh . . . and then, with a hangover you get thoughts, at least I do, that in all sobriety I'd be scared to think of, when in body and soul I'm at my most wretched, but hungover afterthoughts are the right kind, ones that push a person not much, but at least a little farther along the line . . . When it dawns on a hungover sod just who he offended the night before, what a spectacle he made of himself, when horrible cold sweat breaks out on a person for how he ran off at the mouth, at what he threw in friends' and neighbors' faces, when consequently the person has no desire to live, when in his hungover state he contemplates suicide, then the buried line is all of a sudden resurrected, 'What's to become of you?' You see actually, now it occurs to me, my writing, my writing is also a guard against suicide, as if I run from myself in my writing, but at the same time I ask, what's to become of me? The person I was before and who I am right now, the writing helps cure, the way confession cures Catholics, the way the Wailing Wall cures Jews, the way confessing doubts and secrets and worries to a mute old willow would cure our forbears, and when all's said and done, the way relaxing and talking about whatever's on their mind cures Freud's patients . . . Actually that writing of mine is like I run line to line, all so clearly beautiful on the typewriter, I never know what I've written, I'm always chasing some thought, there beyond my reach, I want to catch up to it, but it's always one step ahead of me, just as when I raced to catch the train to Grandma's as a child, as I raced home from school, as I raced out of the house at home, out of myself, along the river, and for that matter as I always did run wherever I happened to be, out and away, ran from girlfriends to buddies to play cards, only to run from the buddies after a while, into the darkness, and when I stopped, I saw I needed to keep running, always from myself, because neither as a child nor as a young man did I ever, ever find any aims, and all my jobs, always jobs that kept me on the run—as an insurance rep, I couldn't wait to be home, once home I had to run out, taverning; as a traveling notions and toy sales rep, on trains and buses I had to run, but where? To sell shopkeepers notions and toys, ride the bus four years up to Poldovka in Kladno, run and work aboard the bus, move material to the smelters on the little train, then back home by bus, then straight to the tavern, where even these days I suddenly pale and have to flee elsewhere, same as today we've been constantly on the move, on the run, always on the road, because we're intimidated. What're we intimidated by? What's to become of us?"

We drew to a halt outside a lighted garden restaurant, under the old chestnut trees were tables, packed tables, a brass band oompahed on a small bandstand, wire-strung lanterns hung in the trees, you could hear laughter and shouts, hushed voices, patrons lofting their glasses and making a toast, through the open doors to the tavern more tables, filled with more people, the evening was warm, coats thrown over chair backs, the aged publican drew beer, people squeezed up to the bar drinking their beer greedily, others with half-empty glasses stood in conversation with neighbors, or stared, dully, dead front . . . And voices and laughter came down from the treetops even, first floor up, people out on the terrace, tables there loaded with people as well, over their heads on wire strings painted lanterns shone from between the branches . . . We entered the garden, the music started and couples rose to dance, the doctor was delighted, he saw a friend . . . And then such shouts, such hugs, and the doctor led his friend over and introduced him.

"This is Ludva, the butcher, for a whole year he and I strove on two opposing work brigades up in Poldovka." I offered this engaging person my hand, I recalled the doctor telling of Ludva, the butcher, who the women chased, it was even graver than the doctor let on, Ludva was gorgeous, his body put together beautifully, he actually did look like a bodybuilder, narrow waist, and up top a huge chest and a neck like a Swiss bull, like Marlon Brando. He smiled at me and even his eyes had a sad beauty, aswim already with the alcohol. He invited us over to his table, a large table, three tables pushed together actually, certainly in the early afternoon the tablecloths had been white, now all beer and wine spattered with upended shot glasses. Ludva took the doctor's fold-up mattress and my little umbrella and hung them on a hook nailed to one of the old chestnuts, he spread out his arms and to the group of men sitting there in shirtsleeves said, "This is the doctor and his young lady; me and the doc, we were up there in Kladno doing the spadework for the homeland, practically brought about currency reform single-handedly . . . And these," he pointed to the group of gentlemen, "all butchers, because this party's put on by the butchers from the Prague abattoir, this is even our music, the brass band music of the Prague butchers . . . And . . ."

And Mr. Ludva didn't have an opportunity to finish, because the brass band began to play, and all the butchers got up and began to sing with great feeling, *I was twenty, no more, and the world was a bore* . . . And it was as if the tables took flight at one and the same time, all the patrons stood and started to sing, even people on the upstairs terrace rose, their faces appearing between the branches of the old chestnuts, children ran in and out between tables . . . And the doctor stood, one arm around Ludva's shoulders, singing with great emotion along with the rest, I got up and merely gazed about me, I beheld nothing but women and men, plain people, but none with any reason whatsoever to run from themselves, forever wishing to be somewhere else, I could see the one thing these people wanted was for this Sunday evening to last as long as it could, so perhaps they wouldn't need to go home at all, so they stood, all looking around at each other, toasting one another over the tables with their glasses, and all singing now with great emotion, almost in tears at that sad song . . . *everything I had is no more, and I've lost the key to love's door* . . . I could see practically every butcher at our table was disabled in some way by abattoir work, one had shortened legs, a second had a scar across his face, a third had hands so red they looked like they'd been scalded, a fourth had a hump shoulder, a fifth had a massive gut . . . only Ludva, as the doctor said, was as gorgeous as a Greek god or Marlon Brando.

The doctor offered me his hand and invited me onto the floor, we made our way past tables, past children, to dance, people dancing the polka, some danced the old, the six polka, and a clutch of youngsters danced separate, swing polka . . . The doctor pressed me into him, I leaned on his shoulder, and then he got into rhythm, good at dancing, turning the circles fully, he got me turning, head turned and breathing lightly he danced and might have gone on endlessly dancing, I could feel he had the muscles, now he took me by the waist, and pressed close, I was able to feel his legs, he did have strong legs . . . and my head spun, the whole garden restaurant went spinning, a lighted merry-go-round, a grand glass Venetian chandelier, several times we collided with other couples, but after each collision recovered, till finally we danced at the outside edge of the floor and the doctor had room and time to tell me, "I was a champion at polka and waltz. I won a prize in the mature/advanced category, you know, I completed two levels of dance, wanted to be the number one of the dance . . . One level at Němeček's, in the suburbs, but not a woman showed, so men only dancing together, odd numbers men, even women . . . but the next year, in the Pension Hall, I won a prize in polka and waltz, for mature/advanced dance. All I remember is, out of all I've ever done, guess what I'm still the best at today?" The doctor placed his cheek to mine and bellowed, "The polka and the waltz!"

And I leaned back as far away as I could, while he kept a grip on me with his mitts to gaze into my eyes, around us whirled the garden restaurant, lanterns spun, tables spun, all the guests, all the glasses, spun in circles to the rhythm of the waltz around us, other dancers passed, distorted faces receding and advancing closer, my head commenced a spin, and I laid my head on the doctor's shoulder and shut my eyes.

The waltz ended, we stumbled our way back, while the other dancers stayed on the floor and shouted, "Play it again, play it again!" And they looked up at the bandstand, at the five musicians sitting up there, butchers with their trumpets, instruments gleaming with brass, faces gleaming with fatigue. And then we gobbled up the goulash and drank our beer. Then Ludva asked me to dance, he didn't make the full circles when we danced the waltz together, he just swayed to the rhythm, held me so tight I was only able to loll in his arms, he was looking at me closely, very closely, the exact opposite of the doctor, who always averted his eyes, as if guilty of something, as he always said about himself, he was shy, because when he was a youth the custom was that young men be shy. But Mr. Ludva knew, that's why he was looking and knowing, once he smiled at me I'd lower my eyes, and begin to blush, and the more I blushed, the more imposing did Mr. Ludva, the butcher from the Holešovice abattoir, become . . . He truly was gorgeous, perhaps it was just me, though, and perhaps just because he had this beautiful blond hair, combed and parted, the hair lightly curling at his neck and his ears, into a single wave, which from time to time he would pinch and shape with his fingers, as if with a curling iron, that kiss curl above his brow, and hair finely scissored at the back, which made him seem not at all like the butcher, but the most junior general in the German infantry, who had danced with me at my sister's wedding during the war, who'd danced and begged I write him, I did write, but he was cut down somewhere in the Ukraine . . . And I also noticed the butcher's hands, thumbs like those someone had bitten off and doctors had sewn back on. By the time we finished dancing, I had turned serious. Mr. Ludva simply smiled, didn't need to say a word, amuse me with stories, for Mr. Ludva, it was sufficient that he just *be*.

As soon as we sat down, we started drinking beer again, the doctor declined the shots Mr. Ludva offered, drank pints of beer instead, in fact, on the young barmaid's rounds, he took two at once.

"What's that on your hand?" I asked.

"That is . . ." Ludva said, and his voice was dark, which intensified the brightness of his straw-colored hair.

"That's . . . where a pig bit me, I was going for him with the snippers, they slipped, the pig did an about-face and chomped on my fist, I almost got the whole lot mauled off," Mr. Ludva said, laughing.

"Do piggies bite?" I asked, quite surprised.

Ludva took hold of the doctor by the sleeve and said, "You like to write, so you'd best know this . . . You havta terrorize the pigs a bit, because soon as they feel at home, they'll turn on you, that's why we have these oak switches, soon as they're let outta the railcar, we start beating . . . in the slaughter, even, we beat so the pigs stay scared. Fear's very effective for teaching manners. You should see," said blond Mr. Ludva dreamily, "sometimes the pigs get into such a panic, even as we beat, they fly straight into the scalding tubs, pigs scorching, steam rising, and us there with our electric snippers, then we murder 'em with a mallet, because we're butchers."

The doctor went quiet, I noticed the butchers even had their wives sitting by, wives gently reminding husbands not to drink so much, take it easy, especially not to mix their drinks . . . but the butchers merely patted them on the hands, eyed their wives, smiled, waving them aside . . . and continued drinking.

"As a future writer, you . . . you should see it too . . . When you open up a railcar of porkers, in nearly every one there's one or two pigs dead . . . Died of terror, heart attack from the fright, same as people exactly . . . According to the statistics, in West Germany, sixty thousand pigs a year die in the railcars of terror . . . In Milan, they came up with this sliding tunnel, at the Milan slaughterhouse, the pigs come out of the railcars onto this sloped metal slide, a funnel, all the little piggies go sliding down, tumble stunned and injured to the bottom, the easier to kill with a hammer . . . and electric snippers!"

So spoke Mr. Ludva and his eyes waxed lovelier and lovelier, he kept hold of the doctor by the elbow, who did nothing except lean forward and drink his beer from a pair of stein glasses, and I could see him dying of the same terror as the piggies in the Milan abattoirs, but since he desired to be a writer, since he had the desire to pick up everything, even against his better judgment, he swallowed and listened, and the music played and the dancers danced, and Ludva preached on to the doctor.

"Gentlest creature in the world is a calf, they bring the adolescent calves in railcars. Sometimes what'll happen is you'll open a railcar that's been traveling all weekend, the calves lying on a siding some-where, and when you open up the car, two inside are suffocated, babies, little grown-up baby calves, suffocated, but don't count that same as you do two on average pigs that die in railcars of terror, heart attacks . . . I saw this in a West German magazine, they bring horses from way over in Romania somewhere, will open a railcar and there inside's your suffocated horse, I saw this one picture in a magazine, of a horse that didn't want out of the railcar after being in transit for three days, so, Doctor, you're for being a writer, you ought to know this, so in the picture there—I'll bring it for you, give it to you—so in the picture and in the article what's going on was, when the horse didn't want out of the railcar, the drover up and cuts its tongue out, and when it still didn't want out, the drover opened its throat right in the railcar . . . Doctor, you're a writer, that's why I'm telling you this, because a writer ought to know the goods." So Ludva spoke and smiled, the wrinkles puckering around the corners of his lips, he had beautiful blue eyes, and when he smiled so, a diminutive blue dot appeared on his eye, diminutive blue at the very top, and it seemed to me that Ludva had an inner something, something saints have, like in the cheap reproductions I saw at the parish church where I'd been placed to work as a cook and milkmaid near the war's end.

"Sometimes," Mr. Ludva shook his head, "sometimes even here it can get on a person's nerves . . . They started up this new assembly line for killing cows, as I'm from Kladno, I'm still required to work a half year in the Kladno slaughterhouse, before I come back home here, to Holešovice . . . so new line, fine, I've still got the go in me, so they get the line moving, cages built to stun six cows at a time in line, but these cages don't function, so we have to start pounding . . . And I'm thumping one cow after the other, with a mallet—can I hit!—each time, a cow goes down, but the two guys supposed to cut the cows' throats go for a smoke, and I'm pounding the twelfth cow when what do I see? The first cows I thumped getting up, the two fellows off having a smoke, and me here whaling away at those poor cows for nothing, so I havta wait for those guys finishing their smoke to give those pie-eyed cows a second round . . . Doctor, the stuff we saw, the stuff we lived through up in Poldovka, eh? Folk scorched, choked, burned to death . . . But anyhow . . ."

He didn't finish, all the butchers rose, time for the gala moment, music played the fanfare, and an elderly lady in a white apron was led over to the regulars' table under the aged chestnuts, the landlady, who a while ago had brought me out a plate of goulash and a basket of bread, who whisked the crumbs off the tablecloth and looked into my eyes, such a nice look she'd given me, and a smile, for she was certain she'd cooked the goulash as best she could and was certain I'd like it . . . And so the organizers brought over the landlord from the taps, then Mr. Ludva hooked the barmaid by the waist, took her tray of beer and set it on a table, and guided the girl over to the band-stand, over to where the landlord sat beside his missus . . . And the music rolled in a fanfare, and the doctor whispered to me, "Applies to all the pubs in Libeň now, husband and wife aren't allowed in the workplace together, they can still serve in the taverns, but they have to be different ones."

And the organizers presented the couple with a bouquet of flowers, everyone hugged, the landlady cried, the barmaid, probably the daughter, stayed impassive, afraid the beer would go flat, she went back to her tray, lifted it handily above her head, and went on with her rounds . . . And then the emcee made a speech . . .

I got up on tiptoe, looking at the tearful former proprietors of this summer restaurant Břežanka, they smiled wistfully and gazed down at the sand, accepted roses from people, good-bye kisses, then more hugging and crying, all the patrons took turns, and then and there I remembered myself standing at the train station, back when I'd been twenty, Daddy had signed all rights to his factory away, relinquished all his properties, just for a permit to leave with Mom and me and my younger brother, Heini, we were standing at the station and the express came in, and all of us about to get on board, when a clerk from the town committee came up and showed us some papers that said only my dad and my mom could go to the West, Heini and I must stay because we were Czech schooled and therefore Czechoslovak citizens . . . And crying in the windows of the express train, my parents started to pull out, and I cried and called to them, "Don't worry, the Red Cross will get us over to you!" But I never saw Daddy again because he died, had a heart attack . . . That's what I mused over while I witnessed these two old proprietors forfeit their garden restaurant Břežanka, bid fond farewell to all, patrons who would never see them again. And now the musicians split into two groups, one under the old chestnuts, while with their trumpets the others crossed the street and those glimmering instruments glittered along the trail, ascending to a grove of acacias up there somewhere, the patrons were all in a state of excitement, even the landlord and his wife stood now, time for the closing ceremony, climax to the entire evening, even the musicians who'd stayed on in the restaurant garden gazed across the street, over to the hill overgrown with acacias, they picked up their instruments . . . everyone went quiet, the only sound, cars in the street and now musicians with their trumpets aimed at the gentle hillside of acacia trees and shrubberies started to blow a mournful tune . . . *To me she gave a gilded ring* . . . and from the hill across the street the other musicians who had recently left joined in . . . and so they played, one group ending, the other opening, one wooing, the other answering and bugling back, and the music carried across the street, and the patrons listened and were touched, in fact, more touched by the exchange between the two troops of musicians than by the couple, who had waited upon their guests for the last time tonight.

The landlady came to my table, patted my hand and looked into my eyes and said, "Did you enjoy?"

And the patrons stood up, their glasses raised to the hill, drank to the musicians cloaked in deep acacia shadow, and sang . . . *And I gave her my heart in return . . .*

■ □ ■ □ ■

CHAPTER TEN

THIS MORNING I LEFT MY ŽIŽKOV APARTMENT A LITTLE EARLY, THAT second mother of mine wasn't speaking to me, at night she lit into me about how I should at least have a bit more gratitude, considering all she's done for me, I'm living at her place on the sly after all, working on the sly too . . . not to mention that when I'm off, I'm never home, I come in at all hours, I've changed somehow, smiling, never listening to anything she says, I stare at the ceiling and smile, as if I had a permit to live in Prague or something, as if the office for work issued me the permit to work at the Hotel Paris . . .

So I set off for the center of town, and when I reached number ten Spálená Street, where the doctor worked, I took a few steps into the passageway, which stank of damp and old paper, the walls were scraped raw, heavy gashes from fallen plaster, probably from cars backing into and out of the courtyard, I could see a huge pile of old paper under the light of a bare bulb in the courtyard, and two garage doors open, shining with light, and in one corner scales, above which an electric lamp shone. And there were schoolkids wading around waist high in piled paper, dumping baskets of wastepaper or plastic bags, and now two gypsy women came into the passageway, wobbling under the weight of a crushed cardboard bundle, everything flapped up out of that bundle, I stepped back against the wall and then fled, my heart pounding, all the way back to the Church of the Holy Trinity, under Saint Tadeus, trying to muster the courage, find the heart, and I lowered my head again, looked at my lovely dress and its green buttons, and I set off, head high to bolster my strength, those red high heels constantly gave me confidence, I opened my little umbrella, held my little blue umbrella up . . . And I walked along briskly, turned into the passageway, but only got as far as the open gate, from there I stood looking at that morass, that horror, those piles of every-color paper, I could now see a truck that had backed into the courtyard parked there, could see a curly headed man coming from one corner bearing bales of compressed paper on his back, his mate near the tailgate sifted through them, pitched them up on one knee then and stacked them one on top of the other, a man in a beret crossed the courtyard, fat man with a trim beard, and he had this somewhat anguished gait . . . And a wave of horror and fear swept over me and I fled again, ran until back at Saint Tadeus again . . . Several women stood there gazing into the saint's sandstone face, the saint whose good word had the power to get things done in heaven, things that wouldn't be done otherwise . . .

I knelt in the pew and people streamed past around and behind me, and I prayed, "Saint Tadeus, put in a word for me, that I might find the strength right now, to be able to take a first step into that courtyard, where the person I love works, I just want to see him, give me the fortitude right now, Saint Tadeus, to walk in and behave naturally there, to not be as petrified as I am now, I only wish to talk to him for a bit, Tadeus, I only want to take a look at that man at work there, who I keep thinking of."

And something tapped me on the head, I turned and there the doctor stood, looking down at me, a pitcher dripping with foam raised, and under his arm a shopping bag containing a large greasy sheet of paper, which steamed lightly. He had torn shoes on, overalls, a ripped shirt, and a long apron, and on his head a cap rolled back over his forehead.

"What a coincidence—come on over and have a look at our establishment!" He smiled and added, "Do you know what coincidence is? Another name for the Holy Ghost . . . Of course, not even the roll of the dice can eliminate coincidence, but come along, come along, so you can have a look at my fine place of employ." And handing the shopping bag to me, he set forth. "Mind you don't stain that beautiful, elegant dress!"

He turned around and laughed again, and he was so confident, so proud of himself, his apron and cap, he turned to keep a watch on me and continuing down the passageway at the same time, giving everybody a wide berth so he wouldn't knock them down, again he turned and forged on into the courtyard; the covered courtyard had a huge gap in one wall, through which a little air and daylight came, here were bales of paper, and the doctor put the pitcher of beer down on one, resting against another was the driver, his back hunched over slightly, his curly hair fell onto his face, which dripped with sweat; the driver's mate lapped a giant rope over the bales in the back of the truck, propped a boot against the tailgate, and tightened the tether so it cut into the bales, then he tied a loop, pulled the tether over the load as tight as a bow, made a sailor's knot, gave it a yank, and now he leaned on the tailgate, breathing hard, red in the face, not red from the work, but red as if in childhood he'd had his cheeks scalded, or as if he suffered from rosacea.

"So, boys, this is my lady friend."

The doctor took the shopping bag off me and on another bale spread out the hot sliced meatloaf, he offered me some, I took a piece, then the driver came over and had a slice, the driver's mate too. Well, they ate on foot, ate hungrily, ate mutely, gulping down one slice after the other, and the meatloaf was none the smaller, a two-kilo, warm meatloaf, definitely.

"Boss," said the doctor with his face full, "come over and have some too, and this is my lady friend here, she came to have a look at the former boss of Čedok, who used to make more than fifty flights a year, until he flew the whole way down to trash collection here, where he's lucky to hold a job as boss." And the boss doffed his beret, gave me a bow, and had a slice of warm meatloaf.

"It's terrible, madame," the boss told me. "They took away everything, even took the house on Celetná Street, where Franz Kafka lived once upon a time, evicted me, but I'm still its owner. Up on the third floor, where I used to be, a painter lives now, down on the second floor, a lady vegetarian; fine, so they took my house, but even though I'm still its owner, I'm a landlord without a flat . . . And now, imagine the nerve, when they called me down to the properties management office and told me, 'Now see here, a parade's going to pass by your building, we're having a festival, National Gymnastics Festival, and the parade's going right by your building at number three Celetná Street, it would be a good idea to fix her up and throw a coat of paint on that building at number three.' So I say, 'Good idea, you go ahead.' And they say back, the nerve of them, 'But the building's not ours, you're its owner.' So I start squawking, 'But I don't take in the rent, I just collect as the landlord and hand it over to you, so who's the owner?' And they shoot back, 'You, and whose building is the parade going by? Yours, at number three Celetná Street. So *we* will fix up the building, at your expense.' So this is what they say to me with great zeal, and they are surprised I wasn't entirely enthusiastic about the parade giving my building the march past, being stuck with the tab to fancy up the building for the big event was little honor for me."

So the boss told us, and keeping a hold on a slice of warm meatloaf going cold, he looked at me and I could tell the doctor had been bragging about me to him already, could tell from what the boss was telling me he knew I came down from thirteen rooms, and as a child had had my own nanny, and we had cooks and a chauffeur . . . He gave me a bow, put the slice in his mouth, cocked his head to one side, then moped across the courtyard to the scales, he pressed a switch, studied the dial, and called back, "Eight kilos . . . now dump it nicely on top of the pile."

Well, the three men had probably consumed close to a kilo of warm meatloaf by now, and they were still hungry and still eager to eat. I ate a third slice, and it really was an excellent meatloaf, just plain old meatloaf, not special, just run-of-the-mill meatloaf, two crowns per hundred grams. And I could see how dirty the men's hands were, dirty from the whole morning already, as though they hadn't seen water in a week.

The doctor said, "Soon as you wash your hands here, soon as you begin the hand washing, they crack so bad they start to bleed, we only wash 'em after a shift. Anyway . . . have you seen the gypsy kids? Dirty to the point of being terrifying, but I never heard any gypsy kids got sick from dirt, is that not so? Mr. Volavka, Mr. Živný?"

And the driver and his mate proceeded eating and nodded, for some reason they wouldn't look at me, they looked away, probably because if they did look they would have stopped eating, lost their appetite . . . And now they picked up the pitcher and took turns drinking from it, and again their eyes turned elsewhere, probably because if they had looked, they would have started to splutter and cough and that would write off the drinking.

"That's the way it is," said the doctor, "excuse me."

And he leaned over, pushed the knuckle of his index finger up to his nostril, and blew out a gob of snot into a scrap of wastepaper, then he blew the other nostril empty, wiped his nose on his shirt-sleeve, and said contentedly, "Man, have we got the handkerchiefs."

And both the driver's mate and the driver laughed so hard they started to choke, and the doctor went on.

"Doctors when they have kids, soon as the kid can read, they stick these signs up, on the bathroom mirror, in the toilet, in the kitchen, so the kids'll notice them everywhere, WASH YOUR HANDS! SO YOU DON'T GET SCARLET FEVER! . . . WASH YOUR HANDS AFTER YOU FLUSH, SO YOU DON'T GET CHOLERA, SO'S YOU DON'T GET DIPHTHERIA! . . . GARGLE DAILY! . . . BATHE EVERY DAY, CLEANLINESS IS HALF THE BATTLE. And in the end the doctors' kids get not just diphtheria, but measles, and scarlet fever, and cholera!"

And a man entered the yard wearing a pair of overalls and a fe-dora, walking as if his heel had a thorn in it, one hand thrust in his pocket, the other he brandished in great agitation. From over by the scales, the boss groused, "Haňt'a, Jindra, for God's sake, pick up the pace a bit, check out that God-awful pile! Heinrich!"

But Haňt'a wouldn't be roused, he just waved him off.

"Heinrich," said the doctor, offering meatloaf, "take some, have a bite to eat."

But Haňt'a/Heinrich/Jindra stood in front of me, nose twitch-ing, the overgrowth on his lips stained yellow, as if lately eating a boiled egg.

"See, soon as I eat, the blood rushes to my brain and the thinking goes down the drain . . . but, Doctor, what *is* this?"

He pointed to me.

"My lady friend," the doctor said.

"Jesus, then we must extend a proper welcome, this is one fine mess. So you're lady friend to . . . this here?" He pointed at the doctor.

I nodded, and the driver and his mate made their way back over to their truck, bowed to me, the driver climbed in, his mate went into the passageway, you could see his silhouette signal the direction, showing the driver his way out, now his figure lighted in the sun out on Spálená Street, Mr. Živný glanced around, gave a little nod, and the truck pulled out of the twilit passageway, scraping the wall here and there, and the bales of colored paper glinted in the sun, the truck turned onto the street, and the driver's mate opened the door and hopped into the cab. Mr. Haňťa/Heinrich held me by the elbow, I tried to pull away, his mouth emitted a disgusting smell of beer and cheese, but Mr. Haňťa droned into my ear, "Tomorrow I'll bring you a little token, some pickled mushrooms, not any old mushrooms, nothing but best orange cups and rough stems, and then, chanterelles pickled in vinegar, gathered in Mořinka—Mořinka the Famous, you understand, where Charles IV changed horse, driving his stallion on up to Karlštejn. Doctor, you know what I discovered? That hellish boy Charles IV staged the entire Hussite uprising, that infernal boy not only added to the cities but the monasteries besides, Doctor, rest assured, if that much property weren't there in the nation, then why revolution? Why an uprising? Regular folk had a chance with each city conquered to steal wholesale, rape women, set fire to buildings . . . and it was Charles IV actually brought all those happenings about, you know what it must have been like to break into those monasteries with no fear of reprisal and rape nuns, murder priests, and then top it off by setting it all ablaze? The people must have loved it . . . and imagine the pleasure your average person must have taken, when he pulled a German knight down off his horse, when he seized the horse along with all the trappings? And when they killed themselves a knight slowly? A person could last out to retirement just off the hardware, boots, and armor by itself . . . But if I'd been alive back then, my greatest pleasure would be cities ablaze, burning monasteries, the churches toppling, that would have been the happening for me, courtesy of Charles IV, the one who changed stallions in Mořinka, while on one of his charges up to Karlštejn, from whence, madame, I am to bring you the picklings of orange cups and rough stems in vinegar, chanterelles pickled in vinegar . . ."

"For the love of God, Haňťa, get to work, down to the cellar and to your work, just get a load of that pile," wailed the boss, and down onto his own knees he got, right there and then in front of Mr. Haňťa. "You know I did a tally for you; make ten bales a day tops, and I'm hunky-dory."

"Not on your life," Mr. Haňt'a protested, "not on your life. You underestimate me, chief—not on your life—I'll do twenty!"

"Plenty if you do ten in a day," the boss persisted and then rose heavily, for over by the scales a pack of schoolkids with bags of paper were watching the boss on his knees in front of one of his employees, in front of a worker . . . And Haňt'a muttered something or other, started up the stairs alongside the garage, turned around as though about to say something, but then waved his arms as though it was pointless and up the stairs he continued, then his footsteps could be heard descending somewhere cellarward, and for the first time I noticed that beside the next garage was an older lady stomping on papers, stomping the paper into a variety of box, it resembled a coffin, or a chest, the paper tamped down, she grabbed hold of the sides and climbed out of there as though out of a bathtub, first one leg, then the other, then she strode over to the mountain of old paper piled ceiling high, scooped with both hands, tossed the paper into the box, got back in, first one leg, as into her tub, then the other, stomping paper, buried in paper, her whole head bound up in a muffler, even I shivered from the cold here, the draft so fierce the entire paper pile flittered in the wind . . . Now I watched the doctor, he was in the garage plucking books off a slanted pile, paperbacks, tearing the covers off and setting the white pages in a box, he was leaning, cap rising and falling again into the box, he was working without gloves, I stepped toward the garage, I couldn't fathom why this person would do this work, and that he actually did like it, perhaps trying to prove something, perhaps in that old paper he is the numero uno, now he straightened, looked for a while at me, I lowered my eyes. The doctor walked over to the bale with the pitcher of beer, one hand on his waist and with the other he gripped the pitcher and took a drink, a long drink. Once he finished drinking, he brought the empty pitcher over.

"In this yard only thing'll warm us is beer. Tea—forget it!"

And then he was brightened by a thought.

"See that woman working over yonder? That mess of a woman? Messed up, true, but only because they evicted her from her villa too, in fact, at her villa she had a gardener, her husband was director of Kladno Cable, but they locked him away, he owned fifty patents for manufacturing cable, they gave him a workshop in the clink, a drawing board, and somewhere out there in lockup land he's dreaming up further improvements, while his wife's in here packing old paper, living only for that moment when her husband's let out, and they are together once again, in a single room where our Miss Mařenka lives now."

And as if she'd caught wind of the doctor, the woman looked up, her face brightening, the face bound in the muffler let out a smile for me, a childlike smile in a middle-aged woman, I gave her a bow and she gave me a nod back. I never would have imagined this woman in a villa once and with a cook, a driver, and a gardener, but that's likely how it was, from how she looked at me I could tell, she clued in first thing to us both in similar shoes, actually all of us here in this yard were somewhere other than where we were supposed to be, in a situation undreamed of, one that it never ever occurred to us that we'd wind up in—so, the boss alone, even while weighing paper or walking across the yard with an armload of it to the office, maintained that slight cock of the head, so all might tell from a distance he used to be head of Čedok, used to occupy the whole building at number three Celetná, the three-story building where the parade would do a march past next year.

"Gentle, melancholy apocalypse," the doctor said, and he lit right up. "Now we can look within ourselves to understand all those revolutions that befell other cultures, except we have an advantage, they didn't liquidate us physically, the way books get liquidated, just look here, I'll bundle ten, twelve bales a day, whatever's no longer 'in,' I even get the aborted ones here in my garage, whole book runs, never read, all those books, the slaughter of the innocents . . . and I'm right in there with all of it, books here by mistake, they get pulped in any case, leftovers from publications that say nothing to people any longer, sometimes even rare books will put in an appearance, those I'll take home, or sell them at the second-hand bookshop with Mr. Haňťa, so we have the wherewithal for lunch and beer, you see, we live in a time ashamed of its past, that's why it's attempting to cover its tracks, as a young girl destroys love letters when she marries someone other than the correspondent who wrote her so beautifully . . . and I'm on top of it, it is passed through my hands . . . actually, I should pay them for letting me work here, because I continue to think of myself as a writer, one day I'll write a book after all, a book to contain the whole sweep of that sweet apocalypse, a book, just one little volume, that will be more than eyewitness account, the facts erupting with poetry."

"I have to be going," I said, sighing.

"Wait . . . This pile of paper, renewing itself every day, to me is a giant Dadaist collage, Kurt Schwitters, a German from Hanover, would be made insane by this beauty here, he spent his entire life montaging pictures of stupefying beauty out of these papers . . . and I'm up on it, scared to look even, sometimes with a yen to stay weekends and copy down one text after the other off this pile, but I don't have the strength or the heart or the pushiness for that line of writing—you have to have real chutzpah . . ."

"I have to be going," I said, again sighing.

"Just a bit longer, just a little bit longer, when you're near I fire on all cylinders, I think clearer . . . I'm finally starting to comprehend why I was so hyped up in Kladno, four years I went there and worked around piles the same, mountains of obsolete tools and machines and junk, which me and Ludva the butcher loaded into bins and watched disappear into the steel smelters, everything mulched, same as these bales of paper in a pulp mill, to get made into new books, new posters, new wrapping paper, and so forth, just like all that old iron and steel and cast iron's resmelted into ingots, ingots into slabs, slabs into products the factories and workshops roll out as new machines, new things . . ."

"I really do have to be going," I took a step forward.

"Just a bit longer; finally it hit me why I sold those trinkets, toys, all that schlock, angel hair to sparklers, scrub brushes to eyelash curlers, for years I lugged two suitcases around, trailed two casefuls of that insane stuff to every drug- and toy store, trying to convince storeowners to buy, cash on the barrel, five percent rebate . . . why open those two suitcases twenty times a day to flaunt at storeowners? Why open those suitcases stuffed with hundreds of free samples, even back in the hotel? Because junk of that sort always touched me, the same as piles of scrap at the steel mill touched me, the same as this paper here moves me, old paper, scrap and tatters . . . Come on."

The doctor took me by the hand and led me up the same set of stairs Haňt'a/Heinrich/Jindra, as they called him here, went up a while ago, we entered a hall, and then the doctor led me down further into the depths of a dark cellar, I held onto him firmly by the hand, and his hand felt good, in fact I squeezed it a little, and he squeezed back, from down there came the crushings of a machine, so I shut my eyes and the doctor kissed me, kissed me for a long time, one long kiss . . . And a door opened and there, under a bare light-bulb, stood Haňt'a/Heinrich, bowing.

"God bless you, good people," he said.

And the doctor led me into the cellar, bales of compacted paper were stacked in rows, and a hydraulic press, in front of which a paper pile escalated as far as a clogged hole in the ceiling, into the yard, where that same pile tiered on up to the light bulbs on the yard's ceiling top, and inside the paper small mice scurried, paper hosed down, damp, and giving off a revolting aroma.

And Mr. Haňt'a stood there like a bannock bun, drenched in sweat, his fedora lay atop a paper bale, a mouse cavorting on it, the sweat was pouring out of Mr. Haňt'a and running and dripping down his nose and chin, he looked groundward and raised an arm.

"I do my best thinking, Doctor, only while I'm hung over, that's every day around eleven A.M., and while I'm at this tyrannical work. When all's said and all those wars and battles, all those revolutions done, they're the only real events for people! We lived through that kind of real event in forty-five! Revolution, revolution, it *was* a revolution too, but mainly about property and defenseless people, when's it ever happen Joe Blow can grab whatever he wants out of a German's flat, grab livestock of any kind out of a barn? Every German shop in Prague and Jihlava and Brno left wide open, and beautiful German *Mädchen* in their dirndls, beautiful nurses in field hospitals, everything laid on a silver platter for that precise instant in history when the last German soldier pulls out and then heaven help the vanquished! And anyone who people thought a collaborator, him they could kill with impunity, Hieronymus Bosch and his hell risen from the dead, Pieter Breughel's slaughtered innocents come to life, all in the name of payback for what Germans had done to us and all those other lands, but all of an event, because for a person there can be nothing more beautiful than when he becomes enraged, when he may commit evil in the name of history . . . and how beautiful, when a person may do whatever he will, whatever he feels, when the sky's the limit, when one may watch the castles and antiques of the

German bourgeoisie and nobility go up in smoke, when you can be creator of such sweet apocalypse of fire and blood and fornication, all with indemnity."

So said Haňt'a with a little smile, his skull shining, it appeared he had a halo around his head, I was unable to move, because everything Mr. Haňt'a talked about, I had lived through, the doctor grew as stiff as a wax mannequin, and Haňt'a proceeded.

"And just as the Reich's army, when it crossed the Soviet border, advanced on flames and fire and ruin and on torched villages and cities and millions of dead, so the Red Army, when the tables were turned, advanced on the retreating dregs of the once-victorious German army, so that when they crossed over the border into Prussia, and Silesia, the whole Red Army, every last soldier, while still alive, had his happening laid out before him, joy at the obliteration of his enemy, joy because the more demolished German cities and villages ablaze, the more dead bodies on their road to Berlin, the more absolutely history would show who was victor, and therefore who the better . . . And the ultimate Happening, Berlin's fall, that smoldering, smoking city, in which not one building was left standing, period, I would love to have been there when the soldier climbed to the tip of the Reichstag and planted the Red Flag . . . and then it's hip hip hooray, and open season then on every building in Germany, every bit of booze, every bedroom, every cellar, pure payback then, no tooth for a tooth time, but whole jaw for one molar, both eyes in your head for the one . . . And know who to blame for all this?" asked Haňt'a merrily.

"Who! That blasted boy, Charles IV, the one who built up the plush German cities, the plush monasteries, that blasted boy, who not only triggered the Hussite revolution, but this, the Second World War even, for once the Reichstag fell the old empire did as well, the one Charles IV cherished as the German and Holy Roman Emperor, and only now does his imperium fall, courtesy of the Red Army . . . Hehehe, Herr Hegel's mind wasn't wandering when he scrawled that Charles IV was feudal . . . *der letzte Universalist auf dem Thron* . . . And Hitler identified with his imperium . . . Now, Doctor, I *am* thinking clearly, I'm over my hangover, and on to happier matters." Mr. Haňt'a changed his stance, planted one hand on his waist, leaned against a bale of paper with the other, and laughed.

"It was close to a month after the war, times were already happier and cherries ripening on the trees, near where I lived, a group of Red Army soldiers passed by, got a hankering for some of the cherries, so they ripped out the fence, as they were used to doing during the war, tore off whole branches . . . and they ate and they laughed . . . and the owner came over, this painter, and he brought a stepladder and explained to them how much work it had taken to raise the cherries, he talked to them in Russian, and drew in the sand, described how a tree like that grows, and the soldiers stopped eating and almost burst into tears, called themselves pigs for managing to destroy such a beautiful tree . . . but the professor consoled them with his drawings, the tree was beyond repair anyway, then he gave them the stepladder and told them to pick as many cherries as they wanted, and to come back again tomorrow . . . And what they did, before leaving, they promised the painter they were going to make it up to him . . . and then not until fourteen days later did one come back, he was laughing, and the painter was out in his garden and the soldier gave him something wrapped in newspaper . . . and he laughed and rode off again on his horse . . . And the painter, when he unwrapped that newspaper out there in the sunshine, what did he see but blood-stained ears with diamond earrings, women's ears, a true treasure, because those ears were six in all."

Haňťa quietly concluded speaking, the doctor standing in front of him. Mr. Haňťa had small breadcrumbs stuck to his lips and in his beard, and out of nowhere the doctor picked out the crumbs and ate them.

My stomach turned and I said, "I really have to be going."

■ □ ■ □ ■

CHAPTER ELEVEN

ALL WEEK LONG LIZA KEPT CALLING ME AT WORK, ASKING ME NOT
to let her down for God's sake, they were heading off to Moravia for
the weekend, for a funeral, and they wanted me to come over to their
place, because they were taking care of Bobby, a Kerry blue, whose
masters had stayed on in Austria and weren't coming back, so they
took Bobby in and that was that, because Liza loved dogs and this
terrier, so sweet, even the doctor fell in love with him and brought
him in to all the pubs . . . She wanted me to sleep at their place, and
Liza begged, "For God's sake, just take that little dog for a walk, give
him something to eat."

So I set off for Libeň first thing in the morning, arrived in time, and
indeed had never seen a prettier dog, we became fast friends, indeed
I was happy Liza asked me to come. Liza and Wulli were piling so
much stuff into the car, for a while I got worried they were moving to
Vienna for good and leaving me with Bobby here. But finally we said
our good-byes and they set off, Bobby stood on guard near the gas
lamp for a while, but when I walked over to him, he gave me a lick and
barked and ran into the hallway, where Mrs. Beranová was washing
down the tiles again with buckets of water, she patted Bobby and said,
"Beautiful beast, isn't he?" And then Mr. Slavíček came downstairs
from the other courtyard, leading a timid-looking boy by the hand,
a young girl came behind, she smiled at me, they patted Bobby, and
when they made it down to the bottom of the stairs, Mrs. Beranová
splashed three buckets of water at their feet, so they had to jump

back, and dressed once more in violet panties and bra, the neat lady grumbled, "Why don't you watch where you're going!"

And Bobby ran into the courtyard and beyond into the washhouse and began to bark madly, joyful mad barking, and from the washhouse the doctor emerged, naked, holding no more than a tiny towel out in front of him, Bobby barking for him, the doctor leaned down and closed his eyes, for Bobby to slobber all over him. As soon as the doctor noticed me, he gave a start and almost dropped the towel, Mrs. Slavíčková was on the toilet, door open, torso and head poking out and calling, "Doctor, aren't you a teeny bit embarrassed? My kids went by a moment ago."

The doctor protested, "I'm covered, madame, I know what's proper, I was brought up correctly," and he turned to me and whispered, "You're going to look after the dog here, they gave you the keys, eh?"

"They did, it's my friend, Liza, but you have keys to their apartment too, don't you? After all, you've been at their place every night for five years, haven't you? You're their friend too, aren't you?"

"Sure, I like Liza, she's who she always was, but Wulli, for God's sake, it's just dawned on me now . . . He used to go round in a folk-dancing costume, rode a horse in the festival of kings, doesn't know a word of German but now the Germans are *uber Alles* to him . . . but anyway! I'm going swimming, not to the Vltava though, but the Labe, you'll come along, yes?"

"I have to mind the doggie," I said.

"Mrs. Beranová will, she's in love with him. Go give him a walk, I'll get dressed in the meantime, shave . . . Go upstairs, his leash is hanging up there."

"Where?" I asked.

"Don't worry, he'll show you."

And there upstairs, good-naturedly pulling up her huge underwear, her Vamberk underwear, and smoothing down her skirt, Mrs. Slavíčková came out of the WC, she smiled at me and leered at the doctor and growled, and then stepped into her flat and slammed the door behind her . . .

I tried to pry open the door to the circular staircase with my knee, on the third try I managed and again was greeted by a cold draft of musty air that reeked of peeling paint, Bobby ran downstairs meantime and was having an exchange with Mrs. Beranová, she patting him and lisping some gobbledygook to him, I reached the balcony and then Liza's apartment, Bobby came running in behind me, barking and leaping at the coatrack, where his red leash hung, I put down my bag and then I blushed, because I'd actually had it in mind to go swimming with the doctor, not only had I brought bread slathered in pork fat, but two packs of schnitzel and roast pork besides, and then went redder than red, because in my bag I even had a pint of beer, and when I leaned over to put the gorgeous coral-red leash on Bobby, I broke into a sweat so severe I had to wipe its drops off my brow with my elbow, for I realized the doctor wasn't alone in this, but everyone in the building here knew Liza and Wulli were away for the weekend, and the only reason for going was for me to stop over, take care of Bobby, Liza borrowed Bobby just so the doctor and I, no others, would keep an eye on him for the two days they were in Moravia for the funeral . . . And Bobby got up and gave a friendly bark, back and forth to the balcony he ran, when I went to the balcony, he ran up and down the stairs, delighted, showing me how glad he was to see me, how glad that I was taking him out for a walk. And I turned the lock to the door and there downstairs Bobby started in, fawning all over the neat woman again.

"Look," said the woman, "look, it's beautiful out, I'll do the looking after of the dog, he'd probably run off on you . . . and I have a couple of pots on the go for the doctor, a little treat. Oh, Lord, a little treat, Bobby, right, Bobby, right? Back when I was a waitress in Hamburg for twenty years, I had a dog like that too." And she took the full bucket of water and splashed it on the tiles and then swept the water with a broom into the gutter.

And I stepped over that huge puddle in my high heels and Bobby barked in the hallway, turned toward me, then barked for the door handle, and when I opened the door carefully, Bobby stepped out onto the sidewalk carefully and gave a bark, I put the red leash on him and Bobby walked ahead, carried himself proudly, and I led proudly, because his red collar and leash were the color of my famous red high heels, and I laughed till teary-eyed, somehow it brought me back through time, at home we used to have an Airedale terrier, Daddy took pride in his dogs and I took them out for walks because Daddy loved them so, loved purebreds like Bobby, whose master and mistress had gone off to the West simply for Bobby and I to go strutting out on Na Hrázi, people turning to take another glance, because we looked so fine. And I gave a little jump for joy, did three polka steps, Bobby barking in time, in fact, an old lady even stopped me and said, "We used to have one like that too, oh, so many tears when he passed on, he died of distemper . . . little Kerry, Kerry blue terrier, I know the breed's from England, for otter hunting, and they have such a good disposition, if the otter gets hold of him before he manages a hold on the otter, even while your otter's dragging him to the bottom, this terrier will keep wagging his tail till the otter drowns him, yes ma'am, drowns." The old lady shook her head and I smiled and nodded and continued on to Ludmila Street. And so Bobby and I reached the train tracks and then continued down to Main Street, strutting forth, Bobby beside me, and my high-heel red and Bobby's leash-and-collar red had an affect that made people jump aside, let us pass, and people passing in the other direction turned to look and I put on this bored demeanor, as though thinking higher thoughts, I walked along as though Bobby and I were the chocolate or Parisian pastry with whipped cream on top. And a young lady came out of Pramen grocery store, she looked like a puppet, so much makeup on she resembled a clown, and the lass took a glance at Bobby and then at me, she gave Bobby a pat and I said, "He's a Kerry blue, a little Kerry, from England, the breed they use for hunting otters, such a good disposition he has, that whenever . . ."

But the puppet-faced lass grimaced and then said with a laugh, "Give the doctor a message from my grandmother, as his landlady, she reminds him he owes her half a year's back rent, *drei hundert Kronen.*"

I said, "And why tell me, why not tell the doctor, personally! And why the *drei hundert Kronen?*"

And I jerked my shoulder away and turned red, but Bobby and I continued on down Main, still the center of attention, and I walked thinking about that clown-faced lady, why she lit into me on the street, why she didn't tell me as much back at number twenty-four, and in any case, who owed rent, me or the doctor? And immediately I pictured Liza's flat, a door near her bed, a locked door that led into the flat where Wulli's aunt lived, and this lassie here was her niece. I saw the locked door and the bed next to it, had seen that bed earlier today, I turned red because I recalled the bed had been freshly made this morning, which would have been no big deal, but this morning the bed had new sheets on, which would have been no big deal either, but a pair of clean Viennese pajamas had been set on the freshly made bed. For me. And I turned all the redder, stomped my foot down so hard Bobby jumped, what would the doctor think? He too had a set of keys for that flat, keys to that flat . . . and I'm expected to sleep there, everything made up for me beforehand, fresh soap and clean towels, blood flooded to my head, so much so I needed to stop, heart pounding . . . thing is, it was a snare, so the doctor would sleep with me, and then, no more cares, not as many at least, because I'd be his blushing bride by then, with a place to live at number twenty-four Na Hrázi Street and even a work permit . . . And so what if it were a snare? piped up my inner voice, because I took after my mother a little, a forest ranger's daughter from Lower Austria, not only hard- but pigheaded too, who could suddenly wheel about and do the opposite of the expected, as a young girl she attended church every last day to pray, but when Hitler turned up she went to watch him in Vienna, and from then on he was her god, right up until the last day in May of forty-five . . . after all, did I not have a right to listen and adhere to an inner voice that said, Yes, let all happen as fate has it drawn for you.

And Bobby was at the door already, up on hind legs, barking for the handle, so in we went, and Bobby ran straight to Mrs. Beranová, sitting on a chair reading *Saturday Ahoy,* Bobby put his head between her fat legs and blissfully closed his eyes, I handed Mrs. Beranová the red leash and said, "Okay then, thanks ever so much, we would probably end up forgetting him somewhere."

And the neat lady gave her head a tilt, her glasses slid down her nose and with her bloodshot eyes she looked right into me and laughed, saying, "No kidding!"

And the doctor came downstairs, stopped, pulled out a little pocket mirror, and examined himself, straightened his fine hair with his fingers, and the neat lady remarked affably, "A real looker, still the looker." And I ran upstairs, unlocked the door, ran into the kitchen in the little room, and sure enough, there by the locked, painted white door, the bed freshly made, and as sure as can be, I was not mistaken, the pair of Viennese pajamas, I grabbed my purse, and sure as fate, as I walked out to the balcony, there above the washbasin, a fresh towel and a new piece of soap, I paused, laughed, shrugged my shoulders, What's to be done? It was too like in *The Bartered Bride*, the whole building, the whole Hotel Paris, the whole host who knew me looked on me as the little bride, so why should I not regard myself a bride too, particularly in the building where the doctor put on his in-house weddings every fortnight . . .

And I locked the door, my red high heels clacking on the wet staircase on the way down, Bobby still had his muzzle between Mrs. Beranová's thighs, he gazed into her eyes, wagged his tail as though being dragged under by an otter, I looked eagerly in the direction of the doctor, waiting for me with his eyes, but he lowered them immediately—his turn to blush then—so we stood in that big puddle drying in the afternoon sun, and the neat lady Beranová, when she saw the doctor go red, simply sighed and waved us off with her hand . . .

Well, we walked abreast down Na Hrázi, the doctor ran over his hair with a pocket brush, he wore an open, light-colored cardigan, gray slacks, walking at a faster clip than I, actually he sped ahead, as though we were in a hurry to catch a train, but he did wait until I caught up, then walked beside me for a bit, but then once again sped up, twice almost I broke my red high heels—never mind the heels, I heard a small crunch in my ankle.

"This," the doctor said, pointing, "this here is a notorious mailbox. First day they fixed it to the wall, I saw a blind man walk past, going his usual route, and run headfirst into the sharp edge of this tin mailbox. And he gushed blood, but then that blind man takes his white cane and runs it over the mailbox twice! Can you picture it? Can you hear it? Anytime I step out with you, you can hear, see it for yourself, how I gush, how I just barrel on . . . probably because you talk little, probably because you're my grateful listener . . . Ach, that Wulli, who looked so fine in his folk-dancing kit, who so dislikes Jews—what am I saying?—he hates the Jews so much he walked blind and into a mailbox too, because he put his whole stake on the Germans, who made short shrift of the Jews, as you well know, that Wulli, while Liza was in the clink . . . in the end it turned out right for her, she was a party member, you must understand, wherever the Germans went they rounded up, not just Jews, but Communists and shot them . . . But here Wulli was at his auntie's place, that landlady of ours I still owe back rent to, out here on the veranda was a huge cage, and inside, Lorry the parrot, 130 years young, raised in Vienna, so she spoke nothing but German, every morning she says, '*Lorry ist schon und brav,*' and consequently when Wulli was here about a month after the war, putting the finishing touches on a letter, Lorry on his shoulder as usual, outside Wulli goes carrying his letter to this here mailbox, and when he throws the letter in, he drums on the mailbox lid, and Lorry screeches, '*Ein! Zwei! Drei! Der Kaiser ist da!*' And it was morning time and the street full of people, imagine hearing orders in German at that hour of the day! And in comes Wulli along with Lorry flying, into that hallway of ours . . . Ach, that Wulli! You know, if his had been a love story, then fine and dandy, but to marry Liza right when over forty thousand Czechs were to be executed for sympathizing with Heydrich's assassination . . . and him, a Sokol, to marry Liza right at that moment, to do that he must have been dead certain the Germans would win, that the Reich might fluff it didn't occur to him, never in his wildest dreams."

I shrugged my shoulders, and just then it struck me that the doctor had it right, I remembered during the Protectorate how Wulli and Liza sat at our place, with soldiers and NSDAP members, Wulli carefully listening in, not knowing a word of German while Liza quietly translated for him, and not only the soldiers but the Nazis too were convinced right up until the last minute that the Reich was going to win, because Hitler had his secret weapon . . . And now we walked along the train tracks, a locomotive went by and filled the street with steam and brown cloud, we stood out in front of a building, a long balcony running along its second floor, blankets over the railings and fat ladies standing, leaning on them. We waited for steam and fume to die and then carried on, on the ground floor there were ten doors, ten doors on the second floor, and you entered the flats by doors like those of a wardrobe. And all the windows and all the doors were open, and old people sitting on chairs in front of them or leaning over the railings, they seemed in a fine festive mood, as though away off in Sazava, leaning out over the railings of a chalet that looked down upon a glittering river, while they sat here in smoke. It took some time before the breeze blew away the smoke and fumes, away to the gates, away to Libeň Station to land on the bushes and thickets alongside the railway tracks. And when the smoke lifted, or crawled away over the ground, we still stood in front of that odd building with the odd occupants, and they still watched the railway tracks and us and enjoyed themselves, like watching a special display, a parade march along that dusty Žertvy Street.

"That's the Peruzz," the doctor said, "where workers from Peruzz Laundry lived, and still live, but as soon as one of them dies no one else wants to anymore, so the only souls moving into the empty flats are . . . Come on in the yard, we've time."

And the doctor turned in under the crumbling arch of the gateway, and we walked through to the yard, there the building looked similar, except even more dilapidated, balconies held up by wooden post and beam and walls peeling and flaking like pastry dough. And here the people seated in front of their flats were also attired in their finery and in holiday mood, they gazed out of the deep shadows into the sunlight, at a red hand pump that shone in the sun, at dozens of small sheds cobbled from slats and boards stretching the length of the yard, and seated inside the open sheds were old folk diligently employed at workbenches, filing, sanding, and fitting things together, while a band of gypsy children disported themselves on a small green field near the hand pump, the children and their clothes shone like gems in the sun, and for the first time I remarked that all the gypsy kids had beautiful hair and eyes and skin, on them anything looked good, even though practically every one had a noodle of snot that dangled down out of his nose . . .

Then we returned to Žertvy Street, the doctor paced ahead of me alongside the railway tracks, walked so swiftly I couldn't keep up, I, in fact, slowed down purposely to force the doctor to turn around and wait until I caught up. And whenever he paced ahead, I could see his legs were a bit bowed, soccer player's legs, when he turned he guessed what I was looking at, blushed a trifle, and when I caught up to him, he said, "The legs wouldn't be that bad, but what really bothers me is losing my hair. I had so much of it till I was thirty, I couldn't put a comb through it even, had to pour oil on it to comb, and even then use a bristle brush. My hair used to be chestnut, little wave over my forehead, regular ducktail . . . such ends, from such beautiful beginnings."

"Same for you as everyone," I said.

And next thing we crossed the main street to the railroad crossing, beside the main street stood the station and a cement-and-lime store, the lime glittered in the sun, and like spring snow, hurt the eyes.

We passed by a coal yard and walked on the tracks until we reached the station, the doctor bought the tickets and then we stood on the platform, through an open ticket master's door you could see desks with telegraph machines, a huge panel of mechanisms constantly rattling; the dispatcher then ran out and threw switches for the signal box, and then took his position on the platform, passengers streamed to the side of the tracks and a train came in, hauled by a steam engine, smoke billowed and settled softly on the passengers, but once the train halted, you could see it was jam-packed, people standing in corridors, open windows so crammed with people their arms had to hang outside, two women conductors finally managed to squeeze out from a carriage, the people from the Libeň Station started to board, squeezing in, pushing through, and you could hear people shouting the length of the train, "Move all the way into the compartments inside!"

The doctor mounted the steps, but rested on the first, then shouted, "Open the lavatory door!" And that's how we managed to board the train, strange holidaymaker's train, I stood pressed to the doctor in the lavatory, thank God for the open window, I was afraid to look down at the cracked, filthy toilet bowl, thank God for that open window . . . holding onto the window with his two hands, the doctor stood squeezed up against me, and I, facing him, his arms about me, and that's how we steamed out on our wonderful outing, headed where, I had no idea, but I did know the doctor and I were pressed together, as though to dance, I raised my own arms and placed my hands on the doctor's shoulders, so even our faces met, the train gathered speed, I could see the smoke land on the crowds standing at the railway crossing on the main street, into that smoke disappeared the main street, the train slowly gathered speed and spewed steam onto the track, and the steam intensified the smell of the smoke falling, I held onto the doctor, it growing dark in those clouds of smoke and steam, as though we had pulled into Wilson Station . . . And then a signal light, and the smoke lifted enough for me to see the long Peruzz balconies through the small window, old ladies leaning on their blankets watching with curiosity as our train passed, some seated at the railings, arms hung over them, as though dislocated . . . and then the train gathered its speed and you could see the streets of Libeň on either side of the tracks, a garden restaurant at Ružka's, and then a tunnel and the train picked up more speed, I had never noticed the lovely hills that surrounded Libeň, cottage rooftops poked out of them, a dotting of fruit trees and bushes on the hills, people everywhere, shirts and T-shirts glinting, some in their shorts and bathing suits lying on deck chairs in the sun.

"That's Hájek," the doctor whispered in my ear.

"Yes?" I raised my eyes, looked him in his shaved chin, could feel his breath.

"And that's Kotlaska, and now we cross the River Rokytka," whispered the doctor into my ear, his lips on my earlobe, it was lovely, the fact we had had to squeeze into this horrible lavatory involuntarily, this lavatory with the open bowl letting a draft of air in off the tracks below. And then we passed by a gasworks, behind which rose a small hill and some tumbledown cliffs, immediately above the tracks a path led up the hillside and people there were walking along the path dressed in their finery, they stopped with their kids and gazed at the packed train, the lady conductor on the steps holding onto the steel handrail, and the train pulled into a station, and there dozens more waited, when the train stopped you could hear the lady conductor pounding on the cars and calling for people to squeeze all the way into the compartments, otherwise the train would stay here in Vysočany . . . But the people were headed out on their trips, beautiful days all planned, the whole car filled with shouts and happy chatter, filled with colorful shirts, T-shirts, purses, handbags, and I froze for fear somebody had to make use of this toilet, somebody with an urgent stomach upset needing to use this lavatory, then the luck that allowed the doctor and I to huddle into this lavatory would run out. And the train started to move again, it jolted forward, the car rocked back and forth so much we were thrust even closer together, in such tight embrace our thighs and stomachs bumped, we held each other by the hand as if dancing a polka, or a waltz, we looked through the window, and the train was passing through groves of birch trees outside, where young mothers lay on blankets in the grass with their children, then we passed a brickworks and more trees alongside the tracks, children and adults lying here and there under the trees . . .

And the toilet bowl was laid open, covered in filth, through the dripping open hole you could see receding, alternating railway ties and the oil-sodden gravel and droplets of condensed steam. And when the train came to a halt, people poured off, passing their children and bags through windows, the lavatory door swung closed and we were alone there, still held onto each other, embraced, pressed onto one another, dancing our polka or our waltz.

"I always feel good when I'm with you," the doctor whispered.

"Me too," I said.

"You see, when I'm with you, I feel . . . you're not even with me," he mumbled.

"I don't understand," I said, "but . . . I get it."

"Well, I simply feel good with you . . . what if you were to move into my place? See, I only have this one room, but it has a door you can go through into the next room and that next room is same as mine, one room a mirror image of the next, and a common hallway, and common WC out in the yard, it's nice, when it's raining or the snow's falling, to walk out barefoot to the WC in the courtyard, and then in the laundry room there's even a bathhouse, with these terrific tubs we could take baths in, and then, you saw yourself, there's a little terrace roof, I could saw up one chair more, just for you," said the doctor, his lips to my ear, my eyes closed and I nodded my head like at confessional in church, and I responded, "Yes, yes, yes."

Then came a knock on the lavatory door, then the doorknob rattled, the door flew open and there stood the lady conductor, calling angrily, "Tickets, please . . . right now! The corridors and compartments now have the spaces, so free the shitter, please, yes?"

"Yes," I said and took the first step out, and the doctor stepped after me, both blushing, but not for shame, but the luck that surely came my way and maybe even the doctor's in that stomach-turning toilet, which then and there resembled the booth for a confessional, and when people saw us pass by stinking of Lysol, they moved back disgusted and I regretted bitterly not staying in there with the doctor for a lot, lot longer . . .

■ □ ■ □ ■

CHAPTER TWELVE

AND THEN WE DESCENDED FROM THE TRAIN AT A SMALL STATION, the doctor appeared somehow in an un-made-up mind, but deeply moved; he scanned the station, stood there indecisively outside the waiting room, the dispatcher went in under the roof affixed to the stationmaster's and threw the switches in the signal box, and coming down from the baggage-car end, the locomotive, was a woman in her railway uniform, pushing a handcart of parcels and luggage before her, and when she spied the doctor, her face lit up, she left the handcart to the attendant and gave the doctor a heartfelt hug, the dispatcher signaled for the train to depart, the woman and the doctor exchanged a kiss, and the dispatcher, returning from the side of the track, went into the office, picked up the phone, and then came back out, he was young and wore yellow shoes, and under the jacket of his uniform his shirt was wide open.

"Chief Dispatcher," the woman called to him, "this here's the dispatcher I worked with during the Protectorate, the one the Germans wanted to shoot."

But the young dispatcher just gave a shrug of his shoulders and went in the office, the woman returned to her handcart but the doctor ran ahead of her to handle the cart himself and wheel it on over to the baggage shed. The doctor, it was as though he forgot all about me, I followed after him, the woman piled parcels and luggage, and then the doctor pointed me out and said, "This is my lady friend . . .

and this woman here . . . I used to work with, but tell me, how did it all end for our old stationmaster?"

And the woman offered me her hand, made a little curtsy, I could still see her as pretty, back then, twelve years ago, she must have been simply beautiful, even now she looked like the Virgin Mary, she smiled at the doctor, who offered me the chair, and then sat down on the handcart. The woman smoothed the doctor's hair and said, "But what's up, you're losing your hair? And Prokop, the stationmaster, how did he end up? Don't even ask. Got locked up for a while right after the revolt, but nothing happened to him, then he worked for a while somewhere near the border and straight into retirement. He learned his lesson . . . But, Doctor, what's up, you're practically bald." She examined the doctor's hair and then looked at me and explained, "See, the stationmaster used to work as a dispatcher on the Ustí–Děčín line, he fell in love with a German woman and married her, back then it was common enough, Germans still visited the Czech restaurants and Czechs the German, they'd sing a Czech song and then a German song, and Czechs would even sing German and the Germans Czech, but then along came Henlein and the beginning of the end . . . but that stationmaster's wife went a little gaga on us, Hitler was her god, once the stationmaster was assigned to us in our station, we had to be on our guard, you see even the stationmaster sided with the Germans, they had a daughter and she was Hitler Youth and oh, the festivities when Hitler took Poland and then France, and oh, the joy when Hitler took on the Russians even, we had to be on our guard around the stationmaster. But! Then Stalingrad, up till then we'd always have these *Schweinfests*, second floor, stationmaster's flat, people singing and partying, but then Stalingrad, the stationmaster's wife donated her furs to the front, but that didn't help any, and then the stationmaster started looking out behind him, once Stalingrad fell, started coming downstairs into the office at night, coming down and even talking to the signalmen and the switchmen about the situation at the front, he stopped listening to the Reich's broadcasts, listening to only the ones from England, the stationmaster's wife and daughter alone kept faith, but by the time you arrived, as a dispatcher, near the end already, the stationmaster knew how the war would go, only the stationmaster's wife kept on believing her Germans were going to win, because

Hitler had his secret weapon . . . But, Doctor, what's up? Is one of your eyes drooping?" And the woman looked concerned at the doctor and waved a hand in front of his eyes and then her own waving hand scared her and she laughed, the dispatcher came out of the office, stood near the station tracks, a freight train thundered through, the dispatcher watched it go by and reentered then, in the roofed space you could hear the signal handles chatter, the doctor raised himself up and watched the freight train, watched it go by and was intent and serious and then returned to his seat on the handcart and stared at the dusty floor.

"Those are my most beautiful dreams," he said, "I keep dreaming I have a fine uniform, polished black shoes, jacket buttoned up to the collar . . . I stand there and express trains and locals and military transports pass through my station, closely watched trains headed to the front, and I switch the tracks and open and close the signal switches, I'm in the office, telephones and telegraphs chattering, the stove is roaring—you were always adding more to it, you were forever smiling, smiling all the time and smiling even in my dreams. You know, if I could have a second time around, I would want to pass my whole life as dispatcher and then stationmaster at a small station, but the stationmaster *was* good to me, I practically ate a whole pig on him."

The woman took over, "No kidding, but only because his gall bladder was shot, and his liver destroyed, and his wife couldn't eat a bite, because Budapest had fallen already, Vratislav fell, that's why!"

The doctor looked at me and for the first time I noticed that one of his eyes truly did droop lower than the other, like the officers who sat around our place and told us about what they survived at the front, even Herr Norden, the one who resembled Marlon Brando, the one who pushed me on the big garden swing, fingers touching mine where I gripped the chain, he too had one eye low and exactly like the doctor appeared off in a dream, as though elsewhere, as though peering into a distance, into the depth of time.

"Yes," the doctor said, "that's it, Breslau had fallen already and the stationmaster slaughtered a pig, he still put a *Schweinfest* on, but those legs of pork he looked ahead to, he couldn't eat the way he did, every night, when I came in on the night shift, I'd hear him come down from his flat and offer me a big plate of kebabs, half a kilo of pork chops, quick-fried in fat, chopped onion on the side, he'd carry it in with his white apron on, his white butcher's apron, and offer up this delicacy he himself could not eat, he'd turn a chair around and sit, chin propped on his folded fingers and sit there just so watching me eat those hot, fast-fried slices of pork, watch me, and actually I was eating for him, because he swallowed like it was him eating those pork hocks. Every night for a whole month I ate that well, the stationmaster bringing on plate after plate, till I demolished both legs of pork for him . . . And then the front got nearer, Ostrava fell, one night up there in the stationmaster's flat the light was on, the stationmaster's wife and little daughter pacing back and forth, and then down they came carrying their suitcases, the wife pale and crying, I helped them onto a hospital express with their bags and then never saw sight of them again."

"But, Mr. Dispatcher, what're you talking about!" the woman said. "That Hilda was no little girl, she was a young woman already, sixteen years old . . . and you didn't know? Come on, after all she was in love with you. And how! The only reason the stationmaster made you kebabs was to buck up your courage and get you up to their place just the once, to see Hilda."

The doctor went red and said, "But Lord's sake, back then I couldn't venture upstairs, back then I couldn't venture a visit with the stationmaster's wife, who believed right until the last the Germans were going to win, they had a secret weapon . . . the concentration camps were bulging, think I'd have had the gall to start something with a German girl? I know, little Hilda would come down, sit here beside the telegraph machine, I'd go out to the trains and in here she'd be reading *The Sorrows of Young Werther,* I know she was sixteen and beautiful, she'd sit here, and whenever I would lean across the telegraph machine, how many times did I practically faint on that fragrant blonde hair of hers, a sparkle in the dimmed lamplight and chatter of telegraphs and telephones . . . I wonder what your fair-haired Hilda's up to now?"

"Somewhere in Holland, she got married there, but Nymburk local's on its way in, Doctor, I have to be at the baggage car. Wait for me, we'll hark back some more."

"No," said the doctor. "I'll make that stop some other time."

The woman smiled at me, proffered her rough hand, her face was lined, but pretty still, she wore lipstick and a clean uniform, now she gave the doctor a concerned glance all over again, brushed a few random hairs from his brow, but the manner of moving her hand was more as if she wiped away some care, a care which probably only she could perceive.

"You've gotten older, Mr. Dispatcher, grown dreadfully serious, what, what's happened to you?" She passed her hand in front of the doctor's eyes once more, and he looked away to the side again, one eye lowered.

And the local pulled in and the woman quickly pushed the handcart out of the baggage shed, the wheels trundled across the tracks, the train came to a halt, the handcart stood by the baggage car, a uniformed man stood in the door opening of the baggage car, giving a salute to the dispatcher and the station porter . . . Sadly the doctor laughed and raised his hand, the station porter loaded three packages on the handcart and then waved the doctor good-bye, I walked behind the doctor, even a little stooped now, in front of the office window he stopped and looked in, squinted for his eyes to see better, to peer in at a long table, the telegraph table, and when he turned, I could tell he had seen Hilda there, the fair-haired girl, and sixteen, the one who came down into the office to read *The Sorrows of Young Werther,* in there he'd seen Hilda, who pretended to be reading, but who wasn't, she was harking to the chatter of the telegraph machine and the telephones' ring, but mainly the tread of the young dispatcher, who back then had probably had loads of hair and been quite fetching, just as I, that time when I was back in our big dining room, pretended to read, the youngest general in the German infantry, von Norden, seated facing me, and my eyes dropped, in a pretense of reading, just like Hilda, hearkening to the blood rush to my head . . .

The on-duty dispatcher stood at the step now, about to go back into the office, but as if against his will, he hesitated, turned around and said, "Do you want to come have a peek into the office? From the time you worked here nothing's changed."

"No actually, or maybe I will?" The doctor laughed. "I might faint, the Germans wanted to shoot me here, twice, once they already had me on the SS steam engine, and I could feel rifles pressed into my back, not till we'd passed Rozkoš did I feel the tips of those rifles pull back and the SS commandant nodded for me to climb down out of the steam engine," said the doctor sourly, but not to the dispatcher, rather right at me, and then I was flushed and shouting, "But it was when I was sixteen! Is that my fault?"

The dispatcher still stood at the first step, and again offered the doctor a peek inside the office, saying nothing had changed from that time.

"But it has changed," the doctor said, "back when I worked here, one time I had one button undone on my uniform, and the railway inspector stepped off the train, I was on the platform, black shoes all polished, and the railway inspector did up that button himself, in front of everybody."

And the dispatcher stood, inspected his yellow shoes on the first step, then fingered his open blue shirt, shrugged, and went back into the office.

"Too bad they didn't shoot you back then," he said.

And then we walked under the clock that hung over one corner of the railway station, we took a turn and walked along by a broken fence, past scattered rails and strewn tools, through an alley of old lindens, we entered an old two-story roadhouse, walked down the passageway and back out into the sun, then around the side of the building and in through the village, we peeked in at a crumbling old estate, a gated estate, once proud, gateposts adorned with two plaster lions, in the yard stood a ruined barn, but on one wall a sundial still shone. The doctor waved a hand and then turned into a small street, three small houses were there, a Spartak parked next to one, and a young man soaping the hood with detergent, digging a sponge into a bucket of suds, dirt dripping off the car in a trickle, and behind the building, two seeding machines planted to rust without their wheels.

"Really, it is too bad they didn't shoot me back then," the doctor repeated, "but it's good it was here we made the stop, I never understood why . . ."

And then, there was only an extended trail through the fields and apple trees growing by all the ditches, and then we stepped through some mud a tractor had deposited there, and the doctor grew angry, "Who says you can't live the way people did, when I lived at the brewery, the farmer, before he'd come in off the fields behind the brewery, he'd scrape every bit of mud and dirt off the tires and using his shovel throw the soil back in the field and then drive out onto the road with the tractor clean." And far away then we heard a bell toll, and continually then the doctor would run on ahead of me and wait, or he'd turn and come back, and I continued picking my way carefully in my high heels, and my purse felt cumbersome, I walked and the dirt was grinding under my high heels, and out of nowhere the doctor said, "My friend Marysko, the poet, you'll meet him, always wanted his own studio, and when he'd spent around ten thousand finally he got that studio, the deed to an old shop. And so we stood in front of this closed metal shutter, and Marysko had the shop's key and the deed, and when we finished a bottle of Botrys, Mr. Marysko unlocked the shutter and I rolled it up, it flew up with a rattle, and when we looked in the display window and through the glass door we saw two beds in the show window and a man asleep, his legs splayed, and a wardrobe in the door. This cook had cut a way in from the adjacent flat and set up an extra room for himself, and because the fella had three children, the people at the housing office even bawled out Marysko as soon as he showed them his title to the shop . . . I think back at our place in Libeň, if we cut our way into the next room, secretly, we'd find ourselves in the same straits as that cook, know what I mean?"

He stood ahead of me, and once I caught up to him, he started backpedaling and looking at me, and I could see one eye was lower. And then we walked in sunshine, the scent of the water closer, and then we reached a row of poplar trees, and then before us lay a gentle river, and so we stood there a while gazing cross-river at a hamlet, and then we strode down to the landing for the ferry, there was a gangway and a raft coupled to a line stretched over to the other riverbank, and on the riverbank the ferryman lay, hat down over his face, and three goats grazed the riverbank, tugging clumps of grass, chins trembling. And the doctor offered me his hand and led me aboard, helped me to a seat, I sat down and breathed a sigh of relief, my feet were starting to ache, I put my bag by me on the seat, but the doctor picked it up and sat down in its place and put the bag on his lap. And subsequently we sat there next to each other, and that trip to the train station, and everything I'd listened to there, left me unable to breathe and spoiled the atmosphere. And then the ferryman woke up and took us over to the other side of the river, I dangled my hand in streaming water and felt abashed. And then we made our way to a small power station, and water rumbled and sprayed into the air and created these pillars of water drops, and the wind whipping between the pillars carried spray water into the distance, and we walked on into those water clouds and the sun shone dim, and then we walked past these little cottages adjacent to the river, every cottage open, exuding the aroma of food, we saw cottagers in bathing suits swim down in the river, sprawled on blankets among the shrub willow, waves piling up sand in the small inlets. And then an inlet with a beautiful sand beach, we walked down to the river, changed into our swimsuits, and went swimming. And after we laid into the schnitzels and bread and drank the beer lukewarm, and I then lay listening in the sun to the water splash and kids yell a ways away, and then eyes closed, fell asleep and simply drifted in and out then for a time, and when I woke and had my eyes open, the doctor was sitting beside me and had a little fire going, the breeze off the water stirred up the fire and the doctor warmed his hands, now he rose and ran along the riverbank gathering dry twigs and branches, I felt really tired, and saddened. And a couple more times we went swimming then, and the fire heated our hands and our feet and it felt nicer, I smiled at the doctor and was glad of his being quiet, and I realized then how the doctor behaved with tact and how he liked me, why he was being quiet, anything he might have said or done to justify himself would have made me all the sadder, because I was a German girl to the doctor, too, and therefore out of the blue I said, "But, Doctor, I have Czech schooling, my parents were moved to the West because of being German, and I stayed on here on account of my Czech schooling, exactly as my brother Heini did, because Czech schooling gave us Czechoslovak citizenship, and so here I am."

The doctor leaned down and put his finger on my lips, I closed my eyes and he kissed me, then he got to his knees in the sand and kissed me, then he lay on his back and raised his arms and gazed up at the sky and I leaned over him and pressed my face to his and kissed him, and he wrapped his arms around me and for the longest time we kissed and then over and over again. And so we lay in the shrub willow and the sun dipped behind the oaks. And then we sat upright to gaze in twilight into the glow of wood embers fanned by the wind.

And we changed our clothes then, our swimsuits chilly already, and ate pork then and bread and finished the rest of the beer. And the doctor then tamped out the fire with sand, and then back we started, but this time to the village, and at a distance circles of light drew close, and we stood then at the bus stop with dozens of other people waiting for a bus to pull in, and then sat next to each other, the doctor had his arm around me and I dropped off to sleep, when I woke, my head on his shoulder, we were entering the outskirts of Prague. And I was tired out, my eyes slowly opening and closing, as though I had fever, as though drifting in and out of sleep, as though falling into unconsciousness and coming to again slowly. So in my head by turns the pictures changed and blended with the pictures of that darkened street through Libeň, as though I were night driving, flipping high beams on and off. The doctor led me by the elbow and all at once I saw the gas-lamp glow, and as soon as we laid a hand on the doorknob, Bobby started barking happily there in the yard, when we opened the doors, he came running out, barking and jumping, and it took a long time before he in any way settled down. And then we walked into the courtyard, Mrs. Beranová was in bed already, reading, she called to us through the window, "Bobby was beautiful, we went out for a walk, his leash is hung on the knob to the doctor's door."

And then the doctor got the stove going, it was cold there inside, I took the big pitcher, put Bobby on the leash, my face was burning, and when I touched my shoulders, they were burning too, the doctor was roasted and his eye glimmered lower even than down by the river. And I went out to the yard with the pitcher, Bobby ran the whole distance to the street doors, then back, like the doctor on that trail through the fields, when I walked by the lighted window, Mrs. Beranová lay there a few feet away, glasses on her nose, calling, "Bobby had his treat! And as soon as you bring the beer back, you go to bed, news said storms were coming, a gale's passing through, there are changes and geomagnetic storms on the sun, so I'd rather lie right here . . . you know, I was born in the Sudetenland too . . . so *Ich bin Wetterkrank auch,*" she yelled through the window and tilted her neck and her glasses threw squiggles under her eyes, and I was in the corridor already, and then out ran Bobby, and then me, wobbling down the street, and someone approaching from the direction

of Ludmila Street, blond-haired curls cascading into his eyes, but
drunk, and then our gypsy lady turned onto the street, pounding on
the man's back, and every one of those blows was enough to drop a
horse, she shoved the man and his fine, straw-colored hair went flying and the gypsy woman said to me, "Here you have, madame, that
jewel of mine. Two days on a bender and the cash gone, yessiree, the
cash all gone."

And then I went into Vaništa's; Bobby raced into the hallway in
the lead, there was a glassed-in taproom off the hall, and men were
standing in their Sunday best drinking a long beer and a short shot,
glasses were lined up on a table in the corner, and behind the glass
partition a fat publican was drawing pints, now and then the pub
door would swing open, and voices and chat and light would spill
into the twilit hallway, men came out to avail themselves of the lavatory in the yard, patrons exited and put on their coats as they headed
for the door, and one man shouted, "It's the doctor's dog!" and staggered off, then the publican, when he took hold of the pitcher, gave
a well-satisfied nod and said, "This is the doctor's pitcher." And he
craned across in his dispensing booth to get a look at me, I craned
over too for him to see me better, and when our eyes met, I stuck
my tongue out at Mr. Vaništa and he let out a laugh. And then he
was about to hand me the pitcher, but had to put it down, a pale
young man came out of the taproom and told the publican, "Hey,
Láď'a, I've had six shots, put it on the slate for me." And the publican
laughed, came out of his glass case, reached into his back pocket,
pulled out a notebook, kept on with his laugh, thumbed through
the notebook, and marked in the total and gave a laugh and a bow to
his customer, who staggered to the door where the booze jerked him
sideways. And now the publican turned serious, notepad in hand
he walked to the door, through which our guest disappeared, and
yelled, "Bloody lot! Drink yeah, but pay, it's like drawing water from
a stone!" And then he came back, rolling his eyes and explaining for
me, "Four hundred here, if you please, two hundred and fifty crowns
there, and up and up." And then he yelled at the door again, "Bloody
lot, drinking's easy, but on whose slate? Mine!" I took the pitcher
and wanted to pay for the three pints of beer, but the publican shook
his head, flipped through his notebook, and marked in the charge
and said, "That's all right, the doctor's my customer and he's a good,

decent, million-dollar client." And a man standing, glass in his hand, clicked his heels together and raised his glass and proclaimed, "I'm the postmaster if you may, I deliver the doctor's letters and postcards personally, to your health!" And he clicked his heels together again and drank his drink . . .

And I went back with beer, and when I got into our building, it was already dark at Mrs. Beranová's, that neat lady was asleep already, I trod heavily up the stairs with the feeling I had been living there for a long time already, upstairs at the Slavíček's the window was open and you could hear voices, the lady and her kids, that little family twittering on, lying in bed in the dark, talking over all the things of interest that occurred that day, everything that moved them, everything that had angered them, I peered through the asparagus hung in the window, the doctor sat at the stove, leaned over, elbows on his knees, hands clasped, and that woman at the station had it right, he appeared aged from the time I'd first spied him here a month ago, scrubbing the floors, he appeared sadder, as if suffering from something, he gazed off into the distance and appeared tremendously far away, but now he reached into his pocket and pulled out the small oval pocket mirror and examined himself from every angle, and probably disliked what he saw, he let out a shout and opened the stove and threw that mirror into the fire and Bobby barked.

And then I went in and set the pitcher of beer on the table, the doctor reached for the pitcher with both hands and took a long drink, he handed me the pitcher and I drank thirstily as well, the beer spilled across my lips and ran down between my breasts, the doctor couldn't wait for me to finish drinking, now he took another long pull, and when he put the pitcher down he smiled at me, and Bobby stretched on the carpet and heaved a profound sigh. And then we ate the roasted pork from the saucepan, and quaffed the beer, we stayed quiet and the doctor appeared to grow younger on the beer and I felt beer hurtle to my head, and when we polished the pitcher off, I went and fetched another three pints, and when I returned, the windows were shut and Bobby off to sleep already, and then we drank more beer and ate more roast pork, spearing pieces of the meat on our knives and eating ravenously and drinking, and the doctor made the bed, and when we were done with the pitcher, both of us perfumed with beer, the doctor switched off the swag light and taking me by the hand, led me to his bed, and the cracked cast-iron stove threw a flicker of shadow on the walls and I was perfumed in beer and the doctor leaned over me, he also in a beer perfume, and then slowly we made love and then again, the only thing I heard was the beat of my heart, the aroma of beer around me, the aroma of beer on my lover, I felt I was swimming in a pool filled with beer, in a huge keg of pilsner, and so in this man's arms I fell asleep locked together with him, my head rested on his shoulder, and when I awoke the first time, I felt a furriness at my feet, and it was Bobby, who'd crawled into bed with us, and so he became the first witness to my own in-house wedding in this building . . . And then from downstairs, from the building's lower depths, the neat lady let out a horrible howl, I sat up with a start, then again someone howled in the heart of the building down there, while upstairs a freshly made bed waited in vain, a fresh pair of Viennese pajamas, a fresh towel, and a bar of scented soap that had yet to be used . . .

CHAPTER THIRTEEN

THIS SUMMER WAS EXTREMELY HOT, AND THE DOCTOR AND I WENT swimming. Down to where the Berounka met the Vltava, and to the Jizera, which flowed into the Labe. The doctor always gathered twigs and dry branches and always lit a fire on the riverbank, a modest fire, we stayed out by the water a long time, so the fire never failed to come in handy. We used to take Bobby, he liked a swim too, and he also liked to sit by the fire, and it was as though that Kerry blue terrier were our child. The doctor would add wood, and one couldn't speak, those fires were a holy Mass for him, the same as was the water, no matter where, the doctor couldn't catch sight of water without scooping a handful and laying it on his face, he would scoop the water slowly and press it to his face, close his eyes, exactly as he would when he peered into the fire. And the doctor could not pass any fountain by either, up at the castle was a fountain in the shape of an *L,* he wet his face with that water too, and at the fountain in the old town square, he'd scoop it up by the handful and go on his way soaked through, he loved when water dried on his face, when his eyelashes matted with water and dried off swiftly in the sun.

So we'd do our daytrips, and Saturdays and Sundays go swimming. During weekdays, while the doctor waited for me to finish work in the afternoon, or when I would pay him a visit in Libeň, we went to the Vltava, down to Maniny there, to its riverside, where poplars rose along the river, where the railway tracks passed and where the sun shone so sweetly in the afternoon. That's where I was at my happiest. There on the bend of the river a set of steps beetled down to the water, there with the sunlight shining in under my skirt I'd sit, step down and sit on the steps, and the river would glitter in the sun and the waves and the water cast their reflections up into my eyes, I read, or did a crossword, Bobby there beside me . . . And the doctor went collecting wood under the old poplars and made his modest fire again, for the longest time gazed with joy once more into the crackling of the fire, and swam again in the disgusting water, which even I took a dip in sometimes; trash drifted in the water there and offal from the abattoir, on occasion even condoms floated by, indeed on one occasion the doctor came up out of the water with a condom dangling from his ear, he tossed that filthy object away from him, not with disgust, but just easy, as though it were an olive branch; olives grew along the river, and when in bloom the doctor would pick them, put them in the laundry, in his bed, he told me next year, when olives bloomed, we'd pick and put them with our clothes, into our chest of drawers. And so the doctor behaved as though we had been together a considerable time already, married for years, he pleaded with me not to talk while he gazed into the fire, pleaded with me not to utter a word when the urge came upon him to stop suddenly at one of the city's fountains to bathe his face . . .

That day it was hot, and we sat on the riverbank, the sun setting behind the clouds, a humid day, a breeze blowing in off the river, and our modest fire burned and gave off its melodic weep and moan, we sat on the steps, I looked into the flowing water, the little fire crackling behind me, my arms wrapped around my knees, I thought about that apartment in Libeň, why on earth it could have taken this long to notice what had been there since my first arrival in that courtyard, old ads over every wall in the doctor's flat, metal billboards spread across the ceiling above the doctor's bed, SHAME ON THE MAN WHO HASN'T TRIED AVION, and then a big poster, WE PAY TOP PRICES FOR OLD GOLD. And then there was a Singer poster out in the courtyard itself, a big green S and art deco girls working on the Singer sewing machine . . . And hung between the vines of wild ivy in the yard, a death mask, face tied up with wire like a broken earthenware pot . . . and then a poster saying, YOU CAN TELL EGO CHOCOLATE TASTES GREAT, and Primeros . . . True, when I'd been to the doctor's that first time, I didn't even remark on the big wardrobe, my primary impression was of everything he had cleared outside while he scrubbed his floors . . . Therefore I sat on into the twilight, which promised rain, normally I would have fled an impending storm, but the doctor sat behind me, quite carefree, gazing into his fire, not oblivious to the storm's approach, he felt it coming right from the time of our meeting, had started to stammer, the afternoon was truly fine, but the doctor was clamming up, because exactly like Mrs. Beranová, he was a *Wetterkrank,* could predict the weather too, because before a storm he always felt he had a nail driven into his head, that's how, with a big ha-ha, he described the pain for me, a nail driven into his head, the type of pain his friend Vladimir got, who looked in through the flat window that once, said hello to me, called me young lady . . . and when I invited him in, told him the doctor was on his way, he declined and never did come back, I never saw a handsomer man, tall as an American basketball player, a volleyballer, he had curly hair and was likely jealous of me, he looked at me askance, and likely left because he started to feel his nail in the head, or perhaps he always did have that nail driven through his handsome head . . . I sat on into the twilight and the doctor babbled so, he began to stammer, "Every . . . day . . . when . . . when we walked from school . . . home, we nipped into this shop . . . Novák's . . . and then . . . They started ads, came up with flyers? And when, yes . . . oh, they were so great . . . we pasted them . . . damn, what do you call them . . . yes, handbills, pasted them into our exercise books."

And he skipped down the steps to the mirror of the twilight sky in the water and went on, "That was a lovely space of time . . . handbills . . . shopkeepers would give you your receipt written on them . . . and put your handbill into the bag . . . along with the bread . . . and butter . . . flour . . . poppy seed and the like . . . And then Dad and I would mount the motorcycle and go around the restaurants, Dad did their . . . what do you call it . . . aha! Taxes! And those metaled billboards all flashed by . . . Singer sewing machines . . . Speedwell oil . . . and motor oil . . . AND IF IT'S OIL, IT'S MOGUL OIL . . ."

I sat there in the profoundest twilight, observing how the sun had long since disappeared behind cloud, how lights on Libeň Bridge flicked on, how lighted trams crossed the bridge, how the trams and the entire bridge were mirrored in the river's deep murk, and on the outskirts of Prague somewhere lightning flashed and thunder rumbled. I sat there and wasn't at all surprised that I thought about all the ads plastered around the doctor's flat and in the yard, and that out of the blue he had started in on this chatter to me about ads.

"As a student, when I attended . . . damn, what do you call them! Lectures, aha . . . up in Vysočany . . . I used to take a train to . . . that's where I got off . . . at where the train stopped . . . and over the rooftops I saw this huge, tall . . . sign, well . . . a billboard that spelled out BEAUTY in letters five meters high . . . translucent . . . BEAUTY shining in the night . . . So I entered Prague the beautiful . . . like a king, me . . . not until later did I find out . . . it was a flophouse . . . Yes, the Hotel Beauty! Who was it lived there . . . way back . . . Ladislav . . . what's his name! Yes, Klíma, Ladislav Klíma. . . and after forty-eight . . . the flophouse was kaput . . . So we wanted to . . . disguised as workmen . . . we wanted to dismantle that sign stuck up on its roof . . . towering over Vysočany . . . you could make it out all the way from Krejcárek. . . from Pražačka . . . from Hájek . . . and Šlosberk . . . each one of us was going to keep a letter apiece . . . A letter five meters tall . . . but when we got to it . . . BEAUTY was gone . . . they took the sign down the day before . . . and hauled it to the scrap merchant's . . . but this is going to be no rain, this is a thunderstorm coming, a deluge, a cloudburst . . . And I can tell."

And the wind quickened, and toward the lights on the bridge we walked, streetcars clattered over, we held each other's hands, walked the steps up onto the bridge, and when we crossed over, the wind rose from way down in the river, hit us, we clung to each other's waists and continued on into Libeň, and the wind blew and carried all it had lifted from way off in Maniny, in Karlín harbor across there, all that rubbish from the peripheries, it whipped up those papers, twigs, boxes, an awning flew across the bridge through the black sky and crashed into a yard of garages, that wind whipped sand and grit into our faces, we clung to one another and thrilled, the doctor bowed his head to the wind, but now and then the wind would let up and the doctor jerked me sideways, only to lean back into the wind again as though into a door closed on him. And then we had crossed the bridge and a number of raindrops plopped onto Main, the lanterns atop the tall lampposts clinked like crazy, people scuttled across from one sidewalk to the other, now a lit tram rattled down the street, the wind off the river blew several rubbish bins out onto Main Street, the stores were already closed, only the display windows shone mutedly, we turned into our street, leaning into the wind by then, bent, the gas lamps rattled, clinked and clanked like a set of loose dentures, and we slipped into the hall and the doctor led me on tiptoe past the windows of our neat lady Beranová, she wasn't in, we ascended into the inner yard, but everywhere was dark, Slavíček's dark, Liza's dark, the doctor unlocked the door and I slipped into the flat, the doctor struck a match and lit the kindling and crumpled newspaper waiting in the stove, he opened a window . . .

I stood by the window lost in thought; behind me the cast-iron stove roared, in front the asparagus and ivy hung from the piano's candelabrum, vaguely profiled against the sky; lightning flashed and it thundered, beautifully; I'd never felt so moved; behind me the fire glittered through the cracked sections of the cast-iron stove, and in front of me the skies flashed on and off in the rainless storm, with each lightning flash the asparagus flared and shimmered silver, with each lightning flash the Singer machine billboard lit up, and in between tangled shoots of climbing ivy flashed the doctor's clay death mask, the one Vladimir made him, in rhythm it flashed as if that climbing ivy were the doctor's hair, wind tossed; the death mask it appeared to me was grinning; the death mask resembled the doctor more than the doctor did himself, more than the man behind me who stood looking at the selfsame thing . . . And right then, heavy droplets began to drop on the yard, audible blows like a hail of ice. And then rain started; in a bolt of lightning the skies simply opened up, and the warm wind that flowed from the yard and into the doctor's flat suddenly chilled, and then it rained; it poured as if out of twenty shower faucets all at once, and soon the yard filled up with water; the small drain couldn't swallow the flood fast enough; the doctor added wood to the stove and left the door open a crack, and I looked up and as stove flame lit the ceiling, I noticed for the first time the ceiling . . . vaulted. And then I leaped back; the rain poured and wind flung hail against the machine shop wall, and now the remaining plaster tore off from the wall and plaster thudded dully onto the angle roof of the shed, the sound of sods of earth dropped onto a coffin over an open grave, and the gutters wheezed and downspouts couldn't keep up with the water falling from the heavens, and behind me the doctor stretched himself and issued a howl, then shouted ceilingward, a gleeful shout, and stretched himself a second time and issued one more delighted howl and then told me with a chuckle, "The most beautiful ad I ever saw was the one Mr. Marysko put together. Down there . . . where Dlouhá Street opens onto Old Town Square . . . used to be a chemist's shop belonging to Mr. Fafejta. And the specialty of the house: Fafejta's Primeros Condoms. He wanted an ad made for the Primeros, so he left it to Mr. Marysko, who placed a two-hundred-crown commission with Mr. Albich, a painter in his third year at the academy, who developed it as per Mr. Fafejta's wishes."

And out in the yard the rising water was up to the first step of the laundry room, lightning flashed again and lit up that lovely flood across the roofs and over the yard, and the doctor, the minute the skies opened, the pressure was off him and that nail in his head gone, that nail pegging and paralyzing his tongue lifted from him, and delightedly the doctor strode around the room, babbling on pleasurably not at anything he said, but the fact his head was free and his tongue able to keep up with his flow of thought, ahead of the storm, he'd been in the same condition the courtyard sheds and gutters were now in, unable to handle the pressure of the water and the rain . . . and the water surged and overflowed, splashing greatly through the courtyard, the same way as when our neat lady Beranová splashed bucketfuls of water under her windowsill . . . And the doctor went on, exulted, "And lo and behold one day, when Mr. Fafejta rolled up the shutters what we saw on his chemist's shop . . . a sign spread the length of his display windows, done in marker and written in fulsome calligraphy by one Mr. Milan Albich, third-year student at the academy . . . FAFEJTA'S PRIMEROS, PEOPLE WHO BUY THEM ARE FAILSAFE, NO DOUBT ABOUT THEM . . . and there were six of these cartoons hung there, pictures: three pictures, drawings of Mr. Fafejta's clients who had employed his Primeros . . . and then three drawings of lovers who had failed to employ the product on offer . . . And you see, along came nineteen forty-eight, and Mr. Fafejta went, same as that beautiful ad and six pictures in the shop window."

And the doctor ran out to the yard, but came back in straightaway, removed his shoes and stripped to his underpants and then returned to the yard, he strolled around in the downpour, muddy water to the knee, by now the lightning had ended, the doctor flipped on the light under the small roof to the laundry room and took down a hose attached to an old hand pump, he unrolled the hose, the full distance from the drain to the top of the stairs leading down to Mrs. Beranová's, he sucked on the end of the hose, as one does when one bottles homemade wine from the barrel.

"Please, come back in, you'll catch cold on me," I said.

And he ran down the steps again, then back up through the rain, then over to the window and repeated through asparagus branches and hanging ivy, "You'll catch cold on me," and eyes wide, he nodded his head up and down, and when he came in the room and stood up to the stove, I took a towel and dried his back, I pulled his soaking underpants down and told him again, "You'll catch cold on me yet . . . those underpants are soaked."

And telling him, I became tongue-tied, suddenly I pressed myself to him, not even him really, the doctor, but this male body, which didn't smell all that nice, which stank of water mingled with soot and plaster, thunder rumbled, dying off somewhere, I kissed his wet body, actually less than a kiss, more I stuck my tongue out and ran wet tongue all the way down wet body, and the doctor turned and I took him in my mouth, and he held me by the hair and drew my head back up, and then again I ran my tongue downward, the one place it kept drawing me was down, and again down, and I emitted a moan, a moan I didn't believe I had in me anymore, the moan a woman gives when the one thing she desires is her man to be inside of her, to take her in his arms and to do whatever he desires, wherever it transports him. And then he lifted me up and carried me to the bed, the rain had ceased, and the door lay open, and the window, and the fire burned in the stove, pine logs blazed and sparks blew out through the cracked sections in the stove, and I rose, arched my back, dug my nails into the body of the man, which lay on me and plunged in repeatedly and I arched my back repeatedly, waiting for the man's plunges to quicken, and I quickened my own in response, and then went as taut as possible, and I felt the seed of the man shoot hot, male seed hot inside me and it felt so fine I began to cry, seed shot in and tears rolled out of my eyes and outside the rain drew quietly to a close and I, open and my man, open, and the window, open and the door, open and the gate to the street, open . . . nobody around, I wished the whole building full, everyone at home in the rain, letting up, I wanted everyone from the building to come in and take a look at us, all the doctor's friends, I wanted all of them to witness what a true in-house wedding looked like, but no one was coming, and no one came . . . I sat on the bed naked, the man lying naked behind me, stretched out, I got up to add wood to the fire, I stared into the fire, beginning to be obsessed by the fire as well, when I turned, the man's eyes were glittery and his voice pleasantly hoarse, he began talking as though he were giving me a lecture, "Most beautiful ad I ever saw though, was an ad for Koh-i-noor Waldes patent buttons . . . I would see the sign on my way into Prague, twenty years ago, when I saw it I knew the Beauty flophouse was in the offing, beauty, which still shadows me through Prague even now, my path through this world, still lit by the icon of that beautiful girl, the girl with a patent metal button set into her eye, a small blue button snapped tight into the eye of imagination . . . Know where they got the beautiful girl for that billboard? This translator told me how he was aboard a ship once with Mr. Waldes, headed from America to Europe, even back then Mr. Waldes had a patent on his Koh-i-noor buttons . . . but they weren't sporting the image of the beautiful girl yet, the one he met aboard ship over a sip of champagne, and when that starlet asked what he did for a living, Mr. Waldes presented her with a box set of patent Koh-i-noor buttons . . . and giddied by the champagne, she put the button in her eye, like a monocle, and giggled, and Mr. Waldes, under the influence of the actress and the champagne, sent for a photographer and he took a picture of the bombshell with his patent button in her eye . . . and at that Mr. Waldes asked her for her permission, and from then on the girl was on his patented Koh-i-noor buttons, and not only she and that billboard shine over Prague today, but on me she still shines, because her entire story is a beacon and highlights my way through life . . . And you know, the two of you look alike . . . and know what I think, we could announce our wedding vows next month."

"Only if you're not making light of me," I said. "And," I added, "And after this much, perhaps we might begin addressing one another in the familiar?"

"No . . . that no," he said. "Not under any circumstance, how can you think of such a thing, using the familiar this soon," he said pensively. "I would be happier addressing you in the third person, as one does in Vienna at the Café Demel when the waitress asks, '*Was wollt Ihr Ihnen?*' Better we use the formal address, we can proceed to the familiar later, after."

"When?" I said.

"After the wedding, because if you started employing the familiar, you might take liberties with me," he said, and I laid myself on the darling man, kissed him, we lay one on the other, a couple of slices of buttered bread and then everything went as shortly before, as our first time . . . And then we rested on our backs and while the fire in the stove went slowly out we sighed and started to fall asleep, the doctor so tired he snored, but my eyes remained open staring at the ceiling, I dreamed of the moment I put on my very best ensemble, the new dark-blue with gold buttons and red lining and red border around the jacket pockets, Italian shoes, coral red, and red purse and a red hat, like Dutch stewardesses wear, I'll put my makeup on, eye shadow and false eyelashes, I will go first to the housing-permit office—they're forever calling me down to that place—I'll have wedding announcements in my purse and just for the hell of it I'll ask the clerk, "Is it possible to get a permit for permanent residence?" And as always, he will tell me only if I furnish an official transfer of address from my last place of residence in Píštany, or show him confirmation of permanent employment from a Prague business . . . And I will pull out the wedding announcements and slide them over and I can't wait to see his eyes roll, for even though the announcement is a check I can only cash in on my wedding day, at least it demonstrates I *am* getting married and that my fiancé's residence, once he's my spouse, will be mine as well . . . Lord, his eyes will roll, and that second mother of mine, Ema, how about hers when I present her with my wedding announcement . . . And then I'll take a hold of my announcement and set off for the central Restaurant and Cafeteria personnel office, a clerk down there detests me and is mean even to Head Chef Bauman at the hotel, I can't wait to go down there and demand that the bitch, for God's sake, finally if you please, give me a permanent employment permit . . . And what she'll do, the stupid moron, as always, is say sweetly, "Of course, what wouldn't I give to help you out, but! Madame, I'll issue you the permit once you furnish me a permit from the housing office stating you have a permanent residence here in Prague!" And I'll just cock my coral-red high heels, cock my hand on my hip, and open up my blue ensemble for her to see the scarlet-red lining, and then, once satisfied she has given me her look of triumph, from my red purse I'll take the wedding announcements and lay them on the counter and say, "Hopefully this will suffice, by way of deposit!" I will wait for her to finish reading, and then I'll file the wedding announcements away and tell her, the bitch, then, "You're so kind, I'll be back within the month with my marriage certificate."

CHAPTER FOURTEEN

THOSE LOVELY DAYS, WHEN I WOULD VISIT MY LOVER IN LIBEŇ ONCE a week, I would carry over a small saucepan for the doctor every time, specially prepared for me by Head Chef himself, and in those days the doctor would simply laugh and laugh repeatedly, with plenty of gusto, which was put on; he supped the Hotel Paris food with a spoon, couldn't say enough about it, sometimes even our neat lady would come over toting a saucepan from the Golden Goose, and every time she handed the saucepan across she'd say, "Here you go, Doctor, a little treat!" And in those days the doctor laughed and smelled relentlessly of beer and hard liquor, he didn't hang about the house too long; Liza told me the doctor was always with his bag walking around Libeň, out shopping he said, but in reality, going from one pub to the other, Bobby at his heel, Bobby was introduced everywhere already, but on every occasion Liza needed to give Bobby a bath, because he too stank of beer and hard liquor. And Liza told me the doctor had set himself on the right path, wasn't putting on those infamous in-house weddings anymore, and his cronies didn't turn up to visit anymore, mainly because once they'd seen me in the yard a number of times, they quickly vamoosed, the doctor's friends didn't take to me for some reason, as soon as I'd look at them they'd redden and launch into a stammer and then wind up tongue-tied.

It was gorgeous back then to visit the dressmaker's, I was having my wedding dress made, nothing special, just the model of dress Mrs. Wallace Simpson wore when she married the prince of England,

I blushed as the dressmaker kneeled in front of me and had to tear parts off my bridal dress, only to have to repin them next time around. Gorgeous, too, the one day when I ordered our wedding rings to measure, I knew the doctor couldn't afford them, and I anguished over how I was going to give him the money, for him to pay for the rings.

And one Sunday we took a trip to Nymburk. When we got out at the station and walked through the town streets, the doctor was petrified with fear of running into someone, I knew immediately, fear of running into an old flame, it was Sunday and the citizenry strolled through their town square, they glanced at their watches and greeted the doctor, and I nodded and smiled at their hellos, and then we crossed the bridge over the river, the wind coiled around me, flowing up from the deep of the bridge, there I had my first good look about me and could see the brewery in the distance, and across the bridge rail, an estate with a little turret, the color of the estate beige, as beige as the brewery in the distance, and only now did my fiancé take my arm, he wore gray trousers and a gray sweater, he sauntered along in his white socks and small suede shoes, and when we crossed the bridge and turned toward the river, we walked along the riverbank and I began to tremble once more, my eyes tear-filled, my face as though on fire, but I clenched the bouquet of flowers and it gave me strength, my fiancé sped down the abutment steps to the river, and, as was his wont, scooped up water in handfuls and splashed them on his face. When he ran back up to the path, he breathed a deep sigh, forced out a laugh, and shrugged his shoulders, like what can a body do . . .

And then I saw a house with a red fence on the riverbank, and then we came to a gate, my fiancé reached over the fence, on the other side there was a key hanging, he unlocked the gate and grew cross, chickens dug about in the fruit and vegetable garden, and a well-coiffed lady ran down the steps, by her high cheekbones I judged this to be my future mother-in-law, instantly, she offered me a hand and smiled, I proffered her the bouquet, and then couldn't help simply starting to cry and we hugged, and my fiancé ran around the garden screeching and chasing chickens, "No chicken belongs in the garden," and he shooed chickens over to the fence, grabbed them and chucked them over into the other yard, and only then ran up behind us on the stairs, and Mother showed me the house, filled with flowers and sunlight, and then ushered me into the dining room and told me this furniture was very special, bought a time ago in Brno at the UP Co., and I told her my father had been a top adviser to the very same company, bought up wood from all over the world for UP, and this dining-room set was probably made of walnut my father purchased somewhere in Lebanon or the Caucasus. And my fiancé followed us nervously around, dodged out to the garden to water and hoe cabbage heads for a spell, then he plucked an apple off one of the trees and trotted back inside to present me with it and a large laugh. "It's a Cox rennet," he said, and just like that took me by the hand and dragged me to that garden and led me from one tree to the next explaining the varieties of apple, which he'd personally planted years ago, he pointed out the savoy cabbage and heads of kale, planted and tended by himself as well, he showed me a peony, which he'd dug from the brewery garden to transplant here, and then he showed me into a yard, where an old man was surrounded by a collection of junk, dozens of little sheds lined along the garden fence, the hulk of an old truck sat in the yard and beside it, an ancient Citroën, I could not tear my eyes away from that Citroën, it appeared to have lain submerged under a pond for five years, seat covers faded and torn and frightfully filthy, the car body coated in rust, and kneeled on the ground in front of the Citroën's grill, a rust woman, she had lipstick on and with a wire brush meticulously scrubbed rust off the metal; my fiancé, as soon as the elderly gentleman looked at him, as soon as the redhead scrubbing and smoking a cigarette, simultaneously, looked up from the rust dust, my fiancé introduced me, "This is my dad, and this my sister-in-law Marta and this is . . . my bride."

And Dad wanted to offer me his hand, but it was masked in oil, Marta kept on scrubbing, she merely smiled up and offered me an elbow and Dad offered me an elbow too, and both went on at their work, Dad tinkering with the dilapidated car, telling me with great relish what a hoot it would be when the Škoda was fixed up again, how great when they repainted the little car dark blue, and how great it would be when Dad set off on a jaunt to his buddies in Kosmonos, mechanics into their retirement already, but who could still bore out valves like nobody's business . . .

And a man with a beret and cane entered the yard, by his face you could tell his best days were pretty well behind him, he'd drunk a lot and loved and had his share of disappointments, he held out a hand and said, "Call me Břeťa, and remember, as Olánek Kolář used to say, 'Anyone who wants into our family will have to adapt.'" So said he and limped over to the Citroën, pointing out with his cane for his wife all the spots she still must brush, he pointed the cane and smiled, while the wife fumed, rolled her eyes, and threatened to do her husband in with the wire brush . . . And following that, I wasn't too surprised when a small man came in the yard, entered very carefully, nose twitching as though he were stepping into water, first one leg and then the other, he sported a fedora, a starch collar, and a bowtie, he placed a brush and shaving cream on a drum full of oil and then he dipped the brush in a jug of water, I now began to get my bearings, heaved a sigh of relief, once I saw how the old gent lathered not only his face, but shirt and collar too, not only carefully lathered his neck, but bowtie too, and no one appeared alarmed, Břeťa merely mentioned, "Pepin, lather your vest too," and pointed with his cane, but Uncle Pepin, yes, here was Uncle Pepin, looking at me and twitching his nose, "And which of them are you?" And I took him by the elbow and said, "Eliška, I came with Bohuš."

"You're that one? Well, a hearty welcome to you, they told me you used to pay visits to Vienna when you were attending school, would that be right? That is *the* most beautiful city in the world, and when I was in the service there, even the more beautiful because I served under the emperor, and he had the most beautiful army, which never lost a battle, because . . ."

"But in the end you lost the war!" said Břeťa, and Uncle Pepin pursued lathering his face and his bowtie and his collar, and no one appeared taken aback by it, in fact my fiancé looked on with great delight, when Uncle Pepin shouted out, "What rot! We won every battle our famous armadas were sent into, we won every one!" So Uncle Pepin shouted, and somewhere in the adjoining lot, where a house sat in the midst of fruit trees, someone angrily slammed a window shut. And Uncle Pepin picked up his razor and began to shave his face, but the soap was dry already, and the razor dull, and Uncle Pepin's hand shook and actually all he accomplished was to draw dry lather down his face, and his gray stubble showed the same as before he had begun. But no one gave it a second thought, no one said a thing, just Břeťa with his cane, a wonder he didn't poke out his uncle's eye in pointing out what parts he should go over a second time with the razor. And my fiancé adored it, he stroked Uncle's face and adored how smooth his uncle was, how closely he knew how to shave. And Uncle Pepin welled up in tears and repeated, "Truth, that's Austrian discipline, the Austrian way!" Mom rescued me by coming out and asking me to come assist her in setting the table for Sunday lunch.

And in the dining room we separated the leaves of the table, Mom opened the sideboard, handed me this exquisite dishware in the sun-drenched dining room, saying proudly, "As one can see, it's Sèvres porcelain, and a twelve-piece set! But one never has it easy with that son of mine, one has one devil of a time . . ." Mom was conversing and setting spoons and forks on either side of the Sèvres plates "be-cause since he was a youngster he was always, still is, elsewhere, home was hell to him, he just came in to sleep, morning to night he'd be out on Polná Street, the entire town knew him, because he was for-ever at somebody else's, always wanting to be somewhere other than where he was. As I said, one can only have one devil of a time with him, as a matter of fact, he ran away on us twice, loafing about down Polná wasn't enough, so he made off one time on a train, and then on a delivery truck! Inside a beer barrel! And out, over there in the brewery, from the time he was six, as soon as he started school, he wrote his homework outside all the time, on a chair, on the roof, any old location but home."

"What're you saying?" The sound of Uncle Pepin's expostulations sailed up from the yard, "The Austrian army won all its battles! Un-der the command of Freiherr von Wucherr, on All Saints' Day, we marched into Přemyšl victorious, liberated the town!"

Mom gave a start and opened the window and called down, "Un-cle, for God's sake, stop yelling, it's Sunday and soon will be noon!" Then Mom ushered me through the dining room and showed me the paintings on the walls and continued with what she had been say-ing, "Now this is *The Tatras* by Antonin Frydl, an original, oil, and as I was saying, one won't have it easy with him, when Uncle Pepin worked the malt house, that son of mine took up with him, to not be at home, when dark came and we couldn't find him, he would be in the stables, at the troughs with oxen breathing down on him, hap-pier hobnobbing with oxen than in his own home, as I say, one will not have it in any way easy with him . . . This pastel is by Professor Vokálka, *Sheaves of Rye by the Forest Edge,* and when he did have to be in, he perpetually scowled, sulked, if it rained, or snowed, or stormed, he *would* stay in, but once we went to bed, we'd not find him all over again, until later, crawled under his bed asleep, we had to drag him out . . . but why tell one any of this? Because for over forty years I put up with that son of mine, and now, as he puts it, time for some *other* one to lose her sleep over him."

And outside in the yard Uncle Pepin began to crow, "What? Hitler got his comeuppance in Russia. But our Austrian armed forces would have defeated the Russian armies too, even taken Stalingrad!"

And Mom leaned out the window quickly, and I could see what gave her the fright wasn't the shouting so much, but *what* Uncle Pepin was yelling about in the yard outside, on a Sunday. "For God's sake, Uncle, we're in hot water as it is, what *are* you shouting about? On top of everything else they'll lock us up, on the strength of your talking treason." And then out into the distance Mom called, as though atoning, her hands cupped to her mouth and her voice magnified, "He caught a wound in the head during the war!" And when Mom emerged from behind the curtains, which billowed in the draft, she reached for a chair, collapsed into it, smoothed out the tablecloth, and said, "One should know, that son of mine, he used to be as malapropos as Uncle Pepin. Every first of May, in the morning, he would unload the doo of the outhouse onto his vegetable patch. And then wonder why he was not appreciated hereabouts. And why, because he's always away in dreamland. As a student he began composing poetry, so around he walked, head permanently in a cloud; even those girlfriends, how ridiculous, those girls arriving at our place believing they were brides-to-be, but away in his dreamworld was their young gent, thoughts gone elsewhere, never in, never there for those fiancées, so every last one went in the end, because, tell me from your end, what are you expected to do with such a man, who walks around like a sleepwalker? . . . And it's how it still is with him, my boy's happiest somewhere other than where he is . . . And it was the same with work and people he knew. With the notary first and then some new position, same with where he lodged, that son of mine, happiest on the run from hotel to hotel, sleeping somewhere new every day, such was his life, but then forty-eight came, the department store he worked for went under and his commercial traveling town to town was a write-off . . . You see, I'll let you in on something, quite frankly, that son of mine takes after me a trifle, I wanted to be an actress, to play in the theater, I was already married, and didn't have the strength, didn't know how to bolt, as my son did . . . but it looks like it's time for lunch."

Mom listened as outside Dad stopped banging on the fender, and out in the yard the wire brush stopped in midscrub on the Citroën . . . Mom rose, she had something to tell me about another painting, but waved her arm and said, "And look out, one has to walk through fire with him, that's his thing, fire, setting fires, nothing but fire all the time, when he was at his grandmother's place in Židenice, he lit the curtains in the windows twice, and here on the brewery premises, he kept a shed in a ravine with a stove and all he did was light fires in that stove, and on the eve of All Souls'? Dad always had to pay the damage, he incinerated the hayloft, piled a bonfire so high he scorched the cherry trees, torched the old dry grass so the woods went up, and on Halloween? Flying around with his broom burning, he'd always char his hat, his shoes . . . always charred, twice he set his hair on fire . . . and to top it all off, how could I forget! One has to live through the *other* with him! Water! That's a thing of his, always down by the water too, almost drowned twice, when the ice was breaking, shoes and clothes always getting soaked, he fell through the ice in his new clothes, six hundred that navy blue jacket cost, through the ice into the river, expensive jacket on, and then he rested the jacket on the heater at the cinema and burned a hole. And how he managed a degree? That I will never know. Always at the water's side, spring through fall, swimming all the time, *Czech Criminal Code* propping up his head, just sunning himself and swimming. How he finished a law degree, I do not know. And one will have to live through still more . . . That imbibing of his! From the time he was four he was prone to return from weddings and funerals drunk . . . and then every drop at home to drink sucked up, as a student it was nothing unless he came back in drunk from a party; when sober, however, he's a kitten, so unassuming, as soon as he gets the third beer in, however, or an ounce of liquor, he's worldwise, a champion whose courage is up, and starts giving offense and intimidating people . . . And what about when he's beyond control, do you know what happens?"

And out in the yard Uncle Pepin's voice rose, "What're you saying? The Austrian armed forces were ever victorious, and an army of that caliber could even trounce the Russians, emerge in victory over the Russians!"

Mom gave a start, pulled the fluttering curtains back with some effort, leaned out, and laid her hands to her mouth and called into the distance, "He means the czars of Russia . . . the czars!"

But Uncle Pepin kept on, "Not at all, the Austrian army would trounce these Russians too, because the emperor's armed forces could rout any army!"

And then Dad entered the dining room followed by Marta, both looked the same as when I had first encountered them in the yard, Marta laughing and covered in rust dust, all she had done was wash her hands, Dad looking as though a tram had run him over, only his hands showed sparkling clean . . . And then Břet'a and my fiancé entered, leading Uncle Pepin in.

Mom ladled the soup and all she would utter was "You were howling like the dragoons again!" And Uncle Pepin was delighted by this pronouncement, he smiled and gave Mom a bow and himself a nod, "Truly?" And dried-up lather flaked away from him, I looked at the doctor, at my fiancé, I was glad Mom had revealed all that about him, glad to have it, even though it would deprive me of the many secrets I may have disclosed for myself over the course of our marriage, which was yet to take place . . . Well, we all wished each other bon appétit, and spoons clinked against Sèvres porcelain and Břet'a was the first one to finish, the soup disappearing into him so fast it was as though he drank it, then Břet'a said softly, "But you wouldn't win!" And Uncle Pepin shouted, "We would," and he coughed, a tiny dumpling stuck in his throat, and my fiancé began to smack him on the back and Uncle Pepin spluttered and sneezed until finally he let out such a sneeze he shot face-first toward the plate of soup, Mom managed to withdraw that rare Sèvres plate in the nick of time. And I gave Mom a look, once more she managed to control herself, she merely waved off Uncle Pepin's screaming, somehow affording me a nice smile, probably because the one thing one could do in this spot was smile, simply smile.

And I remembered the letter from Auntie Pišinka in Vienna and those Parisian pastries with the whipped-cream topping and smiled too, shook my head and looked up and smiled for the handsome brass chandelier with the five brass sconces, and all the anxiety and anger and everything unpleasant fell away. Dad leaped at this opportunity to run out into the yard, one could hear the muffled thud of the hammer as he went on hammering out that bent fender.

I collected the soup plates, my fiancé wiped Uncle Pepin's face with a paper napkin, Mom brought in a steaming bowl of dumplings, she chuckled in the doorway and said it softly, "And you would not win."

And Uncle Pepin bolted out of his chair and yelled, "And we would win! And how!" And knocked into the bowl of dumplings with his shoulder, Mom managed to catch it, but not before half the dumplings in the bowl fell to the carpet, and my fiancé took a pair of prongs to those dumplings and filled his plate, then Mom and I knelt down and retrieved the rest of the dumplings from the carpet, Dad came in, sat down, and sent me a smile, but I could see his thoughts were out in the yard, out with his Škoda, and he didn't want to say anything in fact, for fear of getting involved in a conversation he couldn't flee later. And Mom ladled the dumplings onto everyone's plates as though nothing had happened, when she laid the third dumpling onto my plate I nodded, enough, and then she ladled the gravy and strands of sauerbraten, and then everyone ate hungrily again, Breta was done before I had tucked into my second dumpling, he wiped his lips, got up, and limped to the window. I had to admit what the doctor, my fiancé, had told me was true, the sauerbraten truly was divine; I boldly helped myself to two dumplings more and more gravy, and had I not been too shy to, I fear I may have had a helping more. And then the door opened and a young girl came into the dining room and bowed and asked Mom politely, "Ma'am, would you loan us Uncle Pepin?"

And Mom said indeed she would, but what for?

And the girl said that Uncle Pepin was going to give another lecture for the girls, up at the weir, a lecture concerning sexual hygiene, actually it was a continuation of Uncle Pepin's riverside address from last Sunday, when he'd lectured them on how the key to marital bliss was a well-built body and proportionate sexual organs, and Uncle Pepin had promised that today he was going to hold court on the writings of Master Batista, regarding the consequences of a promiscuous sexual life . . . Mom said it would be okay, as long as the girl led Uncle Pepin by the hand, on account of his not seeing so well anymore, and as long as when the lecture was over, she would escort Uncle home and hand him back directly to Mom. And Uncle Pepin smiled when the girl took him gently by the hand and he said, "And I win. And why do I win again? Because I have Austrian schooling and I served with the finest armed forces in the world and I was a friend of the emperor." And even before Uncle's exit, Dad was out in the yard again hammering that fender, the sister-in-law out too, to get on with the wire brush, scouring the rusty Citroën's grill, Břet'a gazed out the window at the girl leading Uncle through the gate, and my fiancé announced, "Mommy, you're the world champ, I haven't eaten sauerbraten that good in ages and, Mommy, we're going out to take a stroll in the country."

■ □ ■ □ ■

CHAPTER FIFTEEN

WHEN WE WALKED DOWN THE STEPS TO THE GATE, A HAND REACHED
through the railing and, using the key, unlocked the gate from the
other side, and there before us stood a beautiful woman wearing
spectacles, she stood there staring at the doctor, who blushed and
lowered his eyes, that strong beautiful woman blushed in turn, red
blotches actually erupted all over her face, well she stood there like
so, looking at the ground and said, "So you are to be married?"

And my fiancé nodded and said, "Yes."

And that strong woman pointed at me and inquired, "And this is
your bride?"

And my fiancé replied quietly, "Yes."

And that blushing and now tearful lady said, "Well, I guess that's
that, then, well, I wish you a happy marriage, good luck to you
both."

And on the sidewalk she stood looking down at the flagstones,
intensely interested in something she was staring at in those flags, I
knew absolutely how she felt, those flags, every one, was a life pre-
server, the sort a woman clings to when she can't foresee her next
move, I used to stare the same way when that jerk, Jirka, would
shame me in front of the women who fancied him, whenever I stood
and he walked by pretending not to see me, I'd stand and stare at
the ground as though I were struck by lightning, and he would laugh
and saunter off to some café with those floosies, while the only thing
left for me was to go home and weep . . .

And then we reached the river, over on the far side the poplars soared, we walked into the sunshine, and every so often the doctor rinsed his face in the river, we were into September but the sun glittered like April, impossible to look at, over on the far riverbank adults and children swam around, my fiancé, coming back dripping with water, appeared bothered again, I smiled because I'd already been through this, I felt for that woman back there, sickened by how *she* must feel, by her tears, and mainly by those red blotches that erupted on her face once she saw her erstwhile lover. On our reaching the river, I did turn, she still stood by the gate, tears glittering in her eyes, but what can one do? And we walked, skirting a grove of cherries, the dark came on as we went under a railway trestle, a freight train rumbled over our heads and the bridge groaned and shook with a rattle that deafened us, we walked through the shadow, and when we emerged, there was nothing but the sunshine and the water and green willows and the river expanding into the distance.

And my fiancé talked, more to himself really than to me, as though in a confession, so he wouldn't have to brood over that woman in spectacles, he told me of the wind that came up off the river, how sometimes on his way to school, he had to stop and turn back at the brewery, the wind so powerful it would pick him up and carry him into the fields, into the river, where he liked fishing when it was nice out, because he loved to eat the fish, he told me how he could always catch as many carp and bleak as he wished and how Mother would fry them up in batter till the fish were as crispy and nice as pretzels. "I loved it best swimming here close by the willows, there was sand I used to sunbathe on, as a student I'd prop the criminal code under my head and lie there to get a tan, I could just laze, doing nothing but sunning and swimming, the water, when I went in, was always indescribable, and still is, as soon as I get the chance I have to swim, swimming sends me into ecstasy," he said and then down to the river again he ran and lashed water over his face and I smiled, glad I could hear this man and know how to interpret what he said, I knew right off the bat why he talked so, because he was trying to compose himself after seeing the woman in the spectacles up there, I could see he would go on and on, that it might be best for me if he desist, for judging by what he said, he still kept his love for that woman after all . . .

And so after he'd given his face one more rinse, we traversed a dirt road and walked along the edge of a briar patch until we reached the brewery and my fiancé informed me how as a boy at the brewery he used to shoot birds with an air rifle.

"You can see," he shouted to me, "whole brewery's surrounded by a wall and trees grow along the length of the wall and thousands of birds, bluetits and greenfinch, sparrows and blackbirds, redbreasts and in the winter goldfinch used to be up in those trees . . . and I'd shoot them down and not know what for, often I'd just stand, holding the dead bird in my hand and cry over it, only to come back the next day, take aim, and another bird would tumble, never could I believe I managed to pot the bird, and when the shot hit, it just made this tiny *plink!* I couldn't believe the little bird died from that *plink!* and again I would pick it up and mourn over it afresh, you saw for yourself at the gate, I never imagined I could hurt a person so, the way I used to potshot pigeons nested in the malt-house rafters, pigeons who had their young there, and still I'd stand taking aim, had to aim, had to pull on the trigger, and had to watch again as that little pigeon fell, the air rifle not enough to kill them the first time, like the little birds, a pigeon would fall, wounded in the wing like when you wing a partridge, red in the face with shame I had to catch and throttle it, same for all my wounded doves I ran away from, who flew away on me and now come back to roost."

And then we stood in front of the gates to the brewery, I was surprised, for wherever I looked, courtyard or gardens, all I saw was disorder and grief at that brewery, all quite different from what my fiancé related, I thought, given the glowing descriptions, his brewery would be a botanical garden, a palace, everyone at the brewery, noble and good-looking, but when my fiancé told me we were about to scout around inside, the last thing I wanted at that moment was to go in, the brewery disgusted me, not because his past lay there, my fiancé's, but because I was repelled by what I saw. But he saw something quite different, he saw something no longer there, and he probably couldn't view it any other way than through the eyes of memory, it was like his quote from Novalis, who said memories constitute second realities. And then we entered the brewery, me following him, we walked through a garden, past a row of windows, the garden was devastated, as if people had not been in it for ages . . . He pointed out for me where hedges had been, flowers, where walnut trees grew by a fence, under which snowdrops in their thousands and primrose bloomed in spring, he pointed out the windows of the building where he lived once, but by now those windows were different, modern, recently installed, the frames unpainted still, and the wall, formerly beige, now covered only in a coat of whitewash, so we walked by the workers' row houses until we came to where my fiancé claimed the greenhouses, the hothouses were for growing vegetables, and where dwarf trees grew hard by the walls, and hanging ivy, but now old car parts were strewn about, overgrown with weeds, as a matter of fact, every bare patch in that brewery had burst into weed, to overrun the erstwhile vegetable patch. And when we came to the yard where, in my fiancé's account, alleys of peach and grape, alleys of nuts and alleys of apple, and alleys of pear and alleys of cherry throve, only a few old stunted trees remained, arrested in their growth, because parts of some gigantic machine were littered over their roots, like a crashed plane, several engines lay strewn about or jutted from the overrun of weed. But on my fiancé led, he showed me where his mother kept her smokehouse, then where he and Břet'a kept their coop, but none had carrier pigeons in them anymore, such as Břet'a once had, or the Polish lynx, which my fiancé had as a boy, he pointed to what used to be a smokehouse and told me a henhouse was there once, where the maid always fed the ducks and geese, and then all of a sudden that gem of mine got involved in such a piece of nonsense, about how they had this one duck, their maid, before giving the duck her water, would let her out for a waddle, and the duck would make its way over to Bednářova, the brewmaster's wife's windows, and the duck would quack and the brewmaster's wife would open the door for the duck to waddle into the flat, where the lady gave her her treat, and thenceforward every day, up until Mother ordered the maid to slaughter the duck, and the maid plucked the neck feathers off the duck, held it to her breast, and slit its throat, but then she went to see if the water in the washhouse was boiled yet, and meantime, up got the duck, throat not properly slit, and waddled over to Bednářova's, and the brewmaster's wife threw open the door for her and the duck gave its quack in the hall, and when that duck passed through into the flat, that's where she gave up the ghost, and when the brewmaster came home, he found his wife passed out, the badly butchered duck down to its last gasp on the floor in front of her.

I grabbed my hair in my hands and said, "For God's sake, of all things, why tell me this?"

And right then this person in high dudgeon approached, dressed in a guard's uniform, and he was irate. "What are you two up to here?"

And my fiancé lit up, "It's me, Mr. Řepa . . . recognize me? Take a good hard look, I lived my finest years here, and you too, in the row house."

"Well, that's the height of it, I lived in a row house, and you in an apartment, so see here, you have no business in this place, and how you managed to get in at all, and who gave you the permission . . ."

And happy as ever, my fiancé persisted, "But I came to look over the places I loved, still love, after all, I lived here from when I was six, I lived a quarter of a century here."

"You've got no business here, you have a villa of your own, fact of the matter is you're trespassing on state-owned property, you don't happen to have a notion to burn it down, do you? You're not carrying matches? I'll have to search you, for it might so happen I've put a stop to a crime here, let me see, but if you're not willing to, I'll call in the police, let them, the department for public safety, search you."

And looking on, I smiled and was glad when my fiancé raised his arms and the guard patted him down and searched his pockets, checked to see if he had any matches with which he might burn down the brewery, "Now, no matches on you, but see you get out of here, you and your father left here under a cloud once already, so see that you're off, it's not enough for you, coming back here, where you lived like kings and we workers bowed to you, cap in hand?"

And so we went out the brewery gates, my fiancé shaking with shame, I knew he would never set foot in there again, and why should he? I recalled I too returned to look in on our old villa, and how they'd thrown me out too, I had gone to take a look back at Losiny, our villa, now a preschool, and they'd given me the heave-ho too when I told them who I was, I just wanted a look, nothing more than a look and to quietly forget . . .

And when we turned the corner and walked down by the brewery wall back to the river, from afar we could already hear Uncle Pepin at the weir declaiming loudly about sexual hygiene according to Master Batista in his writings, the girls were seated around him, listening,

but we continued on along the cobbled walk, Mother stood outside
the gate talking to someone, the hammer thud came from the yard,
Father, probably onto his second fender by now, I heard the wire
brush scrub furiously at the rust on the Citroën, as we continued
along the walk we passed another villa, the villa next door to the
one the guard had reproached my fiancé for, shortly before, some
detail caught my attention and I turned, and in the window of the
villa someone held open a curtain with a finger and watched us, now
that someone moved and I could see the sad and lovely lady standing
behind the window, now her glasses glinted and silently she stood,
watching me and my fiancé, and I tripped along, I tried to stride as
naturally as possible, in a flash I could see myself, dress, shoes, thank
God I was done up in the latest, lucky to have gone to the hairdresser's
yesterday, and to have had them give me a page-boy cut, the style
women basketball players and girls in the reformatory wore . . .

CHAPTER SIXTEEN

THE SUN WAS SETTING, WE REMAINED QUIET THROUGHOUT DINNER, everyone was tired, the girl had returned Uncle Pepin a while ago, she had actually curtsied and Uncle Pepin was all aglow, head held high, reveling in it.

"No matter, it's a fine thing," he said, "when one person in the family at least is on top of it, when he's got it together, like me. And why? Because I'm a product of the European Renaissance. I have the same design in my head as Goethe or boy Mozart."

Břet'a was seated already, in a clean shirt, hair slicked behind his ears, his beret still on, now I could see that the younger Břet'a must have been quite the handsome man, he knew how to tie a cravat, indeed even his expensive shoes were shined, and his wife, Marta, gussied in a dress the color of apricot ice cream.

Said Břet'a, "Uncle, you know how happy Master Batista would be if he saw you down there by the river lecturing girls from select chapters of his book on sexual hygiene?"

And Uncle Pepin sat, gazing into the distance, tearful and wheedling, "Břet'a, do go on, do talk some more about my latest victory."

And then we said our good-byes, and Mother whispered to me, "If you do have the wedding, I'm afraid I won't be able to attend, I'm afraid the wedding may be too outlandish, I don't have the nerve for it any longer; afterward, we will put on our own wedding in the house here, I only traveled up to Liběň once, visited that son of mine only the one time, and what I saw, I only managed to recuperate from that stove and his yard when I got back to my own, once I had a good cry."

And out into their yard we went, Father flipped a light on and went back to banging on his Škoda, proudly Břeťa opened his Citroën door, Marta went to the gate, there were blankets thrown over the front and back seats of the dilapidated car, my fiancé helped me into my seat, Břeťa squeezed behind the wheel and backed the car out, and Marta, puffing on a cigarette, shutting the gate behind us, squinted as though the smoke were getting into her eyes . . . And then we drove with the headlights on, but not to the railway station, we drove out of town and through a clump of villages, Břeťa telling us about a violin concert he had listened to in the afternoon. The spirit of Jascha Heifetz burgeoned in Břeťa's soul, indeed Břeťa began to weep, so moved he was by Jascha, probably because, as he said, Jews from Odessa were forever full of such sad music, David Oistrach and Yehudi Menuhin were giants, but for Břeťa, the king of the violin was Jascha Heifetz, who played as if he put his complete soul into it, the same as when Břeťa played poker, poker at which he'd won staggering amounts of cash, so staggering he'd grown too big for his britches and spent or lost it all again, and honestly he would cadge money off Father whenever he lost and try to recoup for his losses, but then lose Father's money too . . .

And the Citroën rattled down the road, its headlights poorly aligned, one shone in the ditch and the other off into the trees, my fiancé and I clung to one another, because the seats were so decrepit they threatened to disintegrate at every corner, I was surprised by Břeťa's interest in concert violin, suddenly I recalled that back in our old villa my father also liked to play records, not quite concert but these sad violin pieces, I remember he had a record collection with Helmut Zacharias on violin, I recall Daddy coming home from Vienna once, bringing Olga Čechová, the movie actress, as his guest, she was getting on in years, still beautiful however, she stayed with us for one whole week and Daddy was subtly different from usual, Olga Čechová smoked one cigarette after the other, she had a long ivory holder and sat in the den with Daddy and he put on the same record repeatedly, the one of Helmut Zacharias playing . . . *My heart . . . is like a violin* . . . I listened in on that song, which broke not only Daddy's but Olga Čechová's heart, and even I was profoundly touched, the door to the den lay open, I stood in the dining room listening to Zacharias, and when he had done playing, as I sneaked past so Daddy wouldn't see, from the corner of my eye I saw how moved Daddy was, how his eyes filled with tears, how the record spun and spun, needle hissing and skipping across the vinyl, but Daddy's eyes were tear filled, his hand on Olga Čechová's hand. And then, after Olga had left and Daddy returned too, I picked up the record cover and lo and behold, Stehgeiger Helmuth Zacharias, a Jewish boy in a frock, and he did have sad eyes, big sad eyes, because his heart really was that violin, which he held onto like a mother to a child, like a mother when they want to take her infant away . . .

And the Citroën entered a lit-up town and my fiancé said, "Jascha Heifetz, Jascha Heifetz . . . Břet'a, every Jew has lived through a pogrom, like when the Christians drove them from Spain, across Germany, as far as Odessa, from one century to the next, all those death marches . . . Look, I'll lend you a book of paintings by Marc Chagall, a Jew from Viteb, though he did paint his women and his loves, his uncles sitting by the chimney, those cows and donkeys he has and those giant bushes in bloom and his flowerbeds . . . but Břet'a, in the corner of every painting, a Jew lies dead after a pogrom . . . and everything Chagall knows to say through painting, Jascha Heifetz says with his violin . . . because Jews are as olives, only when crushed, do they give of their best."

And the Citroën came to a stop in a town square girdled by the lighted windows of shops, in front of which people strolled, music came from somewhere, and arc lamps arched low over the roofs of the buildings and small houses, cars drove across the square, red taillights glowing; we sat in the car, my fiancé speaking low into Břet'a's ear and Břet'a listening attentively.

"And there's revolution here, we've all lived it, seen it for ourselves, but Sigmund Freud and psychoanalysis is here, through it Freud, the Jew, proves to Christians scientifically that humanity is established exclusively on the sex gland. And so Sigmund Freud enters the arena guiltless where Christians feel sin. And that's the Jew's revenge for all the Christian pogroms, when establishments exploded and the ceiling fell in, where everything goes topsy-turvy into revolution, like the little hands of Jewish clocks turning time back, like Jascha Heifetz saying it with his violin, that gentle, explosive apocalypse and melancholy of great event . . . Brother, it's a pity we don't have even one ounce of Jewish blood in ours, then we'd rend a hole in the world," my fiancé said with a laugh and slapped Břet'a on the back.

And then we got out of the Citroën and walked across the town square, a statue of Jiří of Poděbrad was fading into the blue of the sky, behind it the illuminated turrets of a large castle thrust upward, it was a beautiful square and beautiful town and I got the feeling the place had been just as it was before the war, then we went into a club, you could hear dance music from the downstairs, at the coat check they greeted Břet'a, Břet'a tossed a hundred crowns to the coat-check girl, who sold tickets for the dance floor, Břet'a waved an arm like he wanted no change and the girl gave him a nod, got up, and hopped down the stairs and we followed, and the waiter, when he saw Břet'a, shook his hand and led us across the floor to a table marked *Reservé* . . . The waiter pulled out our chairs, we sat and I was happy we'd come, so far I hadn't actually been to a club with the doctor. Lights dim and piano and guitar and percussion and in front of a silver counter festooned with buntings, a violinist in tuxedo, and once he saw Břet'a, he smiled, raised his bow, and gave the band its cue, and then started to gently play, I was surprised how softly piano and percussion accompanied the violin, the guitarist strummed and now the violinist made his lingering way to our table, the violinist, his thick hair parted down the middle, leaned over for us, played with great feeling, as Helmuth Zacharias played on our gramophone at home, the waiter stood by our table with a bottle and the cork unpulled, he listened to the melancholy melody, three officers at the table next to ours, they'd been engaged in lively conversation when we'd come in, but now they quieted too, listened to the violin, Marta was smoking and aglow, it made her feel fine, our table the center of attention, the elbow of her left hand in her right palm, smoke rising incessantly from between her fingers and her lips, Břet'a was moved, because the violinist arrived at our table and leaned and played in Břet'a's ear, and when he concluded, Břet'a shook him by the hand and turned to the waiter and said, "And two extra glasses, my treat." And then Břet'a stood, still in his beret, and started talking to the violinist, apparently friends, apparently Břet'a was a regular here, and as I could see, everyone was fond of him . . .

And then the music started, a waltz, and the doctor asked me to dance, the couples on the floor were turning the figures of the waltz. I whispered into the doctor's ear, "I like that brother of yours."

And my fiancé laughed bitterly, saying, "That's because he's been through a lot, he's suffered from that leg of his since he was small, ach, for years . . . bedridden, all we had to do was step on the floor beside his bed and he'd scream with pain, we pulled him about on a go-cart, and while we played soccer, he lay on the cart; this crank Dr. Kafka attempted to make him better by dislocating Břet'a's leg at the hip and resetting it in a cast, and then not only did Břet'a have to stay in bed for half a year and get hauled on a cart, but on top of that, he was wrapped in a twenty-kilo plaster cast, and when they took off the cast, no improvement, they made him this prosthetic that circled his waist and ran down his leg to his ankle, I have the prosthetic at home, hung from the ceiling . . . and then he was able to walk, but only with a cane, and he always fell in love and girls weren't interested, so he turned to cards and poker, the only place he could be number one, the way he played, he'd either win thousands and host the entire bar and the band — he'd treat every last guest — or lose all at the poker, even borrowed money, and he even lost his cravats, play till he hadn't a sou.

"That's why his eyes are so dreamy, that's why he likes those violin performances, and also why, when Zahradníček began repairing hips, Břet'a showed up shaved, ready and waiting for his operation on the hip joint and all of a sudden Břet'a says to Dr. Zahradníček, 'But, Professor, can you guarantee I'll walk?' And Professor Zahradníček pulled off his surgical mask and his gloves and shouted, 'Discharge this man immediately, return him his money immediately, and rid him out of my clinic immediately.' And Břet'a took the money and not till a week later did he venture home, first off he won forty thousand in Prague, but by day three he started to lose and by day five lost the lot, and so he came home minus the money and no operation, and Daddy didn't breathe a word."

The music stopped playing, I held my fiancé tight, looked over to our table, the waiter tapped another bottle, poured, waiting for Břet'a to sample, and then he filled the glasses around the table and chatted with Břet'a, and my fiancé went on in a whisper, "And because Břet'a has loved cars since his boyhood, now he drives a truck delivering everything from stoves to veggies, he's proud of being a truck driver, he makes money, sometimes he's carrying twenty thousand on him, but then the tires'll blow and the twenty thousand's a write-off, see my brother spends money like he deals cards, under the constant impression he had that twenty grand and will have thirty by the time next month rolls around, and that's how he likes to live too, but in the end it always turns out the same, Daddy has to lend him the money for gas . . . And with his Marta, same thing, she had work as a clerk, but had to quit work to stay home, for if Břet'a will bring twenty thousand this month, and next month up to thirty, why on earth would Marta bother with work, especially when he's jealous, he's so horribly jealous of her he goes into fits . . . before Břet'a, Marta went out with a singer, in a choir, but he was young and gorgeously curly headed, like those officers beside us."

"Or, you," I said.

"Right," said my fiancé, and we continued on over the floor. "And Břet'a's jealous of that chorister and Marta has to stay at home, just in case she runs into him, but that said, as you see yourself, Břet'a and myself are both good-lookers, I think if Bob Taylor or Gary Cooper were a tad better looking, they'd almost be a match for me and my brother, Břet'a. And that's saying something."

My fiancé blathered forth and I looked at our table, where Břet'a clinked glasses with the waiter and told jokes and made everyone laugh, even the officers at the next table raised their glasses and drank to Břet'a and Marta, they looked across the dance floor and raised their glasses to me, calling me to come sit down, have a drink. And so taking my fiancé by the hand, I led him to the table, the waiter topped off our glasses and apologized, "Topping off the glass is all the rage now, to let it breathe." And I drank out of thirstiness, I know no other reason to drink except for a thirst, that's why I prefer to drink beer. And so we drank to one another and smiled at the officers at the next table, they shook their heads and flashed their teeth our way, their locks falling in their eyes, ten empty bottles of burgundy lined up in front of them, so far. Then the music switched to a tango, then a waltz, and with every number the violinist came and played for Břet'a and Břet'a was in seventh heaven, and then the officers gathered their courage and two got up and came over to our table and asked Marta and me for a dance, after seeking permission from Břet'a and my fiancé. And Břet'a was the one to laugh, but Marta grew pale and droopy and didn't feel like dancing, she apologized and made eyes at them, but Břet'a called to her and waved his hand and encouraged her, "Go dance, be happy." She was only happy when dancing with younger men, he called to her, that was her shtick . . . And Marta relented, took the officer's arm and then danced the tango with him, I danced with the other officer, his light hair falling into my eyes, that young gentleman smelled of wine and flashed his white teeth at me, he knew he had good teeth, therefore he laughed and I was glad, because I hadn't expected any of it, I hoped we would come to this club again, if we had the time, come again and again . . .

And as I danced, and the world in the dance club spun lightly around me, out of the corner of my eye I noticed the guitarist, how he looked at me, and then the staircase, and then the table, and then the faces and backs of the dancing couples, and suddenly my fiancé's face, serious, suddenly alone, suddenly like he'd just been dropped down out of the sky, he held his glass and threw it back in one shot, and when I'd danced another turn, I saw him pour another glass and knock it back, and then I stood beside Marta and her officer, and Marta was concerned, eyes full of tears, but when she saw how I enjoyed dancing, saw me smiling, she brightened and pressed herself to her partner, who spun her over to the table, to Břet'a, and out of nowhere the dancer leaned over Marta, and it wasn't as though he was giving her a kiss, but he put his moist cheek to Marta's and smothered her face in his curly hair . . . and Břet'a bit his tongue, got up, and then he yelled out, "You're a whore, nothing but a whore!" and raised his cane, but the young officer knocked it out of his hands easily and with a grin reached to pat Břet'a's head and swiped off his beret, and then he froze, even my fiancé froze, and even the waiter went rigid . . . There Břet'a stood and he hadn't much hair, bald, right down the middle, and because of the tanned face and livid white pate, he was like an old clown as he stood there, just stood there, looking down at the table, his face paling, the violinist came up and played into his ear, the waiter picked the beret up and placed it back on Břet'a's head, Marta kneeled by Břet'a, but nothing counted anymore, Břet'a paid the bill, the officers apologized, leaning down to Břeťa, but their curly hair was all around him and it reinforced his envy and sadness and misery all the more . . .

Only my fiancé kept his aplomb, eyes agleam, he merely marveled and looked on, he could not and probably did not even wish to be involved, he made no attempt to say anything, asked for no explanations, more as though privileged by what he had seen, what he had witnessed, he nodded, and I put my arm around Břeťa's shoulders, handed him his cane, the waiter escorted us out, the officers stood stunned, looking at one another, hands hanging by the jackets of their uniforms, perplexed, Marta wept and her eyes spoke to me, I saw it coming, I knew, this is how it always ends up. And Břeťa took the stairs, heavily, the violinist backing up the steps in advance of him, Břeťa's friend backing up and playing a sad melody, the violinist had beautiful, devoted eyes, and he too had thick hair, parted down the middle, pomaded . . . And yes, this was Helmuth Zacharias's melody from the gramophone, from that stars-in-his-eyes Jew, who played his tune, *My heart is like a violin.*

And then, into our return journey in the Citroën, and as we left, violinist still at the door, bowing to Břeťa behind the wheel, not even that sad melody made any difference . . . And Marta beside Břeťa crying, the car started, we made it out of the town, the Citroën threatening to self-destruct, the way Břeťa drove, my fiancé wanted to joke about it, but even he grew somber. Through one village after another the Citroën raced. I begged Břeťa to put on the brakes, I had had enough, but Břeťa kept speeding, the old Citroën kept threatening to self-destruct, and then we got a puncture, but Břeťa drove on, my fiancé and I sat on the back seat, being flung together, I yelled at the doctor, "Do something, for Christ's sake!" But he cowered over to the seat corner, and then it was up to me, me who took after her mother, forest ranger's daughter from Enzendorf, my mother who never let even my father step out of line, that's how hard-boiled and overweening she could be when needed . . . I hit Břeťa on the back, then I hit him again, then I pummeled him with my fists until finally he drove over a pile of gravel, the Citroën almost coming to a stop, I kicked at the door, and as I tumbled out, still managed to grab my fiancé by the sleeve and pull him after. Břeťa recovered himself, ground down a gear and the Citroën spurted gravel, wobbling on its three good tires, swerving and flying on down the road, red taillights disappearing beyond some trees . . . We lay in the ditch on our backs, breathing hard, lay, our arms splayed, the fingers of our outstretched hands touching. The sky was full of stars . . . my fiancé said, "Remember . . . Whoever wants into our family . . . has to learn to adapt . . . like Olánek Kolář said."

CHAPTER SEVENTEEN

THREE DAYS IN ADVANCE OF THE WEDDING MY FIANCÉ GOT SICK FROM the whole to-do. He couldn't sit still, couldn't sleep; the appointment eleven thirty Friday morning at the castle, the notice in plain black and white to confirm the wedding would happen, it all gave him the jitters. As if that day at that hour he was due for an operation, he even took three days off, announcing those three days off work were being taken because of a death in the family. And then all he did was do the rounds of the taverns, a beer for every tavern, then move on, only on the run did he quit thinking of the wedding, as though he were getting drunk as a skunk one day and then spending the next running away from his stinking namesake, he just trotted about the entire time, as a matter of fact he ran, but the drunken skunk always caught him, when he stopped, he was hungover, so only trotting around was he a fiancé, as soon as he stopped, he had the jitters about the day, the day he would marry and officially be my husband, the day was coming on apace and my fiancé no longer ate, he just guzzled and sighed, so out of sorts over the wedding day, he couldn't even string two words together. And I kept on going in to work, the whole hotel was excited and happy about my wedding, from coat-check woman on up to manager, every one interested in the wedding, they came to take a look, I even had to promise, day before the ceremony, when I raised a glass to my marriage with them, I'd wear my wedding dress. But the two happiest people were Maître d' and Head Chef, Head Chef hauled that saddle of frozen venison out of the freezer and began preparing my wedding present, cold game, as though all those years in the deep freeze under Prague Market that buck had been waiting for me. And when I thought how I was going to be married, Friday, at eleven thirty in the morning up at the castle, I got completely jittery, I made mistakes at the register that the maitre d' and the waiters constantly righted for me, and everybody got a huge kick out of the fact that I, at the age of twenty-eight, could get so rattled by a plain old wedding. By Thursday my fiancé could no longer handle it, he picked up the wedding bouquet and wandered around Libeň, from one tavern to the next with it, the barmaids would hand him a pint glass to stick the bouquet in, my fiancé drank his beer, accepted congratulations, made it the entire distance to the Hop Bush Pub with the bouquet, then to Hofmann's in Kobylisy, and then a stop at the Brickworks and up to the Lookout, but couldn't stay longer than it took to down a beer, he started on half-pints only, wearing his wedding clothes, as soon as he and his bouquet were sat down, he opened his wallet, him with a wallet! He who carried all his papers and documents and money crumpled into his trouser pockets now trotted around with a wallet, he would meticulously open it and read aloud, the wedding was to be Friday, eleven thirty, though he had probably read it fifty times over, he still could not believe that one statement by a rep from town council would turn him into a husband. And so he would finish up his beer, take his sopping bouquet, and wander down once more from the Lookout, again stopping at taverns he had never been into before, Čízek's and Souček's, he stopped at Kořáb's, and as he walked he managed to calm himself somewhat, the walking settled him, not as though the walking up to Kobylisy and back down again to Douda's and Schollera's were gaining him any time, au contraire, he was shortening the dreadfully long time until Friday, eleven thirty, when we would stand side by side to become husband and wife. Those final three days prewedding, I thought my fiancé was fooling about, but he wasn't fooling, not trying to be funny, my fiancé, as I learned, was a frightful coward, scared of making a decision, during our whole time together he was incapable of making a single one, he left it to me to decide what to eat, where to go, as if he could never bear the blame for a wrong choice, and delivered everything into other hands, mine. In fact, for those three days he couldn't even look me in the eye, always this scared glance, and then looking off into the distance, staring at the ground and blushing and being as shy as a little girl. I figured he was putting me on, but he was a bigger baby than I thought, this man who could toss hundredweight bales around like a garbage-truck driver, this man who could spend three hours hoeing the garden, sweat pouring, this very same man could be as timid as a chick, a bunny rabbit, a scolded, frightened child. Often as not I had to grab his head and turn his face to me, so standing across from each other, he'd have to look me in the eye, but he'd drop his, I had to pry his eyelids open, it took ages before he'd look and I could look into his eyes, and like a skittish horse, like a tiny frightened animal, try to soothe him. "Now, now, now, now, now . . . what is it, what's the matter?" And like a windshield wiper I'd wave my hand in front of those eyes, try to make the fear leave, the nightmare, like when a child wakes before dawn, out of a bad dream, afraid and crying. And I felt, standing so close, his heart beating, him shaking all over.

"What is it, what's happened to you?" I asked.

"It's nothing, it's nothing. I don't know. It's awful with me," he moaned, "I've been this scared ever since school, always bringing those bad report cards home. I have this never-ending feeling I bring bad report cards home. And then, it's like I've been in flight ever since I was a kid, something always propelling me elsewhere, and then when I *am* someplace else, I want to go back where I was, to start the whole thing up again."

"Now, now, now!" I stroked and whispered in his ear, "Things will stay same as they are, we'll be the same, you do everything as you have, up until now, I go to work, you come down and meet me at the tram, when I'm on afternoon shift . . . and no need to explain a thing to me, if you don't want, we don't have to talk, if you don't want, tell me everything and I'll keep it to myself, you can even do your writing in front of me, I know how to be truly quiet, like not there, perhaps even take up needlepoint again, and you write and do as you please, I just beg you, don't run out on me, I wouldn't want to live other than with you anymore, I would die if you didn't show up at eleven thirty for our wedding up at the castle, for my wedding, our wedding . . . you and I."

Our heads met, our eyes crossed paths, the window to the courtyard lay open, I whispered in his ear and he started crying in my hair, wept like a child, I stroked him, touched by his crying, that he opened up, as he truly was, rent his shirt and exposed his heart like the paintings of Jesus hung over the beds in country houses.

"Do you hear?" I said.

He hiccuped and nodded and repeated time and again, "I hear."

And what I did, three days before the wedding, is put a pot of water onto the stove, the stove roared and the melody of the fire soothed pleasantly . . . On my way back from the afternoon shift, from the Hotel Paris kitchens, utterly messy, saturated with steam and the stink of burnt grease, legs dusty and dirty to my knees, he came and waited for me at the tram stop and we'd walk back through the quiet little streets of Libeň; it was usually near midnight already; we'd walk into our building and then into our future apartment, into that one room, where even I was starting to feel comfortable, especially when a fire roared pleasantly in the cast-iron stove, constantly drawn up the chimney by the powerful draft, a pot of water hissing on the stove, and he'd put a tub near my feet, that old battered tub, if someone had spied us through the window, they would think the man was undressing me to make love, but that fellow, my fiancé, pulled down my stockings and hiked up my skirt only to pour hot water into the tub and mix it with cold until just right, and then he would roll up his sleeves, kneel in front of me, first take the one leg and then the other, lathering my dirty feet and slowly, tenderly, wash them till I closed my eyes and was in bliss, while he took the washcloth and rubbed one foot clean first and then the other, and as the water turned murky from the dirt off my feet, my fiancé would hold my clean foot, dry it in a towel, and place it on the floor, then gently slide it into a slipper . . . and then the other, and then get up, smooth my hair, and walk out into the courtyard and dump out the dirty water with an enormous splash.

But when it was he who sat drooping and exhausted, there in front of me, when he'd done lamenting, I brought over the tub and returned the gift he gave me, I untied the shoes from his listless feet, then tugged off his socks, and I got on my knees in front of him and first the one foot, then the other, I washed, it came to me suddenly this washing of feet was truly the most beautiful thing to happen between us so far, as he humbled himself before me, so I also, before him, and I washed his feet, wishing to do that for as long as ever I could. I wiped his feet carefully, and he, toppling over me from the drink. Then I hauled off his sweater, him falling over on me, it was like undressing a corpse, I got the pants off, then the shorts, threw that body down, naked, onto the Union Jack my fiancé used as a bedspread, he splayed his legs and lay on his back, completely relaxed, and went to sleep.

The stove roared, I added a plank to the fire, looked around that little room, and was happy, I, who hailed from thirteen rooms, where I lived as child and girl, now this one little room was enough for me, I shut my eyes and ran through our old mansion, through open doors, one room to the other, like the playback of a movie, diaphanous empire chairs, the quilt-backed sofas and armchairs, baroque brown dining room with a painting by a Dutch master hung above the sideboard, rooms in which vases glowed full of flowers . . . and I opened my eyes, and sure enough, the swag light glowed above me, and for the first time since I'd been in the flat, I noticed up near the ceiling, its wire looped around a nickel-plated prosthetic with laces to tie it up to the calf and thighs, Břeťa's prosthetic, worn ages before, my future brother-in-law's, and my fiancé's best man for the wedding I was due to undergo in three days time . . .

■ □ ■ □ ■

CHAPTER EIGHTEEN

AND THEN MY WEDDING DAY CAME, BEFORE THE BREAK OF DAWN
my fiancé put on his clothes for the wedding, after dressing though,
he discovered in a huge fluster how he omitted to shave, and so he
lathered his cheeks, and while doing that, managed to soap his shirt
collar for the wedding, and in such a state of nerves, he feared he'd
nick himself, even though he used a safety blade, so he rinsed his
face, got the lather washed off. And his hands shook but kept their
tight hold on the wedding bouquet, the only time he put it down
was to add wood to the cast-iron stove, which had gone out several
times already. And then my fiancé's cousins Milada and Liza turned
up to dress me, and out the doctor went with the bouquet onto Main
Street to get a shave, and I was frozen stiff with dread that he'd do the
same as that other louse, my very first fiancé, did to me, slink off before the ceremony, to marry another. And then it took me time to get
dressed, every piece I picked up jiggled or got stuck on something,
those two bridesmaids of mine had to wedge me upright, one on
either side, I smiled, but I felt like bawling. Then Břet'a and Marta
came into the yard, Břet'a done up to the nines, wearing a heavenly
blue cravat and a fedora, he called me the wee wedding bride and
for the love of God, I implored him, quit it, and Marta smoked and
took nips of liquor with Milada, and Wulli scooted out onto Main
Street and then back in, he'd been to two barbershops to date, but
no sign of my fiancé, and after that my two bridesmaids handed me
my wedding tiara, they had to put it on and help fasten it, for now

I really started quaking, my legs buckling, because the other wedding guests began to arrive in the yard, Milada went to greet them, she pulled a table out of the washhouse, thirty bottles of champagne and hard liquor poked out of the tubs and washbasin, into which water poured constantly, Milada threw a tablecloth over the table and served drinks to the guests, but my fiancé still didn't show up, and then my bridesmaids presented me with my wedding veil, raised it over my eyes which dripped with tears and my rigid smile, a pale-faced Wulli ran in again, arms out wide, to tell me again what I could see for myself, my fiancé still hadn't shown, he was off with his wedding bouquet slinging back shots. And Wulli pulled up his sleeve and showed me the time, time to go, and then, as I lifted my veil and wanted to give up on the whole affair, when I just wanted to run to some corner and have a good cry, who should arrive but Ema, that second mother of mine, bearing a bouquet, and when she gave the yard a look-see, and when she entered our nuptial kitchen, dining room, and bedroom, when she saw me sitting so down at the mouth, truly, that second mother of mine appeared to perk right up, at the fact that everything was set to go, the whole wedding party here, except for groom and wedding bouquet.

And out in the yard Milada and Marta walked around pinning sprigs of myrtle tied in white ribbon to the wedding guests, my bridesmaids slowed the regaling of the wedding guests on purpose, and then our two barmaids ran into the yard, Head Chef at their heel, the barmaids carried a gigantic silver platter covered in a cloth, and as soon as I caught sight of Head Chef, a huge weight lifted, I breathed a sudden sigh of relief, suddenly assured my fiancé would be here, Ema sat next to me and couldn't dissemble her glee over the fact that not only her son but even the doctor had run off on me. And then my fiancé flew into the yard, face aglow and eyes swimming in alcohol, lit up and teary eyed, overjoyed not at the fact we were soon to wed, but overjoyed at how he vanquished his own fear, how he'd found courage . . . And there he was in the midst of our wedding guests, brandishing the wedding bouquet, raising it to toast and eagerly downing the shots, and I brightened and once more felt like that Parisian pastry with whipped-cream topping, I wiped away my tears and stood, slapped my heels down, and then a second time and ran into the yard, and our two barmaids took the cloth by the tail then and pulled, pulled it back, and there was the cold saddle of venison laid out, the meat cooked and sliced, the one thing left, to tuck in, and the barmaids ran to me and we touched foreheads, and those two girls burst into honest-to-goodness tears, and then Head Chef took me by both hands, I lifted my veil to receive his heartfelt kiss on my cheek, but he barely grazed me with his lips, for Wulli started to tap his watch and get white in the face, then finally my fiancé handed over the wedding bouquet, and Wulli gave the signal and led us out of the courtyard, as a witness for my marriage, and then the remainder of the wedding party fell in, my fiancé, thoroughly shaved and perfumed, we went down the stairs, passed by the windows of Mrs. Beranová's flat, from up above the lamp splashed light on the neat lady and her spectacles cast circles onto her face, she ran out into the hall now, gave my fiancé a kiss, shook my hand, and said, "You'll be happy with the doctor, for he's a good man, and tonight from our establishment, the Golden Goose, I'll get you cold rabbit pâté." And the wedding troop blundered down the wet corridor, and the wedding guests, almost every one, when we stepped into the street, tried to wipe the scuff from the wet corridor off their jackets, for the guests, every one, were stumbling drunk from the drink already. After a step or two, several from the wedding party ran back up to the yard to finish off theirs, only to catch up to us by the open gates to Brush and Paint Supply.

And then our troop forged along Kotlaska, the glass doors of Liška's Pub flew open and there the patrons stood and the manager dashed out, handed a fresh-drawn pint of beer to my fiancé, who drank it thirstily, I could see raised glasses glitter in the twilight and smoke of the pub, but I kept my pace, my fiancé caught up and elbow to elbow we walked, the sleeves on my fiancé's jacket were scuffed, Wulli's clothes too, scuffed, I turned and saw the wedding guests, each and every one of them, scuffed with dirt from that horrible corridor of ours, even the women wore its smears on their dresses, I laughed and right then, when I saw our parade of fools, that maskless masquerade, I laughed and raised my eyes to the skies, and my fiancé gathered me by the waist, pressing in, lifting me almost, and gave me the most beautiful kiss, a kiss like never before, and all at once the sky threatened to rain and it turned cold on us, as though about to snow, once we walked off the sidewalk and along by the Rokytka River, my fiancé took a set of steps right down to the water, squatted there on the last step, out of the water which flowed in around rusting stoves and three funeral wreaths that had floated downstream on the spring swells, he scooped handful after handful and then he ran up to us soaking wet . . . And Liza and Wulli were pale faced, yesterday they had reproached me for using the name Eliška on the invitation cards, told me I ought to call myself Elizabeth after my mother, but yesterday I insisted, according to my birth certificate I really was Eliška, and Liza shouted that some chauvinist priest had purposely written that in, and if I weren't about to use Elizabeth, then on the marriage certificate I ought to at least enter that although a citizen of the Czechoslovak Republic, I *was* German by nationality, but I told them I *am* Czech, and by nationality therefore, Czechoslovak. And Ema, when she saw my fiancé walk beside me, so sodden, well, that dear second mother of mine groaned, whereas the other guests chuckled, I discovered our troop had dwindled to less than ten, I was glad my fiancé's friends, the ones who loved to put on those in-house weddings with him, had fled back to the yard to drink their drinks, their glasses of wine, happy they had, for I worried they might fall over or break into song on the spot at the Chateau Libeň's wedding registry.

And then out came the sun and glimmered off the Chateau Libeň ahead, we left the sidewalk and went up steps, then along a sanded path and through a park ornamented with manicured hedges, a huge gold clock glowed on the facade of the chateau, marking five minutes to ten. And my fiancé's breath came heavily, his collar and tie choked him, his eyelashes still in the wet seal of river water, Wulli ran on ahead and pushed open the gate to the Chateau Libeň, inside stood my duo of cooks, over on their motorcycles as promised, in their checkered pants and white smocks and white chef's hats, they grinned and congratulated me, they had likely given their kitchens the slip, I smiled at them, and then a white staircase was leading us up and music raining down, the organ blasted a wedding fanfare, and at the top step, white doors opened and in velvet livery the city clerk stepped out and invited my fiancé, wedding party, and me into her bureau. And then we signed the registry and I saw through the open door members of another wedding, the preceding, exit the lofty doors from the registry, the wedding party swayed down the same staircase we came up, I was glad my fiancé had chosen this spot for our wedding, this little chateau, with its exquisite baroque furniture, and huge, winged doors, principally for those, the type Daddy preferred, and then the city clerk got our wedding party assembled, somewhat surprised at why everyone's sleeves should wear a dirt smudge, and the doors to the wedding registry swept open and I went stock-still, out of the speakers, the sound of an old orchestra emerged, followed by a melody . . . *My heart . . . is like a violin . . .* And right enough, it was Helmuth Zacharias playing that melancholy song, the one so loved by Daddy, the song he played the entire week when Olga Čechová came to visit and Daddy touched her hand and the tears glittered in his eyes, I turned to look for Břet'a and he nodded and sent me a smile, it was he who brought the record and arranged for Helmuth Zacharias to perform at my wedding, red carpet spread before me and by the wall a golden lion glowed and pennants and flowers on a little table, and my witness, Wulli, led me through to a room almost as spacious as our dining room at home, behind me, in step, my fiancé with his brother, Břet'a, I held my bouquet and knew now at last, my wedding was really going to happen, I ceased trembling, opened my eyes, my fiancé was at my side, I could smell the alcohol off him, and now the trembling was his, then the clerk set the wedding registry on the table and from a door in the wall a bespectacled man emerged, a sash across his breast, he took his position behind the table and the city clerk introduced my fiancé and me, and then the gentleman she addressed as Mr. Chairman gave a speech, I looked at his red book, from which a ribbon dangled with a seal, the man spoke to us, he stressed we should love one another, and our love was not only a guarantee but a safeguard, he repeated that we should stand by one another, and then asked us if we knew of any lawful reason why our marriage should not proceed, and both my fiancé and I said we did not, and then he asked us both in turn if we took each other in marriage, willingly, and I said I do, and my fiancé coughed several times, his mouth sticky from the heat, but after all he finally gave his I do. And then the chairman of the town council declared us officially married, and on the strength of that to exchange rings, those gold wedding rings I was compelled to buy myself. And we turned to one another, the secretary offered the rings to us on a tray and thus did we stand face-to-face, for that husband of mine to make repeated attempts with his clumsy fingers to slip my ring on, but finally in the end he managed to slide the ring onto my ring finger, and I playfully slipped on his and then he lifted my veil and kissed me, Helmuth Zacharias reprised the melody one last time . . . *My heart . . . is like a violin . . .* and first the chairman and then the secretary congratulated us, the marriage certificate would be in her office, she whispered to me, and then a kiss from Wulli, which moved him, and then Liza's turn, and then the rest of the wedding guests, I gave Head Chef Bauman my own heartfelt kiss, that good man, who kept me at the Hotel Paris on the sly, who gave me courage, and was the only one to see, back when the doctor buried me in roses during our inaugural *Schweinfest* at the Hotel Paris, that the doctor would take me as his wife, and take me as wife he did.

And so the wedding ceremony came to a conclusion, the last to kiss me was Ema, that second mother of mine, she breathed a prodigious sigh of relief, I could tell by her eyes she was happy to finally be rid of me, not to have me live with her anymore, I thanked her for everything we'd been through with her son, my treasure, whom I traded for a man who would never bore me and who loved me in his own peculiar way, whom I would live with, and whose name I would bear. And the wedding ceremony ended, the doors to the hallway opened, we made our way out, and the wedding fanfare came on again, for up the stairs to the secretary's bureau another wedding party was climbing, pale bride and young groom, accompanied by stiff wedding guests, meanwhile our party went down, relaxed and disorganized already. And then out to the front of the chateau, there stood two cooks and two barmaids to congratulate my fiancé and me; the barmaids cried, and then a number of passersby who knew the doctor congratulated us, then we took pictures, and then headed down the steps to the sidewalk, the duo of cooks kick-started their motorcycles, the barmaids hopped on the back and they waved and hollered and escorted our parade of fools all the way down to Podlipný's statue, where they turned down toward the Rokytka River and crossed Libeň Bridge en route to the Hotel Paris . . . And then an amble along Na Hrázi for us, I undid my jacket for a touch more comfort, there I walked along in my gorgeous wedding dress, holding my wedding bouquet, and from the way everyone said hello and smiled at us, we were causing quite a gleeful stir, on account of the smudge on all our outfits from our hall corridor, and the entire wedding party, staggering; I clutched my wedding bouquet and waved it in acknowledgment, suddenly it dawned on me I was married, it lent me strength, I wanted to go back to the Chateau Libeň and do the walk again, even wanted us to take in Main Street, take my own wedding bouquet tour into every one of the doctor's pubs. And when I turned to see the only two guests disconcerted by our wedding parade, Wulli and Liza, that lent more strength, I removed my jacket and handed it to my husband, and enfolded in white silk, in veil and wedding tiara, I lifted up both my arms and danced Daddy's dance from Moravia, and even Wulli knew how to dance in his Slovak costume before he was lumped with Liza. I lifted up both my arms and danced along Na Hrázi, I could see my husband smile at me, see he was honored by my dance, he gave me such a nice look, smiled with those wide-set eyes, his eyelashes pasted together, from splashing his face in the Rokytka River prior to the wedding, and I ran up to him and hugged him and we kissed under the lamp and I shut my eyes and clutched my flowers, hands wrapped around his neck, and Liza and Wulli stood there looking discombobulated, while the rest of the guests smiled on . . . And then a truck pulled up, the drivers from the garbage collection, and Lord, what a hoot when they saw us like that in each other's arms, and even the boss of the garbage collectors stepped down from the cab to congratulate the doctor and me, so we stood hugging under the lamp, accepting their best wishes, and the doctor invited all the other guests up to our small celebration. And then we squeezed up our corridor, everybody's sleeves messed afresh on the walls, and up I flew into the yard with my bouquet, I turned, spread out my arms, and hailed downstairs, to the neat lady's windows, to where all the people who accompanied me to Chateau Libeň stood.

"Everyone, come take a look at me, everyone, come have a drink, everybody, come and raise a glass, for I'm happy, just sooo happy!"

And my guests came up the stairs, some I didn't even know, doctor's friends, Liza and Wulli went on up to their flat, and when they opened their door, Bobby the Kerry blue terrier came running down, barking and jumping, and the doctor and I patted him, and he licked us and barked and slobbered with joy, and also the guests, he had a little myrtle tied in white ribbon pinned to the curls above his eyes. And sitting in the yard were other guests who'd come for the doctor's wedding, but who preferred the yard, and there they sat, smiling and sloshing drinks over onto the dusty yard. And I showed my guests around, pointing with my bouquet, "This here's our terrace, if you please, our hanging garden." And I pointed to the rooftop on which the doctor liked to write, where he pursued the sun, where he put his sawed-down chairs . . . And then I led the guests to the washhouse, where the bottles of vodka, liquor, and champagne now stood in the tub and washbasins. "This here is my, our, bathroom, if you please." And I led the guests further over . . . to the open toilet. "And if you please, this is our toilet here." And I pointed with my bouquet at the pile of earth, from which two ivy stalks and its sprigs split every which way off wires, up where the billboards shone, and I pointed out the doctor's death mask, wired onto the rafters of the shed. "And if you please, this is our mausoleum garden . . . where we are to have our garden party today." I called and the wedding guests smiled, my husband was the only one taken aback by what I was saying, he couldn't believe his ears, and I hadn't a drink yet . . . today I was in most part simply happy to be a wife, marriage certificate official, happy I hadn't been put off, even though Ema, that second mother of mine, and Wulli and Liza, wanted me sad, wanted me to think about what next as husband and wife, since we'd borrowed from them for this wedding party and had no idea when and how to pay it back . . . And I led our wedding guests in a dance across the yard into our single room, where not even a fire was going, I was cold there, but showed them with a laugh. "And in this corner, if you please, we have our kitchen, and if you please, our bedroom in this, and over here near the window is our den if you will." And with my wedding bouquet I displayed the cast-iron stove, then the cast-iron bed with the Union Jack spread . . . And finally I showed off the stool with tree trunk, festooned with a dead wasp's nest. "And this," I showed them, "this is our dining room!" And I took a bucket and stuck the bouquet in and put it on the table, the table and two chairs under the droplight . . .

And you could sense the whole other room through the wall, that whole future apartment of mine shaking, behind the wall, in the machine shop there, some giant lathe and giant saw was boring through some giant drive shaft . . . And with my little pinkie I pointed, in my wedding veil and tiara turned my head and said, "Do you hear that? That is downright enthralling! Even at night it rattles like so . . . our table moves, our bed rolls . . . but on the other hand, it's so cold here, we have to move out into the courtyard to get warm, or we have to have a fire in every weather." And I struck a match and opened the stove door, the kindling in there already, and the fire got started and presently the stove began to roar, I added wood and ran out, same as the doctor would run out on every occasion where he lit a fire, I ran across the yard, as far as the circular stair that led up to Liza's, then I stood, from there, could see our chimney, smoke beginning to rise . . . The guests followed, shivering from the cold, but I stood in the yard, back to the wall, on tiptoe and showed them all, ever so proudly. "See, see . . . Our smoke, that's it coming out our chimney! That chimney has a draw in it! After all, a blacksmith's forge used to be under that chimney, our apartment was a smithy . . . but now, everyone, come drink to our marriage." And I ran into the washhouse and brought out green bottles of champagne, gave a bottle to everyone, only the drivers wouldn't take one, everyone looked at me and I knew I was seen, now *I* was the girl with the Koh-i-noor patent-button eye, now I was Poldinka, the mistress with the star-seared ringlets, whose imprint traveled the world stamped into every beam of Kladno steel, now I was lady of the house. And I loosened the wire off the champagne cork, I waited, everyone took my lead, except for the few who didn't quite get it, but I could see Head Chef Bauman looking at me, he was happy seeing me as me, the way I truly am, and my husband even looked at me with delight, and the boss garbage man too, and even Marta and my husband's cousin, Milada, who now emerged from the washhouse shot glasses in hand, eyes aswim with strong liquor, and the only ones disturbed by my behavior were Liza and Wulli and Ema, my second mother, all upstairs . . . and Bobby leaped and barked, weaving in and out of everyone's legs . . . And now a sparkling stream of wine broke from my bottle, and five and then ten and then almost twenty champagne bottles popped and the bubbly flowed, Bobby, wherever he would run, had bubbly spilled on him and everyone hoisted their green bottles, and all the guests shouted and laughed, blabbered and cried, but all raised a glass to me and my husband, to our happiness in such a fine apartment, to our fine hanging garden . . .

And then Head Chef Bauman lifted the cloth, and I leaned over the saddle of cold venison and spread my arms and clapped my hands over that beautiful cold game, and with Mr. Bauman holding one side and me the other, we carried the table into the center of the yard and the chef divided out the slices onto paper plates and handed them to the guests, and we all set to, and even Wulli and Liza came downstairs, smiling, the tiff now over, they kissed me and helped themselves to some cold game and uncorked a bottle of champagne, and so all at once we went quiet, listening to the sound of everyone eating, that buck had finally made it to my wedding, I had to retell the tale of how Mr. Brandejs had shot the buck eight years previous, how the buck lay for eight years in the deep freeze under Prague Market, and how Mr. Bauman and I had eventually found it down there, how we drove it to the hotel, and how we had to butcher it first with a hacksaw . . . and how first when Head Chef Bauman had noticed my husband in the Hotel Paris kitchen, he knew instantly that we would be catering for a wedding in this house here and so one saddle of venison he set apart in the freezer . . . And so unexpectedly my wedding turned into an event such as no one had ever seen or attended, at that moment I realized it, when everyone regarded Head Chef Bauman as if the president had come to my wedding in person, or a famous soccer player, everyone looked to him and he smiled and beamed, but then gave a start, because it was time for him to be back at the Hotel Paris, back in his kitchen to prep his specialties, back getting things under control . . . And he gave me a kiss and his thanks, and shook both my husband's hands—that I had never witnessed before, ordinarily Mr. Bauman offered people an elbow—and true enough, he held onto the doctor's hands between his own and then examined the doctor's, felt the calluses, and my husband smiled, for those hands were his pride. And then Head Chef Bauman sprinted down the steps, and the drivers from Spálená Street then said their goodbyes, and even the boss garbage man thanked me, and other guests started to take their leave then, ones who had dropped by briefly, managing to take a bit of time off work . . . And then my husband gathered all the packages and presents, I unwrapped some of them, we drank champagne, and whoever wanted got a shot of Russian vodka to boot, I remembered how Daddy used to relish drinking a champagne cognac, or champagne vodka, he called it a Russian bear, now I drank to Daddy, a champagne vodka, Břet'a was already primed on shots, so he went over to the Russian bear also, we unwrapped more wedding presents, vases and defunct ashtrays, all the gifts I received had been through a series of prior marriages, I knew I would never put them in my apartment, Břet'a commented on every gift, "Hey, that's a rare find, they don't make that anymore, where did you buy it, the flea market?" And he scrutinized the wedding guests, "Oh, yeah, this, you must have dug this out of storage somewhere up at Saint Vojtech's? Well, never have I seen the like, look, Brother, you'll need to have that insured, or look, make sure nobody here steals *that*, throw it straight in the bin." But *that* it so happened was the very gift Liza had given, and she got offended and ran right up to her flat. And my husband unwrapped another gift, and a set of old-fashioned curtains fell out and I immediately pressed them to my heart, because they were exactly the type of curtains Daddy had, to cover his bedroom window top to bottom, for he had hauled those curtains all the way down from his family cottage in Slovakia . . . and I called out, "Ach, these curtains will work wonders for us."

And precisely at that moment, a dull rumble came from behind the tall wall that rose up over our long shed, and then the balance of the plaster tore away from the wall and with a clatter and a roar dropped onto the shed, and the sand and the plaster and the grit slid down off the slant roof; tail tucked between his legs Bobby ran down the steps; sand spilled into the yard and plaster shattered in all directions and the wedding guests bolted for the washhouse and down the steps and stood there, petrified, waiting to see if the whole wall might follow. Only after a time, once the sand clouds and plaster settled somewhat, did they come back in, they stepped over debris, and I took off into our flat and brought out the wedding bouquet, raised it aloft, and cried, "Isn't it splendid, I bet you all envy us our little yard, our lifestyle, eh?" But my guests didn't, their black clothes, grim gray by now, they dusted off, they quaffed their shots and chased them with champagne, I called to our wedding guests, "Everybody, into our place! The living-room area is nicely heated, if we don't all fit, the dining room will do for drinking too, and those who won't fit there, well, a seat in the kitchen nook, but if you find you don't fit in there either, then, if you will, utilize the washhouse connected to the fitness area, we have very comfy lounge chairs." But the wedding guests all threw up their arms to object and shouted, "Anything, but that! We'll catch our death of pneumonia, it'll make us sick!" And they said their good-byes and began to leave, only one bottle of champagne being left in the washbasin, no hard liquor in the tub, and all the saddle of cold venison, long eaten . . . I wagged the wedding bouquet and yelled, "Or down to Hausmann's, to Mr. Vaništa's, my husband will continue his fabulous wedding from three o'clock on, for friends yet to arrive!" But the wedding guests were into their good-byes, wading through the sand and debris, they peered up at that tall wall, where chunks of plaster still threatened a collapse, here and there a segment gave way, shaking loose and spilling down on the wedding guests. They said good-bye to me, most likely happier to go to Vaništa's, my sister-in-law and Milada collared their bottle of booze and went into my flat with me, but once in, they shivered from the cold, so they went out again, bottle and all, and waded over the buried-under yard and up to Liza's, Břeťa lay on the Union Jack and rested his cane beside him and gazed at the ceiling, from which hung the prosthesis with nickel springs and leather straps, the wire from the droplight wound through, and I took the curtains, those curtains with a wealth of meaning for me, I spread them full out, and sure enough, they were the right fit for my windows. I was cold, I gave the stove a rake and added fresh wood and lit the fire and then ran into the yard again, I stumbled over split plaster and several bricks, and then I looked across and yes indeed, our smoke poured out of our chimney, rose to the heavens in a taper, our smoke rose like the slender trunk of a birch heavenward, I went back in, upstairs at Liza's I could hear the remaining guests talk, the ones Liza invited up. I found myself in the yard suddenly alone, I went into the washhouse and turned the water off, nothing was left to keep cool, I pulled out the one surviving bottle of champagne. And on the way back up to our flat, upstairs where the Slavíčková family lived, up there the door to the toilet lay open and Mrs. Slavíčková leaned out, beckoning with her hand for me to come up, she had a thing to tell me, I marshaled my courage and bottle in hand made my way up the circular staircase, up to where I had not been before, suddenly wanting to be up there, for I wished to see the kind of place we ourselves might have one day, I made the landing, my tiara slipping askew, so I flipped it back into place on my hair, but when I looked up, Mrs. Slavíčková actually was seated, benignly, on the toilet, and beside her, as far as the ceiling, shelves lined with jars of stewed fruit, and then Mrs. Slavíčková got up heavily, pulled up her huge bloomers, we had a name, *bomber drawers,* for them, and she let down her dress and chugged the chain behind her, and this, I said to myself, we do not have in our bathroom yet. And Mrs. Slavíčková came out of the toilet toward me, offered her hand, and I was concerned in case she would scold me over my husband peeing into the gutter in the yard last night, and he, then still my fiancé, its ferocious splash could have woken her children. But she congratulated me on my marriage and then ushered me into her flat, and for certain, that's how I wanted my kitchen, and certainly, how our room would be when I put the kitchen in, the style of kitchen I had in Píštany, that Daddy built, when they moved us from our many rooms and evicted us. And with a wink Mrs. Slavíčková pointed at the freshly made bed in the room, but I wasn't following, so the lady turned back the coverlet, and swaddled in blankets I saw my husband's head, saw him asleep, arms behind his head, and Bobby beside him asleep, pinned to his fur, the myrtle and white ribbon. Mrs. Slavíčková said quietly, "He ran up here a short while earlier, and the minute he saw the bed, in he went! And Bobby in after. And now they're sleeping like a pair of newborns . . . but, young lady, come on into the kitchen and we'll talk about the things that have happened, the celebrated story of our lives, our families . . . you know, till I was ten I hadn't a word of Czech either, did you not hear tell, I was born in Berlin?"

■ □ ■ □ ■

ABOUT THE AUTHOR

BOHUMIL HRABAL (1914–97) is considered one of the greatest Czech novelists of the twentieth century. He won international acclaim for the novels *Closely Watched Trains, I Served the King of England,* and *Too Loud a Solitude.*

■ □ ■ □ ■

WRITINGS FROM AN UNBOUND EUROPE

For a complete list of titles, see the Writings from an Unbound Europe Web site at www.nupress.northwestern.edu/ue.